THE GILDED CITY OF DREAMS

ALSO BY LUANNE G. SMITH

The Vine Witch Series

The Vine Witch

The Glamourist

The Conjurer

A Conspiracy of Magic Series

The Raven Spell

The Raven Song

The Golden Age of Magic Series

The Golden Age of Magic

The Gilded City of Dreams

PRAISE FOR LUANNE G. SMITH

The Vine Witch

A *Washington Post* and Amazon Charts Bestseller

"Cleverly crafted . . . *The Vine Witch* is a grown-up fairy tale with a twisty-turn-y storyline of magic, love, and betrayal that holds your attention . . . Pure escapism."

—*Forbes*

"An ambitious debut from a promising author."

—*Publishers Weekly*

The Raven Spell

An Amazon Best Book of the Month: Science Fiction & Fantasy

"This fun, atmospheric outing is ideal for fans of C. L. Polk's Kingston Cycle."

—*Publishers Weekly*

"Smith wraps up the plot neatly while leaving a clear hook to entice delighted readers back for the next book."

—*Booklist*

The Witch's Lens

"A delicious foray into a new series that melds history with the supernatural . . . Smith's fans, as well as new readers, will delight in the heady mixture of historical fiction, fantasy, and horror."

—*Library Journal*

"Smith's thorough descriptions make this first novel in the Order of the Seven Stars series an immersive experience for readers."

—*Booklist*

"Smith puts the historical horrors of the 'war to end all wars' through a prism that both amplifies and elucidates the degree of evil that war unleashes on the world, all while telling a spellbinding, captivating story. As antidote to this dark theme, Smith portrays the redeeming idea of loyalty and sacrifice that transcends evil."

—*Historical Novels Review*

The Golden Age of Magic

"An enjoyable spin on the classic fairy godmother's trope . . . The allure of Hollywoodland comes alive."

—*Historical Novels Review*

THE GILDED CITY OF DREAMS

A NOVEL

LUANNE G. SMITH

This is a work of fiction. Names, characters, organizations, places, events, and incidents are either products of the author's imagination or are used fictitiously. Otherwise, any resemblance to actual persons, living or dead, is purely coincidental.

Published by 47North, Seattle

www.apub.com

EU product safety contact:
Amazon Media EU S. à r.l.
38, avenue John F. Kennedy, L-1855 Luxembourg
amazonpublishing-gpsr@amazon.com

ISBN-13: 9781662524981 (paperback)
ISBN-13: 9781662524998 (digital)

Cover design by Kimberly Glyder
Cover image: © Sybille Sterk / ArcAngel Images; © TamakiKou, © francois-roux / Getty; © AnyaLis / Shutterstock

Printed in the United States of America

THE GILDED CITY OF DREAMS

CHAPTER ONE

The Big Apple Takes a Bite

It was difficult to grasp just how wide the expanse between America's coasts was until one crossed the nation's heartland by train. Even for Celeste, a Fée Gardienne with newly acquired powers, the trip was a test of endurance. More so when the heart was still attached to a land enchanted with orange groves, palm trees, and movie studios run by charming producers. A place that grew farther away with each passing mile. After three days of standing on the rear platform watching the land change from desert to mountain to endless fields of corn and wheat, she no longer doubted there was a correlation between the distance traveled overland and the gnawing discomfort in her stomach that told her she was moving in the wrong direction. But she was a full Gardienne now, and she had a duty to uphold.

Celeste left the rear platform to enter the private parlor car coupled to the back of the eastbound 20th Century Limited. The space could have used a good fumigating from the reek of stubbed-out cigarettes and spilled gin that trailed behind Celeste's travel partner. She supposed after three days of riding the rails with a stir-crazy Anaïs, the mess was a mostly harmless by-product, considering the possible alternatives the woman was capable of conjuring. Fortunately, the odor wasn't quite strong enough to obliterate the ozone-like essence of well-spent magic that normally inhabited the space—the telltale scent of talent and ambition riding bareback on the tail of a shooting star. The quintessential scent of Fée Gardienne magic had been infused into the upholstery, the floorboards, and even the malachite paint on the walls of the parlor car that had belonged to her mentor, Dorée.

Celeste sat curled up on a velvet-cushioned seat by the window, her body flush with mixed emotions as she and Anaïs completed the final leg of their overland journey through the green landscape of the eastern United States. They'd left Los Angeles and were headed toward New York City to catch a steamship back to France. The pair had no choice but to return to Europe after being made temporary caretakers of the sisterhood's ancient staff, to be bequeathed to the next eldest Gardienne, now that Dorée had passed. Celeste could only guess at the full power the rather ordinary-looking relic contained, but judging by the paranoia Anaïs had exhibited every time the train stopped at a new depot, it must have been substantial. During its time in their possession, Anaïs had transformed the nearly one-thousand-year-old staff into a walking stick, a suitcase, a floor lamp, and finally a clarinet in a beat-up case, which she claimed would be the most convenient disguise once they landed in the bustling Big Apple. From there they were to spend two nights in a hotel before their steamship sailed for Le Havre and they could pass the staff off to Gertrude, its new rightful caretaker.

"Cocktail?" Anaïs stood at the bar, pouring herself a drink as the parlor car rocked gently over the rails. In the coach cars ahead, a train full of passengers ate, slept, and counted down the hours to their destination, unaware of the hitchhikers riding at the back of the train cloaked in the glamour that hid them from the world.

"This one is called the Bee's Knees," Anaïs said, handing Celeste a glass of a gin-and-lemon drink drizzled with honey. She'd been keeping her boredom at bay on the trip by concocting every drink she could remember ordering at the Folies Bergère in Paris.

Celeste would never be the cocktail connoisseur Anaïs was, but she accepted the glass to be polite. Taking a sip, she gazed out the window at the layers of blue sky and green fields zooming past her. After setting her first protégé on her star path, Celeste had inherited the full power of the Gardiennes. No more relying on gemstones to refill her magic. No more need for an incantation to seal the bond of energy to her aura. She could harness the wind, bend the light, and even manipulate gravity to a degree with a touch of the blue sapphire pendant she wore around her neck.

Her connection with Sebastian had also deepened. She could feel the little stoat's heartbeat echo within the chambers of her own, interpret his thoughts in the back of her mind, and nearly trace the thread of magic that bound them together with a touch of her finger. Once fragile and temporary, the connection had transformed into a solid tether that only death could sever.

"This gin and lemon mixes together pretty good," Anaïs said. "Remind me to add a lemon tree and beehive to my garden when we get home."

Celeste nearly commented on the apt combination of bitter and sweet in her glass but kept the remark to herself as she caught her reflection in the window. How eager she'd been to be on her own in America when she'd first arrived on the continent. To find her first protégé and make her sister Gardiennes proud of her. That final aspiration felt somewhat hollow now, knowing the level of trickery they'd employed to compel her to flee to America. The real reason they'd forced Celeste to seek her future in California—poor, innocent, naive Celeste—was to flush out a Skulk who'd fallen so far outside the rules of fair play he'd committed murder. The Gardiennes had dealt with him, and now the two women who'd been pitted against each other were destined to be roommates for the foreseeable future.

"I love embarking on the last leg of the journey to an exciting destination," Anaïs said, flipping through a magazine with an illustration of a woman with butterfly wings on its cover. She sipped her froufrou drink and licked her lips, pleased with her concoction. "I could absolutely subsist on the excitement and anticipation. Couldn't you?"

Celeste was less enthused. "I suppose, and yet leaving a place behind sometimes comes with its own bittersweet remorse."

Anaïs pouted at her empty glass and went back to the bar. "You gotta put that man out of your mind, hon. Flying solo is how it goes for our kind. Settling down just isn't in the cards."

"Gertrude figured it out."

"Yes, but she's different. Gertrude prefers not to travel much anymore. She's at the comfortable age when she can sit home and let the potential protégés come to her. It took years to build up her backstory and reputation at her salon. And not without a hefty dose of glamour infused into that apartment of hers to keep it going. But the rest of us? Take a lover or two and have fun, but you'd be wise to put any notions of lasting love out of your head."

It was true, Celeste had been mooning over Nick West ever since they'd left California behind. She knew better than to keep dwelling on the movie studio owner. It had been only one kiss, after all. But while she'd had to erase the memory of her from his mind, she found he occupied nearly all her thoughts. Celeste cast off Anaïs's warning, watching the cornfields roll by as every mile took her farther from California and Nick West.

It was only when they pulled into New York City that Celeste grew distracted long enough by the change in scenery to forget about Nick and what she'd been forced to leave behind. New York dazzled the mind with its skyscrapers and gilded domes shimmering ahead. While Hollywood had felt like a prized rosebud on the brink of bursting to life under the warm sun, the skyline of the eastern city of industrialists had already taken on the worn look of old jewelry. Beautiful and well made, but beginning to show a little tarnish.

The train pulled into Grand Central Terminal. Celeste, of course, had mixed emotions about returning to France. She missed all the best of home: the croissants, cheese, bread, and a c'est la vie attitude. But she couldn't help feeling a part of her heart had taken root in the soil of this enormous, wild country. Ripping those fragile tendrils out now might forever sever whatever it was she'd thought she'd found on her brief adventure—independence, belonging . . . love?

"Come on," Anaïs said, ducking to look out the window. "This is where we get off. Time to fold up the parlor car."

The Fée Gardienne had changed into a sublime ruby-red dress with a drop waist, ruffled skirt, and plunging neckline, which she adorned with a string of pearls that fell in a perfect V between her breasts. Her picture hat, which framed her face in the most flattering manner with its wide brim, had been dyed a matching shade of red. At the last minute, Anaïs had attached an enormous rhinestone brooch and feather to the silk hatband for added flair. Just the sort of thing to earn a disapproving second glance from the old biddy on the platform who glared at everyone exiting the train.

"Have you got it?" Celeste asked with a glance back at their private car before it disappeared.

"Of course I have it." Anaïs raised the clarinet case in her hand as proof.

They were both understandably nervous about transporting the magical relic through a crowded and unfamiliar city. Celeste knew from her studies growing up that the staff was more than a mere symbol of power and position. The ancient relic helped the eldest wield the wisdom and temperance of their magic in its most refined and concentrated energy. Naturally, it was impossible for anyone to know what they carried, disguised as it was, and yet *they* knew what they had, and that knowledge made them jittery.

By the time Anaïs had adjusted her silk shawl so it sat perfectly angled on her bare shoulders, Celeste was already tipping the porter for having unloaded their trunks from the luggage car. When Anaïs stepped into the station's grand hall, she unashamedly soaked up the bulge-eyed attention that naturally swerved her way. The looks came from men mostly, but women also stared, as though wondering how anyone could be so glamourous. Anaïs had apparently been warned when she was younger that it might be best to tone down her style to avoid attracting such attention. After all, so much of a Gardienne's work was done in the shadows and out of the limelight. But it simply wasn't in her nature to be a shrinking violet. Or even a common brown sunflower. She was a beautiful, bursting chrysanthemum, and so she sashayed across the marble floor in full verve to find a cab to take them to their hotel.

"I have a little side errand I need to take care of while we're here." Anaïs looked up at the sky, where her rook, Gideon, circled above, then raised her left hand to flag down a cabbie.

"Oh?" After three days of travel, this was the first mention of a deviation from their plan. Celeste had been under the impression they were on a strict schedule once the train arrived at Grand Central Terminal. Anaïs had arranged for their passage home on the next ship leaving for Le Havre. She'd sent a telegram to the ticket office that had been embedded with the same sort of scheming enchantment she'd used on the postcard that had tricked Celeste into traveling to Hollywood. Only this time, the magic had hoodwinked the purser's office into setting aside two staterooms for them on the ocean liner. But that ship didn't leave until the day after tomorrow. Until then, they were supposed to keep a low profile so as not to draw attention to themselves or the clarinet case. So far, she thought they'd missed the mark on that point.

"An early protégé of mine is visiting the city for the summer," Anaïs explained. "I haven't seen her in a while, so I'd like to check up on her before we head off."

Celeste understood that following up on a protégé's progress was a large part of a Gardienne's duty. She was taught not to smother them with attention, but a checkup now and then was the responsible thing to do. Knowing she'd have to return to California to catch up with Rose again one day gave her a hopeful shiver of optimism. And while she also understood Anaïs's earlier point about a Gardienne needing to be free of serious romantic entanglements, a part of her heart had been put under a spell by a certain Hollywood producer's smile.

A cab stopped soon after Anaïs raised her hand. The driver grinned at the two women, eager to get the trunks into the back of his vehicle before they could change their minds and get a ride from someone else. He was slightly oily around the edges, pale from sitting in his car all day, and somewhat malnourished-looking beneath the scraggly beard and mustache, but Celeste read his heart to be trustworthy. Even if his eyes lingered too long on the shape of Anaïs's legs.

Celeste looked away from the spectacle, preferring to observe the crowd of people going in and out of the train station. The constant motion was almost disorienting. Faces coming and going. Bodies rushing to get to wherever it was they were headed. Yet in the madness her eye caught on a single face in profile. The firm jaw, the immaculate hairline, the casual tilt of the head—it was all too familiar. *Nick?* It couldn't be.

Her heartbeat raced as she stood on tiptoe to get a better view, but then the man turned to meet an acquaintance. It wasn't Nick at all. Just a businessman with a great head of hair. Her heels touched the ground again aside the flickering hope that had been doused into disappointment.

"Where to, ladies?" the cabbie asked after Celeste slid onto the back seat beside Anaïs, eager to get away from the noise of six million people going about the business of living in a cramped city built up fifty stories high.

"The Hotel Chelsea on West Twenty-Third." Anaïs gripped her ruby pendant and locked her gaze on the driver through the rearview mirror. "And stay on Fifth Avenue, please."

"How many times have you been to New York?" Celeste cautiously watched for Anaïs's trademark smirk.

"Only twice," the Gardienne said. "But I know it well enough to know a woman has to be very direct to get what she wants." She finally took her eyes off the cab driver, then leaned toward Celeste, still clutching the clarinet case in her lap. "You never want to leave the impression that you can be taken advantage of easily." Anaïs leaned back in her seat while Manhattan's skyscrapers encroached from both sides.

After a twenty-minute crawl down Fifth Avenue, the cab turned west, passing an unusual wedge-shaped building whose narrowest point couldn't have been more than seven feet wide. Celeste craned her neck to look up, wondering how such a skinny building stayed upright. Maybe it had a little magical innovation stirred into its mortar and steel. She'd barely shaken off the notion as absurd when they approached the Hotel Chelsea, a multistory brick building with the pride of the last century's Gothic aesthetic plastered all over it, with its steepled gables, wrought iron railings, and arched windows.

The two women jumped out of the car and straightened their hems. "What was all that staring in the mirror business about?" Certainly, they didn't have anything to fear from a random cab driver besides a few unwanted looks.

Anaïs patted the clarinet case while the cabbie retrieved their trunks. "I'm covering our tracks by erasing any memory of us from the driver's thoughts. Believe me, the last thing I need is another man having too much information about our Gardienne business." She shook off an uncharacteristic shiver.

"All he did was drive us across town. What could he glean from that?"

Anaïs spun on her heels. "Listen, we're tasked with getting this thing home safe and sound. The staff is priceless. Over nine hundred years old. Without it, the eldest can't see into the future, can't tell if a protégé has made it onto their star path. It would make her work feel like flying in the dark with a blindfold on." Anaïs took an uncomfortably close step forward. "No one can know what we're carrying. Just you and me, kid. No one else. So if I have to rearrange a little gray matter inside some stranger's skull to make him forget he saw us, I will."

Anaïs didn't say so out loud, but there was a warning of something more dangerous in her tone. And while the Gardienne had proved a steadfast ally in their battle with the Skulk out in California, Celeste couldn't help harboring a few lingering suspicions about the woman's loyalties. "Makes perfect sense," she replied, appearing agreeable to disguise her growing unease.

Anaïs headed toward the front door of the redbrick building, swinging the clarinet case in one hand and her purse in the other. Celeste noticed how men's eyes traveled over her ruby-red dress and embroidered shawl as they passed her. She also noticed how Anaïs held her chin up, unafraid to meet their leering looks. The woman might be deceitful, but she sure had grit.

Celeste stayed with the trunks, opening her purse to tip the driver. Sebastian lazily tossed up a few coins from the bottom of the bag with his hind legs. The stoat had grown fat on their overland journey in the private parlor car. Anaïs had indulged his every craving, from mice to rabbits, stunning them at depot stops along the way with her pendant and then letting the stoat do his thing. Such a spoiled experience compared to their trip through the American West, when the poor creature had been forced to subsist on leftovers from Celeste's breakfast plate. Then, her furry companion had arrived lean and in fighting form. Now he lounged on his back with a bloated belly, content to snooze all day until woken up for his next meal.

Celeste had just handed the coins to the cab driver when the squeal of car brakes made her whip her head around. Not twenty feet away, a black-and-maroon Vauxhall four-seater appeared to lose control. It jumped the sidewalk, barely missing a woman walking a pug-nosed terrier. Celeste braced herself against the cab as the Vauxhall rolled up the steps and crashed into the brick wall of the building next to the hotel. The car hit with enough force that its nose was smashed in and the front wheels were left spinning in the air after getting hung up on the mangled wrought iron railing. The dog walker screamed, falling backward into a sculpted boxwood while her dog yapped and tugged against the leash.

Anaïs ran up beside Celeste, breathless and wide-eyed, still carrying the clarinet case in her grip. "What the hell happened?"

"He just came out of nowhere." Celeste ran to the car. Steam bellowed from its radiator as the driver sat hunched against the steering wheel, eyes shut. A cut on his forehead gushed blood, and broken glass covered his suit. She gave the injured man's shoulder a shake. He groaned. He was still alive. "Help me," she said to Anaïs as she unlatched the door. The Gardienne hesitantly set the clarinet case down on the sidewalk and helped pry the driver's side door wide open, while the cab driver ran inside the hotel to call an ambulance.

"Give me your shawl." Celeste held out her hand, not waiting for an objection. Anaïs gave her one anyway via a narrow-eyed warning but obliged in the end, slipping the silk off her shoulders. Celeste manipulated the shawl into a thick pad of gauze that she pressed against the wound. She was no healer, but a little enchantment to stop the blood was within her range of talents. When the blood stopped trickling from the man's cut, he opened his eyes just as a siren wailed down the street.

"Good thinking," Anaïs admitted, rubbing her hand over her bare arm.

A small crowd had gathered to gawk at the spectacle and formed a circle around the accident scene. Celeste attempted to ask the man if anything was broken, but he closed his eyes and leaned his head against the steering wheel again, groaning in pain. The woman with the dog began screeching about how she'd nearly been killed while a young man pulled her from the topiary.

"That's some introduction to the city, huh?" Celeste said to Anaïs as she held the gauze firmly against the man's head.

Not a moment too soon, a big black ambulance pulled up. Two men in dark suits and bushy mustaches dashed out and elbowed their way through the crowd. "Everyone, take a step back. That's it. Give us some room to work. Go on about your business. We'll take it from here."

The Gardiennes quickly stepped out of the way when the medical help arrived, happy to leave the man in their care. The worst of the emergency over, Celeste went to wipe her forehead with the back of her arm but stopped when she saw a red smear on her sleeve. She held her arms out at her sides, turning them back and forth, to inspect the rest.

"Come on, we better get checked into the hotel and clean up," Anaïs said, seeing the mess. She bent to retrieve the clarinet case she'd left at her feet, but there was nothing. "Where'd it go?" Startled, she spun left and right, searching the ground around her. "I left the case right here. Where is it?"

The panic in Anaïs's voice was palpable. Celeste, too, felt a flutter of dread when she bent to look under the wrecked car and still didn't see the disguised staff. She lifted her head to search the crowd and saw a young boy in baggy trousers running down the street with the case tucked under his arm. "There!" she said and pointed.

Anaïs had spotted the boy too. She pushed through the crowd, elbowing stragglers out of her way without apology. Celeste followed, attempting to make amends as she squeezed through, but she knew if they didn't catch that boy, more trouble would come down on them than anything a disgruntled New Yorker could deliver.

The boy, perhaps nine or ten years old, ran down the pavement, dodging people and lampposts with impressive agility. His legs pumped and his head turned once, revealing big bright eyes that betrayed his fear. They tracked him for two blocks, but oddly enough he didn't run into the park across the street, where he might have hidden more easily. Instead, he chose to stay on the crowded sidewalk.

The Fées Gardiennes chased the boy as ladylike as they could manage for another block before he turned a corner on his right and they lost him. By the time Celeste and Anaïs rounded the building at the intersection, the boy had completely vanished. There were shops and apartment buildings on either side of the street, but which one had he found refuge in?

"Where did he go?" Celeste asked, panting for breath.

Instead of canvassing the street with her eyes, Anaïs looked up. Gideon, her rook companion, who was never far away, flapped his wings as he settled on top of a glass-and-limestone building across the street. He cawed and pointed with his beak toward the shop below him.

"Clever bird," Anaïs said. "Come on, this way. That little thief isn't getting away. He simply doesn't understand who he's picked a fight with."

Celeste took a deep breath. She was uneasy about following Anaïs across the busy street. They'd come to the dazzling city of skyscrapers, wealthy industrialists, and gilded dreams as a place to rest and lie low for a couple of nights. They were supposed to be awaiting their big journey across the ocean back to France to return the elder staff to its rightful caretaker. Now, not one hour in the city and they were chasing some ragamuffin urchin down a dirty street to recover the one thing they were tasked with keeping safe.

Instead of taking a bite out of the Big Apple, the city seemed intent on eating them for lunch.

CHAPTER TWO

Dust and Bitter Lemon

The Gardiennes entered the site where Gideon indicated the boy had gone. The shop turned out to be a quiet bookstore that smelled of musty paper and wood rot. Thick Oriental rugs covered the wooden floors and dark shutters hung over the windows, letting in withered ribbons of light. There didn't appear to be anyone inside other than a man in a black suit, who looked up at them expectantly from behind a cash register. His round glasses reflected the pinched sunlight desperately trying to get in through the front door.

"May I help you?" he asked.

Anaïs thought the store clerk's voice came out too deep and guttural for someone of such a slight build, before banishing the unfair observation from her mind. Then again, one ought never dismiss a first impression too quickly.

"We're looking for a boy about yea high," Celeste said. She held her hand out at waist height and stretched her neck to look behind a large bookcase in the center of the shop.

"Well, I'm afraid all we sell here are books, ma'am." The man cleared his throat slightly after his joke landed with a thud.

"We know he came in here." Anaïs strode to the back of the store to take a more thorough look behind the bookshelves.

"I'm sorry." The man folded his long, slender fingers in front of him on the counter. "I've been here all morning. Haven't seen a boy. Maybe try the sweet shop about three blocks south of here. That's where I'd go, if I were a youngster."

"Are you sure you didn't see him?" Celeste asked. "Scruffy brown hair, bright blue eyes, baggy gray trousers with suspenders. Perhaps he ran by your windows."

"Oh, I don't see much out of those dirty old things." He gave a flat smile before glancing toward the back of the store, where Anaïs had disappeared. "We carry many rare books," he called to her. "Is there something I can help you find? Besides the boy, I mean." His lip quivered as he perhaps realized the joke had long gone cold.

Anaïs returned his flat smile and pulled a few books off the shelf before putting them back unopened. After a final glance around the shelves, she returned to the front of the store, rubbing her fingers against her thumb. Dust, and lots of it. Celeste watched her with that doe-eyed stare of hers. She was going to blow it if she opened her mouth to argue with the man, so Anaïs sucked in her cheeks, gave her hands a final wipe against each other, then hooked her handbag in her elbow. "Yes, I can see that you're right," she said. "There's no boy here. We must have been mistaken about which shop he entered. Sorry to take up your time." The Gardienne raised a telling brow at Celeste, and the pair walked out onto the busy sidewalk.

"What was that all about?" Celeste asked.

"Keep walking." Anaïs waited until they were out of view of the shop to pull Celeste into the alcove of the business next door.

"What about the boy and the clarinet case?" Celeste leaned her head out to get a view past the alcove, still watching the shop.

Anaïs pulled her back as an electric pulse of fear threatened to short-circuit her heart. "Listen, there's something not right about that place. I don't doubt for a second the boy went in there. Gideon doesn't miss a trick with his eyes, which means the owner is hiding something."

"But how could a boy just disappear?" Celeste's voice, always so infused with golden optimism, was showing its first cracks of desperation, just as Anaïs feared.

"There was a back office," Anaïs replied, distracted by something nagging at her intuition. "The door was open, so I took a quick look inside, but the boy wasn't there either. And yet he had to be somewhere." She rubbed her thumb over her bottom lip, thinking. There was some anomaly at play. Some inconsistent itch that begged to be scratched. "The dust," she said at last.

"Dust?"

"Yes, that's what's bothering me." Anaïs looked at her fingers. "It was everywhere. Along the shelves, the books, even the cash register. Like no one ever went in the shop to browse the bookshelves or purchase books. In fact, I'd wager those books haven't been touched in months. Not even by a shop owner eager to make a good impression by taking a feather duster to them."

"There was a musty smell coming from the rugs too, now that you mention it," Celeste said.

"Of course." Anaïs felt her throat flush pink and angry. She fumed, cursing her stupidity, before ducking out of the alcove. "Excuse me," she said to the first woman to pass by. "You wouldn't happen to know where the nearest bookstore is, would you?"

The woman, mid-forties and wrapped in a blue cotton dress and fake pearls, stopped long enough to give it some thought, then pointed over her shoulder. "Your best bet is to try Fourth Avenue on the other side of Union Square. That's where all the best bookshops are. Must be a dozen of them. Maybe a ten-minute walk from here," she said with a friendly nod.

Anaïs thanked the woman. She touched her ruby pendant and raised her right eyebrow to offer the woman a token of appreciation by way of a discarded chewing gum wrapper transformed into a dropped coin on the sidewalk. The woman picked up the quarter in front of the bookshop and waved back at them to show off her good luck, oblivious to the purveyor of dusty tomes open for business right under her nose.

Celeste stepped out of the alcove. "She can't see it."

"I don't think any of them can," Anaïs said after watching passersby come and go at the other shops and buildings, as normal as could be, while ignoring the bookshop.

"It has to be veiled in some kind of glamour." Celeste peered at the store in that innocent way of hers. Not quite naive, just inexperienced in all the shapes and forms of magic and treachery at work in the world. Regretfully, the elder Gardiennes declined to teach about the occultists, necromancers, and magicians roaming the city streets. They found them inferior and therefore inconsequential, since their intuitions were led not by service or benevolence but more often by greed and a lust for power. Anaïs had naturally been drawn in like a fluttering moth to their dangerous glow in the dark whenever her rebellious streak surfaced. They weren't all as irrelevant as the Gardiennes painted them to be. Some were quite clever at manipulating the physical and metaphysical spheres.

"There was a shop in Cairo that was rumored to operate in the same manner during the war." Anaïs left out the part about hearing the information from Edward, the man who'd both stolen her heart and betrayed her, and paid the price with his life. "Only magical folk could see the storefront. Inside, there was another realm. A place where antiquities were auctioned off to the highest bidder. Magical relics like scarabs, books, amulets, and incense bowls."

Celeste pressed her hand to her lips. Judging by the expanded whites of her eyes, she understood the gravity of what may have happened to the elder staff. "But we went in the shop," she said, lowering her hand. "There wasn't anything like that inside. Just books."

Anaïs stared at the shop's dirty windows. "At first I thought the boy had stolen the clarinet case because he hoped to pawn it, but now I'm beginning to wonder if he knew exactly what he was stealing. If he went in the shop like Gideon said, and the shop is veiled, then there's more to him than meets the eye. More to the owner of that shop as well. Come on, we need to rethink our strategy."

"But what about the elder staff? Are you sure we should leave? What if the boy comes out?"

Anaïs looked up at her rook squatting over the shop's door. "Gideon will keep watch. I'll check in with him often. Until something happens, there's not much we can do without drawing a whole cartload of unwanted attention."

"And one must always avoid drawing unwanted attention to oneself," Celeste said, reciting the number one lesson all young Gardiennes learned while at the cottage, even though Anaïs enjoyed exploring the boundaries of that particular guideline. Celeste bit her lip, as though trying to see a way around their predicament, but the truth was their unique existence required a level of anonymity. They had enormous talents and abilities they could call upon, but with those came the responsibility of knowing when and how to use them to benefit their protégés.

Knowing they'd been outmaneuvered, the Gardiennes abandoned the chase and headed back to the hotel, passing by the scene of the earlier car accident. The ambulance and injured driver were gone, and the crowd had dispersed. A single police officer oversaw a wrecker with a giant hook on its back rolling up to remove the crumpled vehicle. Anaïs closed her eyes briefly as they passed, probing for any supernatural influence. It seemed a little too convenient that a car had crashed just outside their hotel the moment they'd arrived, providing the perfect opportunity for a thief to grab the elder staff. Their only thought when the accident first happened had been to come to the man's aid, but now Anaïs could see through the perfect distraction.

"It's in the air—bitter lemon," Celeste said, having done her own reading.

Anaïs nodded. "The scent of deception."

But whose deception was it? And how did this boy know that she and Celeste were carrying the priceless relic when they'd only just arrived in the city?

The Gardiennes each took another reading on the area, probing for the depth of mischief. Whatever spells may have been cast over the accident scene, the remains had already drifted onto the pavement and been scattered by the gawkers. With nothing left to detect, they entered the hotel.

To their relief, the travel trunks were waiting for them inside the lobby, stacked beside the front desk. The clerk looked up when they approached. "Checking in?"

Celeste had become quite adept at altering ledgers to ensure a proper room was available, so Anaïs left her and her stoat to it while she took a closer look at their luggage. Both trunks had been meticulously sealed with enchantments for the journey, though that was no guarantee against a determined thief, as Edward had so brazenly demonstrated back in California. As an occultist, he'd sorted out how to get around the enchantments by breaking the magical bond with one of his chemical concoctions, and then he'd stolen Celeste's gemstones with the idea of hotfooting it to Buenos Aires. The poor sucker hadn't even made it past Mulholland Drive before Anaïs and Gideon took their revenge.

Celeste waved a pair of keys. "I got us two adjoining rooms on the top floor." By the time they rode the elevator up to the twelfth floor, her stoat had done the rest by transforming the room's basics into big fluffy beds, sparkling glass chandeliers, and a fully stocked bar—at least in Anaïs's room. Americans were still in their prudish phase, so the bar had been disguised as a full-size radio console. Each room was given a bathtub and vanity, satin sheets, and a velvet settee angled underneath a lamp with a fringed shade to round out their comfort. Not a bad effort for a pair just out of training.

Anaïs sank into the velvet settee as an exhausted Celeste retired to her own room to clean up. Finally, some time to think! Anaïs wasn't prone to overreaction, but the fibrillation she'd been feeling in her chest ever since the ancient rod was stolen had her experiencing an uncharacteristic dread of the unknown. Something wasn't adding up. The theft just couldn't have been random. Especially since the only other person who knew about the staff was the young woman in the next room. The same young woman who'd very recently been betrayed by her own sister Gardiennes. For a greater good, yes, but lied to all the same. Could a young woman's hurt feelings carry over into a lust for revenge? Could she have arranged something so diabolical as stealing the elder staff in the space of a few days? Anaïs had to keep from letting her thoughts seep out through an ironic howl of laughter, knowing that was the very scenario they'd used to scare Celeste into fleeing to America in the first place. You couldn't make this stuff up, she thought, staring up at the ceiling and wondering what the hell she was going to do next.

CHAPTER THREE

Cognac and Dragon's Breath

Celeste closed the adjoining door quietly behind her and pressed her hand over her mouth to keep from screaming. After stifling the urge, she fled to the bed, where she buried her head in the pillows. Sebastian crawled up on the coverlet with her, but instead of comforting her, he complained about his empty stomach.

"Can't you see we're in trouble, Sebastian? Real trouble." The stoat twitched his whiskers, testing the air to detect the trouble she spoke about. Celeste pointed her finger against her palm in the direction of Anaïs next door. "A random boy doesn't just find us on a street in New York City, swipe the very specific artifact we're carrying, and then go hide in a shop veiled in glamour." Celeste shuddered and pulled the covers around her. "This is no coincidence, Sebastian. It's an inside job, and now we're cooked."

Celeste held her pendant and dimmed the lights in the room until only a single lamp remained on. She sat back against the pillows, rewinding in her mind the events surrounding her journey to America. Anaïs had known what would happen to Dorée when Celeste successfully set her first protégé on her star path. She knew that the eldest must perish for the youngest to ascend. Under normal circumstances the magical staff would have been taken up by the next living eldest in the moment of transition. But this time? The next eldest was conveniently thousands of miles away on another continent, which left Celeste and Anaïs the de facto caretakers of the ancient staff while they were in America. The perfect opportunity for mischief.

Feeling a cold chill creep over her skin, Celeste left her bed and conjured up her own well-stocked bar before pouring herself a cognac. The hotel had turned off the room's antiquated radiator for the summer, so with a touch of her sapphire pendant, she inserted a fireplace into the corner by transforming the potted plant next to a velvet chair. This was no time to let the cold invade her blood. Heat and spark must guide her thoughts.

Celeste sat in the soft chair with her legs tucked under her, Sebastian curled up on her lap, and the firelight dancing in her eyes. "We'll have to keep our wits about us," she said, breathing in the cognac's aroma before taking a sip. "But I'm not sure I even understand the potential danger of what would happen with the elder staff in her hands. I mean, how much control could it give her? How much illegitimate power could she claim?"

It was then Celeste began to doubt her suspicions again, wavering on the beveled edge of misgivings and doubt. Gaining her full powers as a Fée Gardienne had given her an unexpected feeling of humility. As though her instincts knew to be careful with the potency of a thought, an emotion, a desire. Gardiennes had the power to alter a human protégé's life by clearing the obstacles that impeded their destiny. They could move minds, money, and mountains to make their protégé's future come into alignment with their deepest hopes and desires. And in return the Gardiennes got to claim the life of their dreams too, surrounded by as much or as little luxury as they desired. So why would a junior Gardienne need a stolen relic?

Celeste stroked Sebastian's neck, dipping into his thoughts to gauge his mood. The poor fellow had been complaining of hunger ever since they'd arrived in the city. She doubted he'd heard a word she'd said as the drumbeat of his appetite for vermin drowned out all other noises.

"Go on, then," she said. "But be careful out there. We don't know who's who or what's what in this town."

Sebastian nodded and slipped out under the door. With him gone, Celeste truly was all alone in a city of millions. The American metropolis wasn't known for magic, not like the capitals of Europe, where the mortar and stone of castle walls, cobbled streets, and Gothic arches were steeped in the charm and enchantment of centuries of alchemy and incantation. And yet they'd barely disembarked their train at Grand Central Terminal before they found themselves embroiled in a powerful spell aimed at stealing the oldest and most powerful artifact the Fées Gardiennes possessed. The theft just had to be a setup. Which only shifted her suspicions yet again to Anaïs.

The staff was older than the gemstone pendants they wore. Older than the dusty old tomes that outlined the laws and duties each Gardienne must uphold. The only things that predated it in Gardienne lore were the willow wands used by their predecessors centuries earlier.

But thinking of books gave Celeste an idea. She opened her trunk and dug through the pile of clothes, racks of bottles, and stack of books. Before leaving Los Angeles, she and Sebastian had gone back to retrieve her possessions and fix the lock on her trunk. The bungalow they'd created at the Beverly Hills Hotel had disintegrated after her magic had temporarily dwindled, but her trunk was there, tucked in among the banana plants and ferns, still protected by a few residual charms. While they were recovering her belongings, her heart had made a wistful plea to one day return to the city.

Celeste caught herself slipping into a daydream about her time in California and had to force herself to refocus. She pulled an old book about fairy-godmother lore, a hand-me-down tome from the cottage's library entitled the *History of Gardiennes*, out of the bottom of the trunk. Its binding was frayed, and the cover illustration of an ancient Gardienne wielding a wooden wand had faded like a ghost from all the hands that had held the volume over the years. Celeste had already skimmed through most of the pages when she was still in training for her life as a Gardienne, but the dry descriptions had never drawn her in.

There'd been only one memorable section she'd taken the time to read in full, a chapter describing how a Fée Gardienne had devised a way to put a princess to sleep, wake her up again with a kiss from an eligible prince, and then marry her off to the young king in waiting. The tale, while semiromantic in the telling, had always irked her. For the better part of the Gardiennes' history, arranged marriages had become their main mission. Alliances—the kind they had the specific talent to bring about with their magic—could seal peace between nations, redistribute the wealth of kingdoms, and launch bloodlines with distinguishable physical traits that would slither serpentlike through generations to resurface in an heir's narrow-set eyes, prominent nose, or receding hairline. There was nothing wrong with the tradition of arranging marriages, she supposed, but so many opportunities were opening up for men and women after the Great War that she found the practice quaint, unimaginative, and an unreliable substitute for true love. There were more creative ways a Gardienne could influence a life besides arranging a favorable marriage, especially considering the downfall effect that would inherently gnaw at the bonds of the relationship. It was a new age, a new world, and she was ready to be a part of the future. *If* she could survive the mess she currently found herself in.

Celeste cracked the frail book open to see if there was anything to be gleaned about the elder staff. After being ignored for so long, the spine complained as she thumbed through the pages. She knew there was a chapter on their history, a written record left by some ancient Gardienne by the name of Wilhelmina over three centuries earlier. Perhaps she was the woman on the cover? "Ah, found it," she said, recognizing a chapter entitled "The Life and Legacy of the Fées Gardiennes." Her finger traced over the words, skimming the information again to find what she needed. Two pages in, she stumbled on the pertinent passage.

In the age prior to the Ascension, the thirteen Wisewomen still wrapped themselves in homespun capes that dragged behind them in the mud. They lived in the forest, where the canopy of stars served as their roof, the trees their walls, and the mossy ground beneath their feet the hearth inside a home where sunlight was always welcome. They did not seek protégés in that long-ago age as they do now. Their magic was still too raw, too wild. They'd only just learned to focus their power with the aid of willow wands that allowed the magic to flow from thought to manifestation. They soon mastered the manipulation of objects like pumpkins into pushcarts and mice into work mules. They bettered the land, communed with their neighbors, and infiltrated the villagers' dreams with visions of art, music, and poetry. Their reputation as benevolent Wisewomen of the woods grew. For years they were considered harmless women with good intentions, even if they did follow odd habits under the full moon.

But when one lives in a house absent of true walls, ignorant eyes can infiltrate to furnish the place with suspicion and accusation. Eventually, the uncanny magic they wielded was interpreted as unnatural and deemed the work of the Devil, whom they surely cavorted with under the full moon.

The women were called out as witches, demons, malevolent fey. Will-o-the-wisps that haunted the foggy bog. Bloodsuckers who strolled the fens at midnight. When the accusations grew too loud to ignore, the sisters were forced to retreat deeper into the forest from men bearing torches and leading packs of baying dogs fevered with the scent of their blood and hair. (Most historians of the sisterhood credit this turn of events to interference by the Infortunii, who'd come to resent the rise of the Wisewomen's good name in the woods.)

Celeste shook her head at the vileness of Skulks before reading the next section out loud to herself as the wood in the fireplace popped and crackled. "As creatures dependent on warmth and light, the dark of the forest nearly became the Wisewomen's tomb as they shivered in the recesses of a cave they'd taken shelter in. That is, until a man who'd heard of their otherworldly gifts approached them with an offer."

"Hugh Capet, duke of the Franks," Anaïs said.

Celeste spun around. She'd been so engrossed in revisiting the history she hadn't realized Anaïs had entered the room and was reading along over her shoulder.

Anaïs knelt beside Celeste's chair. She'd changed into a sleeveless party dress that glittered black and gold in the firelight. "He was the first king to strike a deal." She craned her neck to read the passage above Celeste's finger. "He's also the one we have to thank for the gift of the forest land. He and his men built the cottage as payment after signing the agreement with the Gardiennes."

"A cottage for a kingdom?" Celeste asked. "It never struck me as much of a bargain."

"Not just a kingdom. The sisterhood arranged for an eight-hundred-year-long bloodline for the duke and his kingly heirs. And they didn't just get the cottage. In addition to his assured protection, our predecessors ascended out of the mud hand in hand with Capet when he assumed the throne. No more barking dogs, no more pitchforks, no more threats of death. After they secured his crown for him, the Gardiennes were invited to royal weddings, coronations—"

"Christenings . . ." Celeste added a little bite to her voice, given the Gardiennes had used the occasion of a child's naming ceremony to convince her Anaïs had cursed a poor babe to death.

Anaïs acknowledged the show of teeth with a reciprocal smirk. "And christenings." She picked up the book and turned the page. "We were finally able to do what we'd been born to do."

"How do you know all this?"

Anaïs squirmed with uncharacteristic shyness. "I've been doing some research here and there. I plan on writing a history book of my own one day. Strip off all that medieval tarnish and get to the truth about the women who've been part of this sisterhood over the centuries. Where we come from, what we do, how we choose our protégés."

Celeste hadn't pictured Anaïs as the historian for their age, but she clearly saw herself that way. She did often seem to be the caretaker of information others rarely had at their fingertips, wearing a smug smile of satisfaction.

Anaïs perused the next paragraph with a raised brow. "You're trying to figure out the history of the elder staff, aren't you?"

"Somebody must believe it has value outside of the sisterhood," Celeste said diplomatically. She could hardly say she was curious to know what the ancient relic could do in the hands of a Gardienne who wasn't the eldest. "For it to be stolen so quickly the moment we arrived in the city."

Anaïs gave her a peculiar look, almost as though Celeste was the one under suspicion. "The staff was a gift from the king. He called it a shadow scepter to his own. I think he intuitively knew that crossing the Wisewomen after what they'd done for him would only end in ruin, so he often honored them with symbolic gestures. The staff was carved from alder wood and inlaid with veins of pure gold, unlike the thirteen original wands. Years later, after the Gardiennes' gift of succession held true and Capet's heir became king as well, they were offered the thirteen gemstones as a token of gratitude. I read somewhere they were originally much larger than these that we wear now."

"But where does the wooden staff's power come from?" Celeste asked. "The Gardienne who carries it?"

"Possibly. Probably." Anaïs tapped her index finger against her chin, thinking. She exhaled, apparently coming to a decision. "Listen, if you're thinking you can wield the staff now that you've got your full powers, you've bitten off way more than you can chew. There's a reason it goes to the one with the most experience. Just get the staff back from whoever you're working with and I'm sure all will be forgiven."

"Me?" Celeste nearly spit out her teeth. "You! You're the one with the motivation to steal it for your own power. You're the one who would have known how to set up some mystical storefront for the boy to hide in so you could retrieve the staff later."

Anaïs sat back with her mouth open. "*Me?* Why would *I* steal it? I'm the one trying to protect the damn thing." She narrowed her eyes and pointed at Celeste. "But you, on the other hand, might steal it out of spite because you still can't see that Dorée and I had to deceive you to catch that filthy Skulk in the act."

"You caught him in the act, all right. Dolores Diaz is dead because you weren't honest with me from the start."

The pair got to their feet and stared at each other, fuming. Celeste dropped the book. One twitch of that skinny eyebrow of Anaïs's and she was ready to turn the bottle of cognac into a Chinese star and send it hurling.

"Be very careful, Celeste." Anaïs held her palms up. "I can see why you might still entertain certain opinions about me. I know what people say. I accept that my reputation paints me in various shades of gray. But I swear to you I'm only trying to get the staff back to France and in the hands of the eldest again." She lowered her arms. "And, yes, I admit I suspected you too, but I realize now you simply couldn't have known ahead of time about the fate of the staff when you didn't even know that Dorée, as the eldest, would pass away for you to be elevated as a Gardienne. So how could you have arranged for someone to steal it here in New York days later?"

Celeste's posture unwound as she exhaled, releasing the tension she'd been holding. "Which means someone outside of the sisterhood really did steal it."

"But how did they know?" Anaïs flopped down in the velvet chair left vacant by Celeste. "Certainly, the gold ingrained in the wood has some value, but not enough to be worth the risk, I wouldn't think. So what do they hope to do with it?"

Celeste retrieved the book off the floor. "That's what I was trying to figure out. It says here that the king had the rod carved from a single alder branch. He chose alder because it represented protection, specifically against malevolent forces. But he also considered it woman's wood. Because of the way it bleeds when cut, it was apparently associated with fertility and birth."

Anaïs looked up at that. "May I see?" she asked, reaching for the book. "I was taught the alder represented balance. Male *and* female energy. Which I always thought was a little odd, given we're strictly a sisterhood." She tipped the page to see it better in the firelight. "The symbology isn't random. There's power in blood, especially in a woman's hands." Anaïs rubbed the underside of her chin with the back of her hand as her dark bob cut a sharp line against her jawbone. "But what about in a man's hands, I wonder," she said, letting her eyes drift back to the fire.

"I'm still curious to find out exactly what the wooden staff does," Celeste said. "I mean, why does the eldest still carry it with her? I know Dorée showed the future of my protégé on the wall of a whirlwind, but it must do more than that. Why else would someone steal it?"

"That's one use, but I've also seen it used to amplify a Gardienne's power. It isn't just a ceremonial prop. I recall learning that our powers were much more, um, flighty in the days of wands, before we received the grounding influence of these modern cut gemstones. Their aim wasn't always so precise. The shadow scepter helped the first Gardiennes concentrate their power so that it became more reliable than wands alone. Which, of course, only helped the king and his heirs with their agenda for supremacy even more. But if we're convinced this wasn't a random street theft, then whoever took the staff must have at least as much knowledge of what it's capable of as we do."

"But how could an outsider know?" Celeste felt a whisper of doubt brush across her neck again. The day of their arrival in New York City wasn't planned. Them being caretakers of the relic wasn't planned. She glanced at Anaïs out of the corner of her eye, suspicion still swirling in the air like too much perfume. Wasn't the simplest explanation generally the correct one?

"Depends on who stole it," Anaïs said with that same slight tone of accusation in her voice again before giving a small shrug. "We're not the only beings who can manipulate energy, you know. There are plenty of Merlin types in the world with insights of their own."

Celeste stared into the flames as if in a trance. The power of fire transported her thoughts back to those dangerous days of kingdoms on the rise, battles fought in cold mud amid the clang of clashing steel, and the swirling cauldron of magic newly birthed into the world on the breath of mythical dragons. Who in America could know about their history? Their dawn as Gardiennes? Was there another rogue Skulk on the prowl? She hadn't yet cleared her veins of the chill from her encounter with the one in California, so she had no desire to face another member of the Infortunii anytime soon.

Celeste blinked, returning to the here and now, wondering again why her fellow Gardienne had changed into an evening dress that sparkled like a midnight sky after their long day of travel. Was she going out? Alone? Where was she planning to go? Who was she planning to meet? Celeste's curiosity must have shown, because Anaïs suddenly jumped out of her chair after checking her watch, agitated by the late hour.

"Well, look at that, I've got to go," Anaïs said abruptly. "I've made dinner plans so I can observe that protégé I told you about in her day-to-day life. You can sort yourself out for the evening, can't you, dear? I'm sure you'll be happy to stay in after such a long day on the train."

Celeste took the history book back and hugged it to her chest. "Yes, of course. I'll be fine here by the fire. I still have plenty of reading to do. Besides, I'm sure there's always room service if I get hungry."

"That's the spirit." Anaïs returned to her room with a wink and a wave.

Celeste stared at the door after it closed. Something about the soft click of the latch bolt made her suck in her cheeks and narrow her eyes. Anaïs hadn't shut it in her usual confident pronouncement that she'd exited a room. Instead, the soft close was full of deception. A lie lying in wait. So, was it truly a dinner date? Or something else?

Celeste set her book down, then put her ear to the wall. The door leading to the hallway in Anaïs's room clicked just as softly, as though she'd deliberately sneaked out, and with her went all of Celeste's newly repaired trust.

Celeste backed away, hands on hips. She was in a foreign city, it was dark, possibly dangerous, and she was liable to get lost if she ventured too far from the hotel, but if she didn't leave now, she'd never be able to keep up. So she dimmed the lights, sent a heartbeat SOS to Sebastian to meet her on the street, then shut her own hotel door behind her with a firm click.

Outside, the moon hung suspended between two skyscrapers like a tightrope walker slowly making her way from one building to the other. Or from safety to danger, she thought, depending on her footing. An involuntary shiver tiptoed over her skin at the resemblance to her own possible circumstances. Ahead, she caught a glimpse of Anaïs's glittering silhouette and picked up the pace.

Her sister Gardienne hadn't conjured up a car or called out for a cab. She was walking, which meant she wasn't going far. Certainly not in those shoes. Celeste slid her thumbnail between her bottom teeth as she considered her own shoes. She was still dressed in her travel clothes, minus the bloodstained jacket, but this skulking business required something a little more comfortable and a little less visible. Best to keep her attire simple, dark, and, most importantly, functional. A pair of swishy black trousers, a matching jacket, and some low-heeled Mary Janes would do. She ducked into an alley and used her glamour to change her silk into cotton, then topped her outfit off with a black cloche to cover her hair. When she emerged again, Anaïs was rounding the corner of the next street. The same corner they'd negotiated at top speed while following the boy thief.

Celeste suspected Anaïs might go back to the bookstore without her. But why the party dress? Why the charade of meeting up with a former protégé? Unless she was actually meeting her accomplice? Celeste's eyes teared up as she watched Anaïs duck into the shadows across the street from the shop. Wild scenarios crisscrossed her brain. Was the bookstore clerk her partner in crime? Did the pair plan on celebrating the theft of the elder staff together? Were they going to unite to take over the sisterhood? Or something even more sinister? Why else would she be dressed up and sneaking about?

Celeste clutched her purse and pressed her back to the wall. How had she let herself get mixed up in another predicament with this woman? She'd wanted to believe her earlier, she really did, but then Anaïs had to go and lie to her about where she was going. And now she'd come straight to the shop, the last place they could trace the staff's whereabouts. Come to think of it, perhaps Anaïs hadn't really searched the inside of the shop all that well when they were there earlier. *Just another bald-faced lie.*

Sebastian chittered at her from behind a trash bin as Celeste wondered what to do next. The stoat's stomach was bloated from some city rat he'd dispatched in a stairwell, and now he was having a hard time keeping up while they tailed Anaïs. "For goodness' sake, just get in," she whispered, crouching down to hold her purse open. Ahead, Anaïs still watched and waited from a dark alcove across from the bookshop. Soon Gideon's sleek black form dropped out of the sky to join her. Celeste didn't think the rook had spotted her. His beak and eyes had remained pointed forward and focused on his mistress, so she stayed crouched in the alley. Funny how quickly hiding from Anaïs's rook brought back that old familiar feeling of being spied on in Paris, but it only solidified her resolve to nail the crooked Gardienne to the wall if she turned out to be the thief. Now, she just had to wait and watch to see the truth with her own eyes.

CHAPTER FOUR

Woofle Dust

"Hang back, there's a car slowing down." Anaïs held her arm out to keep Gideon in the shadows behind her while they watched the front of the bookshop. A dim light gave off a smudgy glow in the dirty window, but she couldn't see anyone moving inside. Perhaps she should have invited Celeste along as a second pair of eyes, but she preferred to do this kind of work on her own with her rook companion at her side. She recognized how her skipping out alone at night must've appeared to Celeste. Suspicion had skittered on a trip wire between them, threatening to explode at any moment. One faulty move by either one of them could have lost the sisterhood the elder staff forever. And she simply couldn't let that happen.

Anaïs was rather proud of the plausible excuse that had rushed to her lips when she'd jolted at the vision Gideon had shared with her while she was still in Celeste's company. The boy had left the shop. And he'd been empty-handed. Which meant the staff was still inside the building. And that building was no bookshop. She'd stake her reputation on it, even if it was a bit tarnished at the moment.

The rumble of a car engine grew louder. "It's a roadster," Anaïs whispered. Her rook ruffled his feathers, tickling the back of her arm as she enveloped them in a veil of glamour so as not to be seen by the approaching vehicle. "And look. They're stopping right in front of the shop."

A young man in a dark suit with slicked-back hair sprinted out of the bookstore, hurrying to open the roadster's passenger-side door. A woman in a long black coat with a white fur collar, a glittering diamond headpiece with three feathers sticking up on the side, and a long cigarette holder balanced in her right hand emerged from the vehicle. Her skin shimmered translucent under the moonlight as she slipped past the valet and darted inside the building. The driver stepped out next, straight-backed and lean. He tossed his keys to the man with the slicked-back hair, then slipped him a few dollars before following the woman inside. Both had a jaunty pep in their step, as though they were heading for a party.

"People can see the shop now," Anaïs said as the young valet hit the accelerator on the roadster and drove away. "It was nonexistent to them before, but something's changed." She watched the slick young man park the car two blocks away among a dozen other vehicles on the street, then hop out to return to the shop at a jog. "Look, there's another car coming. I need to get closer, but I think it's best if you stay here and keep watch."

Gideon flew to the roof, while Anaïs crossed the road before the next couple could get out of their car and enter the shop without her. The poor rook was tired and hungry, but she'd reward him well once she emerged with the elder staff. That is, if everything went according to the rough outline of a plan she'd come up with five minutes earlier.

Anaïs's glamour hid her from view as she tagged along with the pair of fur-clad women who'd exited a chauffeured Bugatti Royale. The whiff of money trailed off their skin as they passed by her without notice. Inside, a different man than earlier stood behind the counter, only this fella was wearing a tuxedo. He took no notice of Anaïs as she shadowed the two women, whose stockings had been rolled below their knees, their lips painted red, and their eyes rimmed in black liner to make them appear bigger. But where had all the other people disappeared to?

Aside from the two women, the bookshop was empty of customers. She had her suspicions, but it wasn't until one of the women uttered the magic word that she knew for sure what she was in for.

"Woofle dust!" The woman, already tipsy, giggled at her own outburst.

"Woofle dust?" The other woman nearly fell to her knees with laughter. "Millie, you're already completely zozzled! He'll never let us in now."

"No, I swear, that's what Jack told me to say." Millie looked at the man in the tuxedo. "That's it, right?"

The clerk behind the counter smiled wanly and tilted his head toward the back of the shop, letting them pass. He must have pushed a button somewhere behind his counter because one of the bookshelves along the far wall swung inward to reveal a secret passageway. The smell of cigarettes and booze wafted up as a quick succession of fiery notes played on a trumpet blasted through the corridor.

A hidden speakeasy. Anaïs had suspected as much, but she'd been confused by the veil of magic hiding the store in the daytime. Wasn't the bookshop enough of a disguise? The veil appeared to be removed now, letting anyone and everyone wander in, provided they knew the right code word to get them past the bouncer and through the secret door. She hurried to keep up, slipping through the opening with the tipsy women just before the bookshelf closed behind her.

The corridor they'd entered was dark and smelled of damp concrete, but the music drew the partygoers forward. A staccato beat played a rhythm beneath the horns and bass as the two women practically stumbled down the stairway trying to dance while walking. They giggled all the way down until they passed through a beaded curtain. A string of piano notes sidled up to the melody as Anaïs emerged into the spangled light of a raucous nightclub. It was like being birthed into a seedy underground world of smoke and gin. The band was set up center stage—Black musicians on the instruments, a white woman in a silver gown at the microphone. The music settled as the woman opened her mouth and started singing about packing up her cares and woes.

Anaïs wondered if maybe she should do like the song said and pack it up. There was a strange vibration in the room. Not like the speakeasy she'd visited in California. That one had been full of carefree dancers up to their eyeballs in cheap liquor and expensive cigars. But here there was something skittering just beneath the surface. Something controlled, tense, calculated. People seemed to be having a good time, but it was almost as if they were still acting on their best behavior. A performance? A new place everyone was still getting used to? She thought about leaving again, but her curiosity won out and she decided to see her plan through. Besides, the men were handsome and the night was young.

"Come on, let's sit down and order a drink," Millie said to her bedazzled friend.

Anaïs thought that was a pretty good idea, so she shed her veil while passing behind a Grecian column made of plaster, then grabbed a small table at the back where she could observe the room's different angles. The lights were brightest near the stage, causing black and gray shadows to sink around the people in the audience. A few couples danced under the lights, holding on hip to hip, cheek to cheek, hands sliding ever lower on their partners. A small pang of guilt attempted to perch on Anaïs's heart over Edward, but she batted the feeling away as quickly as it landed. No regrets. Not tonight.

She ordered a gin and tonic, which the waiter brought right away. He hovered a moment, tray in hand, while she deciphered his desire to be paid for the drink. Unlike Celeste's stoat, who'd become quite good at producing bills from whatever bit of fluff resided at the bottom of that purse of hers, Anaïs had to dig around for some small item she could transform herself. She hated to give up her lipstick, but the man did need to be paid, so she changed the tube into a roll of bills and peeled one off to hand to him. The waiter accepted the money, served her a wide grin, and promised he'd check up on her often.

The band shifted into a jauntier number. The trumpeter stood, making his instrument wail like an elephant in heat, loud and lusty. His cheeks puffed until Anaïs was certain he'd pass out cross-eyed, but then he lowered the instrument from his lips and grinned, snapping his fingers with the rhythm of the bass and drums.

While Anaïs tapped her foot, a man in a tuxedo approached her table. His hair was slicked back like all the men's, but unlike the rest his cheekbones were sharp enough to cut glass. If they didn't get the job done, the dark eyes would. He smelled of spicy bay rum and witch hazel as he politely asked if he could join her. Gideon began to object in their shared thoughts, but Anaïs cast his complaint aside with a lift of her chin. She wasn't there to be a shrinking violet, she was there to save the sisterhood from downfall. And if that meant getting chummy with the local flora and fauna to find some answers, so be it. "Yes, of course," she said, hoping her new friend was a talker.

"The name is Anthony," he said, tossing his coattails back to take his seat. "But people call me Tony. What a pleasure to meet a free spirit secure enough in herself to arrive alone. You are alone, I hope? No annoying boyfriend or fiancé lurking around the corner?"

"I'm Ann Marie," she said and extended her hand. "All alone and very thirsty."

"Ann Marie, of course." He nodded, squinting at Anaïs in a curious way that made her regret her choice of pseudonyms. His scrutiny didn't last long as he raised his hand to order a drink from the passing waiter. "And one more for the lady." He removed a few large bills from a slim leather wallet and effortlessly dropped them on the waiter's silver tray to hurry him along. "So, what brings you to the French Drop tonight?"

"The *French* Drop?" The Gardienne could barely hide her amused contempt. Taking a second glance at the place, Anaïs recognized the owner's clumsy attempt at French decor with the additions of lace curtains hung over the false windows, the small bistro tables for two, and a scene painted on the far wall depicting the Moulin Rouge. Such a shabby re-creation. The red paint was more suitable for the side of a barn, and the flashing lights were a touch overboard. Then again, people were mostly there for the booze. But perhaps something else too. The air still hummed with the thrill of peril, as though some threat loomed just behind everyone's shoulders. And she didn't think it was merely the illegality of consuming alcohol in a backward, prudish country. As she understood it, most places paid the police a hefty bribe to look the other way.

"I've been exploring the city," Anaïs said in answer to his question. "Sightseeing. Visiting old friends. Searching for lost souvenirs."

Tony lit a cigarette and peered through the smoke at her. "I'm so curious. How did you learn about this place? Has it gotten so popular that tourists hear about it on the street now?"

Anaïs swirled her gin and winked. "Things were a little obvious from the traffic outside."

The music shifted again to a lively rendition of "Fascinating Rhythm." Anaïs recognized the song immediately, swinging her shoulders to the beat. The tune had become quite popular in the Paris cabarets. Oh, to be back in the city of light, sipping champagne at Le Bal Blomet again, where the jazz ricocheted off the cavernous walls to shoot straight into the hips. She nearly sighed out loud at how much she missed the ambiance of home.

Tony crossed his legs, bouncing his foot to the beat. He leaned back as the waiter arrived and set down the drinks he'd ordered.

"What about you?" Anaïs asked. "Flying solo?" She'd watched for any signs that he was missed from another table, but aside from a few stolen glances and tittering whispers by a gaggle of inebriated blondes across the room, there were none.

"Well, yes and no."

To her consternation, he left it at that and sipped his drink. This one was going to be as tough as a clam to pry open, but her instincts told her he came there often and might just know a thing or two about the owner and why a child might steal a valuable relic and return it to this place. It was just going to take a little time.

Anaïs rested her hand in her chin and decided to read his dreams and desires to get a more thorough temperature of the man who'd singled her out. She took a breath and let down her mental guard ever so slightly. She began by focusing on the hairline at Tony's temple. To her surprise an astonishing golden scaffold of ideas, hopes, and plans began building upward from his most basic wants to his deepest-held aspirations. This one had ambition! He was a climber with big ideas about overseeing, well, everything, though the details of what that entailed grew a little murkier in the shadow of his ego. She was so impressed with his bright dreams she nearly considered taking him on as a protégé. But she wasn't sure what talents and aspirations he possessed other than ambition. Then again, with cheekbones like those, who cared. Maybe she could ship him off to California and get him in the movies.

"Let's dance," she said and downed the rest of her gin.

"Why not." Tony held his hand out to her, and the pair glided onto the dance floor as he signaled the band to play a new song.

The notes of "I'll See You in My Dreams" bounced off the musicians' instruments as Tony wrapped one arm around Anaïs's waist. With his other, he led her around the room, hand in hand, while the music swirled in her ears and the lights glittered in her eyes. For a split second she thought she saw the boy peering at her from behind the band, but just as quickly he was gone. She wanted to stop, to chase after the phantom she'd seen. She had so many questions she needed to ask Tony to get to the truth, but her tongue grew heavy in her mouth, as though it were encased in lead. The paralysis spread from her tongue to her arms to her feet as gravity seized her by the shoulders and pulled. The only reason she hadn't hit the floor was due to the firm arm of a handsome man still gripping her waist. One who'd suddenly lost his smile as she dropped.

Damn. She hated being bested by the handsome ones.

CHAPTER FIVE

The Last Fumes of Hope

Celeste remained in shadow as several cars pulled up and stopped in front of the bookshop. People dressed in party clothes were going inside. But how could they see the shop now when they couldn't before? Why remove the veil only at night? *Ah,* she reasoned, *it must be one of those semisecret American bars that's hidden from the public and the police.* She couldn't see anything unusual through the grimy windows, so somewhere inside there must be another room that couldn't be detected even when one was standing in the middle of the shop. Exactly the sort of place Anaïs would escape to, elder staff or not.

Celeste had just worked up the courage to confront Anaïs about her intentions when the Gardienne darted across the street in her full glamour. The outline of her body shimmered like the northern lights as she slipped inside the door on the heels of two giggling women in fur coats. Sebastian poked his head out of her purse, making a small clicking noise. "Yes, we're at an inflection point," Celeste agreed. "If we follow, we may be walking into a trap. If we do nothing, we may lose the elder staff forever. Not to mention our lives, if her reputation is still a measuring stick to go by."

The stoat stared clear-eyed at the shop, offering a third possibility. A scenario Celeste had barely kept alive on the last fumes of hope that remained. Was it possible Anaïs was acting the part of the hero, returning to the shop to retrieve the staff on her own? "A very foolhardy thing to do," Celeste remarked as she watched the door with growing concern.

Above, on the shop building's roof, barely silhouetted against the night sky, Anaïs's rook shook and cawed. Gideon hadn't gone inside with his mistress. Odd. Was he a lookout instead? And was that agitation in the way he dipped his head and shifted his weight from one foot to the other? Celeste was on the verge of revealing herself to Gideon to get some answers when a long Duesenberg car with black and maroon paint stopped in front of the bookshop. The young valet with the slicked-back hair rushed outside to greet the new arrival, as he had with the others, but this time his eagerness gave way to something resembling fear. He didn't approach the car right away. He stood on the sidewalk with his hands tucked behind his back while he waited for the driver to get out and open the back passenger door for someone.

A man in a long gray coat with a matching homburg stepped out of the car. He carried a black walking stick with a crystal knob that caught the light from the streetlamps. He was tall and muscular, with heavily lidded eyes like a predator's. When he glanced in Celeste's direction, she sucked in a breath and squeezed her body against the wall. She was certain he couldn't see her in the dark, but he struck her as the sort of man you never wanted to be noticed by. Something in his demeanor telegraphed a threat. An expression he wielded like a weapon.

Two more men got out of the back seat, mini versions of the first man in both stature and projected self-importance. One of them opened the passenger-side door, where a young woman emerged wearing a black cloak long out of fashion. A leftover from before the Great War. She pushed the hood back, revealing copper-red hair that she wore in ringlets that had gone out of style with the cloak. It was only when the woman turned to frown at the man in the gray homburg that Celeste saw the baby cradled in her arms.

The valet held the bookstore's door open while the group disappeared inside its murky interior. Celeste was all for letting Anaïs face the consequences for whatever stupid actions she'd taken regarding the elder staff, but something about the man's appearance jabbed her intuition in the ribs. Hard. He wasn't a nice man. In fact, he was a very bad man, judging by the malevolent mist that trailed his aura. Sebastian thought so too, as he shivered inside her bag. She checked in on Gideon to get a reading on the rook's opinion of the newest arrivals, only to find he'd flown off.

Something wasn't right. Despite her earlier suspicions, Celeste didn't like the idea of Anaïs being in the same room with that man. Even Anaïs wouldn't have made an alliance with someone tinged with the gray smoke of macabre crimes she sensed. Like the tumblers on a safe all falling into line so the lock could open, her subconscious recognized the peril Anaïs was in. She hadn't been lying. Not exactly. She'd been trying to salvage the elder staff the entire time, and she'd tried to do it without Celeste. And now Celeste was going to have to save her from her poor decision. That is, if she could figure out how to get inside, sneak past the bouncer, and avoid being detected by the goon in the gray homburg.

CHAPTER SIX

Wisecracks on Ice

Anaïs's tongue fuzzed in her mouth, and her shoulder and hip ached from being pressed up against a cold, hard surface. She opened her eyes a crack. The light cut across her corneas, making her squeeze her eyelids shut again. She tried to speak, to tell whoever was sitting across from her that the light was too bright, but the fuzziness she'd felt turned out to be not a swollen tongue but a piece of wool that had been stuffed in her mouth instead.

"I'm sorry, darling, did you say something?"

Tony. He'd done this. And now he mocked her with pet names. Once her head finally stopped spinning, she'd boil him in his own blood. But first she had to figure out why her body was shivering inside a glass cage only slightly bigger than a phone booth.

"Don't try to move too quickly. I'm told it will only make things worse." Tony adjusted the light, ridding Anaïs of the red glare assaulting her eyelids. "There, is that better? I don't need you to be comfortable, but there's no need to start things off on a sour note."

Anaïs squinted, testing the light again. She saw him clearly now, sitting in a chair with his legs stretched out, his tie undone, taking a bite from an egg sandwich that he held in one hand. They were in a backroom of some kind with crates and boxes, a coffee service on a table, a filing cabinet, and a desk in the corner. She heard music. The band from the club. They were still inside the French Drop. The smell of damp concrete reached her nose as she lifted her head and spit out the wad of wool. "You drugged me," she said. She felt for injury in her nether regions but didn't think anyone had violated her while she was unconscious.

Tony took another bite of his sandwich as he tipped his chair back, balancing it on two legs. "She said it would be the safest way to handle . . . whatever you are."

Anaïs scooted onto her hip. She was in a glass cage with riveted metal on all of the seams and joints. And a metal grate covered the top. Was it bolted down? There was something both familiar and mysterious about the contraption, as though the energy of false magic reverberated off the glass. Intense cold seeped in from somewhere below, making her tremble.

Tony watched her from the other side of the glass with one foot propped against the side. "It's made with reinforced steel. The glass is about an inch thick. The tank holds a few hundred gallons of water when full."

"Keep it around for the goldfish, do you?" Anaïs's head was beginning to clear of the aftereffects of the drug.

Tony laughed. "Water torture test," he said. "Back in our vaudeville days, all of us magicians were trying to equal Houdini's success. It's a damn death trap that almost killed me one night. Who knew it would come in handy again." He pointed her attention to the tank's base, which had been packed in ice within a round metal trough of some kind. "Sorry about the ice, but she told me it was necessary."

How did anyone in this place know about the cold and its effect on her?

"Who is this 'she' you take orders from?" Anaïs asked with a flick of her brow. She'd meant to knock the chair out from under his cocky ass, but the legs only rocked slightly, making him adjust his balance. Her hand reached for the familiar chain around her neck. They'd taken her ruby pendant, despite her enchantments to keep it in place.

Tony put his feet firmly on the floor to look her in the eye. "I don't take orders from any woman."

"Well, she seems to have you skipping to her tune in order to keep me contained. When do I get to meet this commanding woman?"

"You don't seem very concerned about your predicament." He leaned forward so the gun holstered to his chest became visible.

"Why should I be?" she lied. "We both know why I'm here. Let's negotiate and be on our way."

"Yes, let's have that conversation," said a deep voice so void of empathy it nearly sucked the sarcasm right out of Anaïs's mouth.

A tall, clean-shaven man in a gray coat came into view. He was alarmingly muscular with sharp, hawkish eyes that stared out from under heavy, dark brows. There was a near hypnotic quality in the way he gazed at her before removing his homburg and placing it carefully on a hook above the desk.

Tony jumped out of his chair and smoothed down the wrinkles on his tuxedo jacket. "Evening, boss man. Got her put on ice like we agreed."

The tall man brushed Tony aside and took over his chair. He sat straight-backed as he stared at Anaïs through the glass. After a brief assessment he waggled a finger at her and turned to ask someone who remained out of view in the doorway, "You sure this is the one we want?"

There was a pause before a woman replied, "Yes, she's one of the women I saw." A baby fussed, and the woman clucked her tongue to quiet the child.

Anaïs didn't recognize the voice. Who was she? How did she know her? And how the hell had they known to put her on ice? "Look, I don't know who or what you think I am, but you've got the wrong gal. I just came in for a quick drink and to listen to that great band play a few of my favorites." She tried to stop herself, but she sent a scathing glare in Tony's direction anyway.

"Oh, I don't think so," the man said.

The woman finally stepped into view holding the fussy baby in her arms. Long red locks trailed over the hood of a worn-out cloak. She stood behind the man, and together they formed an oddly shaped aura that mystified Anaïs.

"Good work, Tony. Go get Stanley and tell him to bring in the clarinet case."

"Sure thing, boss man." Tony took a last bite of his sandwich, then dumped the rest in the trash can.

The handsome ape left, which Anaïs instantly regretted. While he was clearly a misogynistic villain who got his kicks by drugging single women and locking them up in frozen cages, he somehow exuded the persona of someone she could trust. Or at least reason with. The disparity in her emotions nearly made her head spin as the "boss man" folded his arms to wait for Stanley to show up. What was this all about? They had the elder staff. What did they need to kidnap her for? And why put her on ice? Well, maybe they had good reason for that.

A minute later the boy who'd stolen the elder staff entered the room carrying the clarinet case. Up close, his face was dirty, his clothes soiled and too big for him. The city streets had already taken their toll on the child. He might have been ten years old, but the expression in his eyes put him closer to thirty. He handed the clarinet case to the boss man and smirked at Anaïs. "Just a clarinet," he said, exerting his own brand of expertise. "That's what Broadway Billy said too." He jerked his head toward the source of the music playing, suggesting he'd had one of the musicians give the disguised staff the once-over.

Good luck with that one, kid.

The boss man took the case and laid it on his lap. "I'll be the final judge of that, Stanley." He flipped open the latches and assessed the contents. The clarinet had been disassembled to fit in the case, but the stiff in the gray suit skillfully put the parts together in a matter of moments. "Now, how does it work?" he asked after inspecting all the pieces.

Anaïs wasn't sure if he was asking her or the woman. "You blow hard," she said, unable to pass up the opportunity to wrap an insult inside an innocent reply.

The hawkish eyes turned on Anaïs. Her solar plexus felt a jab as though she'd been psychically punched. *What the hell was that?* She coughed and reeled in her sarcasm as the man stood. He wet a reed, attached it to the mouthpiece, then held the instrument to his lips. His fingers moved against the keys on the clarinet as a low, mournful sound bellowed forth. His effort was sweet and surprisingly melodic. A stark contrast to his heavy-handed entrance. Even the baby thought so, as the child cooed softly to the music.

When he stopped playing, the man held the clarinet out vertically by one hand and asked again in a snakelike hiss, "Now, how does it really work?"

Anaïs's intestines coiled tight. Did he understand what he held in his hands? How could he know about the staff? She wished now she'd stayed with Celeste and her book so she could delve deeper into the history of the sisterhood for a clue as to what this man—this thief!—had in mind. Nevertheless, she had no intention of helping him understand anything he didn't already grasp. "Seems like you did a fair job of making it work already. I don't know why you keep asking me about it. You clearly know how to play."

"She's lying." The woman propped the baby up on her shoulder. "She knows what it is and what it can do."

"There's no need for the charade," the man said. "I understand it's a tool capable of stirring magic, but why is it in the shape of a clarinet?"

"I don't know what you're talking about."

"Is that so?" The man narrowed his eyes, locking his gaze on Anaïs. Some strange magnetic force emanated from his stare that wouldn't allow her to look away. The whites of his eyes grew large and animated, and soon the sensation of ice water penetrated her chest, filling her stomach and veins with frigid cold until she thought she might pass out. "That feeling you're experiencing is the stir of *my* magic." He raised his right hand and pressed it against his throat. She tried to resist, but her hand mimicked his, following a will of its own—or rather *his*—as it gripped her neck, pressing and squeezing until a strangled gurgle emerged from her throat.

What was happening? What sorcery was this? Anaïs wasn't accustomed to feeling vulnerable. *She* doled out the hard facts. *She* controlled the room with wit and magic. But this man had her dancing like a marionette. Tears flooded the rims of her eyes until he let go and she collapsed onto the metal floor of the tank, heaving for breath.

"Keep her locked up on ice until she decides to be useful." The man pulled on a rope, and a black curtain fell from the ceiling to cover the water tank, leaving Anaïs alone in the cold and dark.

CHAPTER SEVEN

The French Drop

Celeste opened her purse to talk to Sebastian. The stoat was a little more alert now that he'd sensed the same possible danger she had. "This place has been cloaked in magic. There's no telling who might see through our glamour. We need to find a back way in. The less we're noticed, the better. Come on."

The stoat crawled out of the handbag and crept across the road, only slightly dragging his full belly. Celeste held her pendant to hide herself from any humdrum mortal eyes that might happen to glance out an upstairs window while she crossed the street. She followed the stoat to the alley, hoping to locate a rear entrance to the nightclub she was certain must exist within the bookshop. Instead, she found Gideon clawing at the bricks in the alley. She sighed at the rook's bedraggled state.

"Has something happened to Anaïs?" Celeste asked. Gideon gave up his pecking and clawing to hop toward her. He bobbed his head, mimicking a broken wing. "Is she hurt?" Again, he nodded, sending Sebastian into a fit of nervous chittering. She cautioned silence with a finger over her lips while she knelt to engage with the rook eye to eye. "Can she see me now? Can she hear me?" The rook shook out his feathers. A firm no.

Music sifted up through the walls ever so faintly. It sounded like it was coming from the basement. There had to be a way in. She suggested Gideon go stand watch atop the fire escape behind them while she walked the length of the alley searching for an opening. If she couldn't find one, she'd have to make one, something that might attract too much attention. But then she came upon an alcove midway down the alley that revealed a steel door with the words DELIVERIES ONLY stenciled in white paint across its face. Celeste gripped her pendant, ready to melt the hinges off, when the door burst open and a man in a tuxedo walked outside, releasing an exasperated breath. He propped the door open with a wooden crate, then leaned his shoulder against the wall while he pulled out a pack of Lucky Strikes. Before he lit his cigarette and sullied the air, she caught a distinct whiff of bay rum and witch hazel on him. A scent made to lure in women, though those cheekbones and brooding eyes alone would have worked on most. Especially Anaïs.

With the door propped open, Celeste was eager to squeeze past Mr. Cheekbones and get inside unnoticed. Vision was the most underdeveloped sense in humans. Their limited eyesight made it easy to fool them with the slightest manipulation of angles of light. Sounds and smells, however, were a little trickier. While the man wouldn't be able to detect the sight of her physical body moving past him, he might still hear her footsteps against the brick or pick up on the disembodied scent of gardenias, which seemed to follow all Gardiennes in their wake.

She waited for him to exhale his cigarette smoke before she made her move. She was halfway through the opening when the man pulled a small object out of his pocket to study. Something that caught the sparkle of city lights through the smoke as he held it up by its chain.

Anaïs's ruby pendant.

"Where did you get that?" She clasped a hand over her mouth, appalled that she'd spoken out loud.

The man turned his head toward her voice. "Who's there?"

Discovered, Celeste squeezed back out of the doorway and threw off her veil of glamour. "I said, where did you get that?"

The man startled and tossed his cigarette away. "Where did you come from?"

Mr. Cheekbones hadn't automatically reached for the gun that was obviously sitting against the left side of his rib cage, so she took it as a positive sign. "That necklace belongs to a friend of mine," she said, pointing at the pendant. "Why do you have it?"

"You know, if we keep answering each other's questions with a question, we're not going to get very far." He closed his fingers around the pendant, chain and all. He passed his other hand over his closed fist in an overly dramatic way by fanning out his fingers, then opened both hands to reveal empty palms. "Have what?"

Celeste was confused. He hadn't hidden the pendant with glamour or she would have seen the shimmer. He hadn't altered the necklace's form to hide it, like they'd done with the elder staff. And he certainly hadn't dropped Anaïs's ruby, so what kind of magic was this that could make a gemstone disappear into thin air? Gideon swooped down from his hiding place on the fire escape on the opposite wall. He, too, it seemed, had been fooled by the trick, but not by the intention. He dived at the man, pecking at his head and shoulders, trying to get his mistress's necklace back.

"What the hell?" The man ducked and raised his arms over his head.

In his effort to defend himself, the pendant dropped out of its hiding place in his sleeve and onto the ground. Sebastian picked up the ruby with his teeth, then ran behind Celeste. The man swatted harder at the rook with his hands, as though genuinely afraid of being ripped to pieces. She supposed she ought to call Gideon off, but part of her completely understood the bird's reaction. It was only after the man finally pulled his gun out, wildly threatening to shoot the rook, that she interceded. "Enough, Gideon. We need him alive to answer some questions."

The rook hopped off and Mr. Cheekbones jumped back a foot, flapping his arms. "He tried to peck my eyes out."

"He likely would have, yes." Celeste bent down to retrieve the pendant from Sebastian's teeth. "You see, he belongs to the woman whose jewelry you stole."

He smoothed his sleeves down but held on to the gun. He slowly raised the barrel, pointing it at Celeste. "Who are you?"

"I'm going to ask one more time." Celeste held up the pendant, letting it dangle on its chain. "Where did you get this?"

"Here we go again, answering a question with a question." The man rolled his eyes. "You do realize I'm pointing a gun at you." He wiped a spot of blood away from his chiseled cheekbone where Gideon had broken the skin. The strangeness of their encounter was beginning to dawn on him. "You don't seem very afraid, if you don't mind me saying so." He looked at the rook, the stoat, and the young woman who didn't cower before him and came to an incomprehensible conclusion. "Ah, you must be the other one."

"Other one?" What did that mean?

"Yeah, the other one." The man looked both ways down the alley, then made a show of putting the revolver away in its holster. He held his palms up in a display meant to show he wouldn't harm her. Celeste wasn't sure she could make the same promise.

"So, it was just some sort of trick," she said, wrapping the pendant's chain around her finger. "Making it disappear like that."

He shrugged. "I'm a magician. It's what we do." He slid a coin out of his pocket, showed it sitting in his palm, then made it disappear in the same manner by swiping one hand over the other. "Name is Tony. *The Great*, in some circles."

"Do you often steal things by making them disappear, Tony the Great?" Celeste knew he hadn't stolen the elder staff himself, but it didn't mean he couldn't have ordered the boy to do it for him.

"Steal? Oh, you mean the necklace." Tony took a step nearer, extending his hand toward the left side of her face. He pulled it away again, revealing the coin held between his fingers as though he'd found it lodged behind her ear. "That was just a bonus, seeing how Frank got to keep the ripe tomato and the other thing for himself."

Other thing?

"She's still in there, you know." Tony eyed the open door before checking the alley again, presumably for stray wanderers. "Your friend *and* the clarinet," he said, dangling the words like bait.

Celeste didn't have to ask if Anaïs was okay. She knew she wasn't, or this man, and whoever this Frank fellow was, wouldn't still be breathing. Which meant Anaïs was either unconscious or being held in a frozen state of suspension somewhere inside. Somewhere cold enough to make sludge out of the magic in her veins. But how did they know about a Gardienne's vulnerability? Or any of the rest of it, for that matter?

Celeste faced a conundrum. She sensed Tony harbored secret motives separate from those of his boss by the way he kept checking over his shoulder to see if he was being watched. He seemed to be a man who hid his ultimate intentions from everyone but himself, but a quick dip into his dreams and desires revealed him for what he was: an opportunist with big ambitions.

She could see in his dreams how he viewed the city. Its streets were defined by grids and boundaries. Territories. The bankers and builders made their "legitimate" money aboveground, but beneath the city, where the bars and gambling halls were semihidden, was where the serious money crossed palms for men like him. And where there was money, there was power, with each lord of a borough or neighborhood scrambling to control more streets and increase the grid he controlled. Tony's dream was to be in the game. Not as a player but as a boss himself. Because money was freedom and his ticket to being rid of whatever was holding him down. He wanted it bad enough he was on the cusp of trusting a stranger with his deepest ambition, as long as it meant getting what he yearned for in the end. Now Celeste had to decide if granting the man his innermost desire was worth the risk of getting what she wanted.

"I can get you inside," Tony said with a glance at the door. The wheels in his head were spinning fast, trying to find the angle that would put her in his debt. "Help you help your friend. That's where you were going, wasn't it?"

"I can get in by myself."

"You won't get far. Not without me." His eyes glittered in the dark as he looked her over. "I don't know who or what you two are exactly, but that man inside who has your friend is willing to kill and worse to get what he wants. He's gone to great effort to get his hands on a very special object. One that he thinks is worth its weight in gold. Something he believes can make him a very rich man. Only he hasn't got a clue how it works, which is the only reason your friend is still breathing. Got any ideas about that?"

"The clarinet." Celeste wasn't willing to give anything away yet, but her heart contracted at hearing the situation was even more precarious than she'd feared.

Tony nodded. "I'd hate to see you face the same fate if you were to get caught going in there by yourself. But that doesn't have to happen. Not if you listen to me."

The man had criminal leanings, certainly, but he didn't have the heart of a killer. Money was his main motivator, whether it was earned legally or otherwise. But it was more than greed. It was expressly tied to his freedom. That much she deduced from the bridge of dreams and schemes he'd built for himself. So perhaps there was a deal to be made.

First, Celeste needed to draw a little truth out of him. "Why aren't you taking me to your boss? I mean, if he's so desperate to understand what it is he stole, seems he'd be very appreciative if you were to deliver the 'other one' to him at gunpoint."

"He would, but I'm thinking there might be another way that works for both of us." Tony tilted his face so the streetlamp at the end of the alley cast his face in half light and half shadow. "Show me who you are, who you *really* are, and I'll get you inside without raising any questions." He spread his palms open in a gesture of offering. "After all, I showed my magic to you."

Celeste was momentarily taken aback by his request. "I'm not a magician. I don't do tricks for people."

He put his hand on his chest where the gun bulged through his jacket. "We can do it the other way, if you prefer." He held the door open wide for her to walk through. "I just need to be certain you really are who they say you are before I risk my neck."

An intense objective wrapped in a dream lifted off him. The ambition was tangible enough Celeste nearly reached up to catch it in her hands. For a moment she considered evaluating him as a potential protégé. But no. There was something amiss. Sebastian thought so too, as his back arched in protest. And she had to wonder again how this man knew anything about her or Anaïs. No, not protégé material, but perhaps a way inside, as he'd said.

"Very well." Making the calculation the magician could handle the truth, she veiled herself with glamour and shimmered out of sight. She supposed the slight gasp that escaped his throat was worth the humiliation of having to reveal her magical credentials in such a crude manner, but if it got her inside unnoticed, got Anaïs and the elder staff safely out, then it would be worth the price.

CHAPTER EIGHT

Delusions of Grandeur

This couldn't be happening again. Anaïs had lost the feeling in her fingers and toes from the frozen lake surrounding the glass cage, but at least she was still conscious. She supposed they could have tried to keep her drugged. That would have really put a damper on things. But as long as she could stay awake and keep her mind occupied, she didn't think she'd succumb fully to the effect of the cold on her Gardienne blood.

Anaïs's eyes fluttered closed briefly, but she didn't feel any desperate need to lie down in the corner. Not yet anyway. Of course, she hadn't remotely considered that anyone in New York City, let alone anyone inside a dingy underground club, would have had knowledge about the effect of extreme cold on her kind. While her mind wrestled with how to get out of this mess, the insidious voice inside her head that insisted she survive this fiasco also kept suggesting the easiest way to do that would be to give up what she knew about the elder staff. Let the man have it. See how the alder wood might respond in his hands. But her loyalty to the Gardiennes roared back. She would rather die than betray the sisterhood by giving that man access to a piece of their magical heritage.

At the thought of magic, Anaïs's stomach clenched, remembering the gut punch the boss man had given her with a mere thought cast in her direction. But how had he done it? How had he made her feel ice water drain through her veins and lungs? She shivered at the recollection and pulled her legs up, hugging them with her arms to conserve body heat.

While the jazz musicians kept the party going on the other side of the door, Anaïs played a game to stay awake. She had to ask herself a question she didn't know the answer to, but she had to respond no matter what. First up: Who was the creep in the homburg? Sherlock Holmes wasn't the only one who could make deductions, so what could she glean from his appearance? The hat was well made. The crown was perfectly molded, and the brim had just the right curl. Both the coat and hat had been personally tailored, which meant he was a man of means, however ill-gotten. Oh, yes, he was a criminal, but not just any criminal. He ran the operation. Men—hired guns—did his bidding out of fear. And criminal bosses were always looking for leverage they could use to get more. Always more. Greed had glinted in his eyes when he'd played the clarinet hoping for a preconceived outcome that would have given him the key to more power. Yes, such disappointment in his eyes when all that came out of the instrument was a few fluttering notes.

Second question: What kind of illicit enterprise was the man involved with, aside from the speakeasy, and where did his magic come from? Anaïs had to make a bargain with herself that two-parters were allowed in the game. Because she had to know the answer to the second part to fully understand the first. The sorcerers and occultists she'd mingled with in her youth had all dipped a toe in the murky criminal waters at one time or another. There'd always been the temptation to go to the gambling halls and win a game of chance by securing the outcome with a little spell or concoction. But rarely did she witness magical folk parlay their talents into a full-time career of crime. There was generally no need to do things the hard way when one could conjure whatever they coveted. So why did this man put himself at such risk?

No, she had to come up with an answer, not ask another question. That was the deal. Anaïs forced her eyes open. There was a small crack in the curtain covering her cage that let in a ray of light. Her eyes had adjusted to the darkness so that the thin beam was enough to provide a layer of incandescence equal to a candle. She leaned her back against the glass and looked up as the outline of the box's grated ceiling came into focus. She stared at the bars, trying to recall when or if she'd ever seen anyone use just their eyes to manipulate energy. For a Gardienne, it was a natural extension of their powers. But a mortal man? She'd only ever witnessed the *impression* of manipulated energy when a common conjurer was doing the wielding. Magician's work. But it wasn't real.

It wasn't real!

Anaïs's mouth fell open. "The grifting tomcat hypnotized me. He never punched me at all." She stood up so quickly at the revelation, she made herself dizzy enough to stumble into the glass. She rubbed a sore spot on her shoulder as she heard a thump outside. Someone turned a crank, lifting the curtain up, letting in light and a gush of warm air. Anaïs inhaled deeply, hoping to thaw a vein long enough to manipulate a little energy of her own. Barely a spark generated off her finger. Just a little more heat and light was all she needed.

Standing outside the tank was the red-haired woman, who would have been the subject of question number three, had Anaïs not had her epiphany when she did. She supposed she could still play the game and answer at least in part who the redhead was, while the woman set the child down on the floor to remove her cloak. The boss's woman? No, not in those hand-me-down clothes. A business partner? More of a subordinate, if she was involved with the club at all.

Then Anaïs hit on another possibility. They knew about magic. They knew about the elder staff, at least partially. So could she be a sorceress of some kind? *Yes, of course.* Anaïs leaned even stronger toward the last possibility when she got an up-close look at the woman's green eyes while she stood on a footstool to lower a glass of water inside the tank. Those eyes, with their uncanny luminescence, held in them the power to see into another world.

"You shouldn't be so stubborn," the woman said, after Anaïs accepted the water. "He'll get the answers he wants out of you eventually. It doesn't have to be painful."

Anaïs swirled the water in the glass and took a sniff. "Did he send you here to soften me up?"

The woman smiled. "Yes, but it was my idea." She watched Anaïs refuse to drink. "It isn't poisoned, you know."

"You don't mind if I hold on to my skepticism a little longer. After all, you people did drug me once already."

The woman sat in the chair opposite the glass tank. "Tony did, yes. But it was the safest way to get you in here. We just told the audience that you'd fainted and would be right as rain with a little rest."

"Tony." Anaïs regretted the handsome man in the tuxedo was part of this. His charm hadn't been manufactured. They could have had some real fun, if he hadn't doped her drink and swept her off the dance floor like a cat in a burlap sack. She shivered and rubbed her shoulders. "I don't suppose I could borrow that cloak of yours."

"Afraid not." The woman peered at her. "Why does the cold affect your abilities the way it does?"

They don't know? This was getting confusing. They understood how to subdue her magic with cold yet didn't know why it worked?

The woman stood. "Perhaps we need to establish a stronger level of trust before you decide to open up."

Anaïs scoffed. "Sure, that will make all the difference."

"How about something warm to drink instead of water?"

The woman disappeared from Anaïs's sight for a moment while the baby sat on a blanket slobbering on a saltine cracker. When she returned, she exchanged the glass of water for a cup of warm, black liquid that smelled faintly of chicory. "Even if you don't drink it, you can warm your hands with it," she said, then picked up her baby and held the child on her lap as she sat again. "I'm Nellie, by the way, and this is Hazel." She waved the baby's hand at Anaïs. "She turns one year old tomorrow."

The simple gesture of the baby waving at Anaïs struck a match of instinct inside her. A wary sense of déjà vu she couldn't yet explain. If only she could get her blood warmed up, she might be able to think straight again, so she did as the woman said and cupped the mug in her hands, though she only pretended to take a sip. Hmm, maybe she did need to open up a little. Perhaps an establishment of trust could work both ways. "It's a matter of viscosity," she said. "My 'abilities,' as you call them, require a higher level of friction in the blood than I'm experiencing right now to flow properly."

Nellie nodded. "And how did you come about this ability, if you don't mind my asking? It's just that I'm so curious to know more."

The sentiment emanating off the woman felt genuine, as the baby cooed and smiled in her arms. "First, a question for you," Anaïs said, still hugging her cup, which, along with the semistale air from the room, was helping to thaw her magic. "We've never met. We've never crossed paths that I can recall. So how could you know anything about me?"

Nellie pressed her lips together, and her eyes flattened in sullenness as though anticipating predictable criticism. "Let's just say I see things."

Anaïs had surmised as much. "You're clairvoyant. That's how you knew to grab me in the club. You knew who I was, and I presume you knew I was coming."

Nellie gave a curt nod. She wasn't used to being accepted for her gift. Cynics and skeptics had seemingly already worn her down. "My spiritual guides showed me both you and your companion arriving in the city. I knew to expect you."

So they knew about Celeste too. Had she been compromised? Was she still safe? "Where is my friend?"

"That, I don't know. I only foresaw the pair of you arriving by train. You brought something with you. Something"—her eyes tensed for a moment, as her mind was seemingly transported to another world behind them—"miraculous."

Was that what she'd told the boss goon? That they carried a miracle? Anaïs kept the give-and-take going with a nod. "But if you can see such things, why do you need me to tell you about the—"

She stopped herself. Maybe they didn't know as much as they thought about the apparent miracle, so best not to give away too much.

"The clarinet?" Nellie's brow pinched together as though it were a sore subject. "It was an odd choice to use for camouflage, wasn't it? I could barely keep from laughing when he began playing the instrument, thinking something magical would happen."

The conversation was getting a little chummier. "Oh, I don't know. I thought he was quite good." Anaïs pretended to take another sip of coffee.

Nellie smirked, revealing so much more than just her taste in music. *She wasn't his.* Not by choice anyway. Not with the ridicule that had nestled so obviously in the expression. So what was her role in all this?

"Nellie, what's going on here?" Anaïs leaned closer to the glass. "You and the baby aren't part of this place. Why are you helping the boss man?"

Nellie wrapped her arms around her child and kissed the top of her head as tears welled in her eyes. "It's all part of the designs and schemes of the heavens," she said. "He gets what he wants, and you get what you want . . . eventually."

Nellie's response left her baffled. Anaïs had made a calculated guess about the woman's abilities and her part in the heist. She'd suspected she was a psychic for hire who'd had a vision she'd sold to a gangster, hoping to make easy money by telling him how to steal a "miracle." Or maybe Nellie had been coerced by threats, like she'd been, to give up her visions. But she didn't expect to be caught up in the woman's delusions of grandeur. Did Nellie believe there was more going on than just the heist of an ancient magical relic? That could complicate matters more than she liked to think.

The door to the office opened. A rush of fresh music and cigar smoke trailed in behind the boss. Anaïs didn't know for sure how long she'd been held in the office, but the party was still going in the French Drop. She almost laughed at how absurd the name of the place was. As a Gardienne, she'd certainly been dropped. Right in the crapper.

"So, is our guest *warming up* to us yet?" the boss man asked. He'd changed clothes, trading his suit and homburg for a tuxedo and top hat. Kohl liner rimmed his eyes, showing off a slight shimmer at play in his irises. It also showed Anaïs his true identity as an entertainer.

Nellie stood with her child. “She’s very determined to be free, as you might expect.”

Anaïs sat down, hiding the warm mug of chicory coffee behind her. She could almost feel the life coming back into her hands. The magic in her veins had loosened up. There was nearly enough there to spark a little mischief. On the other hand, her backside was already feeling the sting from sitting on the tank’s frozen floor again.

“You’re just a common vaudeville mesmerizer,” Anaïs said, taking in his tuxedoed appearance. “One of those cabaret performers who makes some poor sap in the audience cluck like a chicken for laughs.”

Nellie gave her a nearly imperceptible shake of the head before receding to the back of the room with her daughter.

“Common, am I?” He gestured to the surroundings. “I’d say I’ve done all right for myself, opening this place. But, of course, who would say no to a bigger piece of the pie, if the world was offering?” He reached under the desk and withdrew the clarinet case. “Now, where were we.”

Anaïs nearly kicked herself for not noticing the case earlier. Could she have used the small spark she’d hoarded in her palms to force the lock on the top and make a run for it when it was just her and Nellie? Too late now, so she slid one hand back around the mug of coffee to keep it warm. She wouldn’t be able to hold off the brute’s attempts to know more for long, not while she was packed on ice. Something had to give. She hoped it was the lock on her cage. “I believe you were about to impress me with another demonstration of the clarinet lessons your mother made you take when you were ten years old.”

A size 12 oxford sole smashed against the cage’s glass. Anaïs scooted back to keep clear just in case the glass wasn’t as thick as Tony had suggested, mindful not to upset the hidden mug of coffee.

The baby cried at the sudden outburst, so Nellie collected her things and headed for the door. “Be careful, Frank.”

“So, is it Frank the Magnificent? Frank the Mystical Magical Man? Or maybe Frank the Madman Misogynist who likes to lock women up in cages. A mesmerist ought to have a good stage name, after all.”

"You think you're very clever, don't you." The office door clicked shut behind Nellie, and it was just the two of them. "It might be a good time to let you know I'm clever too. How's your stomach feeling, by the way?"

Anaïs took the reminder as a warning and held her tongue.

"Now, let's try this again." Frank leaned forward with his strangely hypnotic eyes peering into Anaïs's until she wasn't sure she could look away of her own free will. "Nellie says you're some kind of witch. That you can do things. That this"—he took the pieces of the clarinet out of the case to put them together, breaking their gaze—"works like some kind of magic wand. Now, just so happens I could use a gadget like that. See, you might think I'm a common entertainer, but people from all over the world come to me for my services. Wanting help bringing their wildest dreams to life."

Anaïs felt an itch at the back of her brain, some tidbit of information she'd been carrying around for years but never had any need to think of again. Until now.

"Because I'm the man that can make those dreams come true," he said, tapping his temple. "Get paid pretty good for it too. 'Go see the dream merchant,' they say. 'He'll make you feel like a kid again.' Or a king. Or tyrant. Believe me, I've seen it all. But I can't help wondering what more I could do with this." Frank hefted the reassembled clarinet in his hand as though it were a baton instead of a musical instrument, waving it around. "See, this feels like it might be a shortcut to getting an even bigger payday. If it does what Nellie says it can."

This guy? This bull in a tuxedo was the man who could transform people's dreams into reality for them? Anaïs had heard rumors there was such a person floating around in New York, but she'd never known anyone who could personally vouch for his existence. No one was ever too eager to talk about his talent in the open. Mortification seemed to work like glue to keep their lips sealed tight, since it was rumored the dreamwork often involved delving into a client's sexual fantasies. Little peccadilloes that could prove embarrassing. So, this hypnotism thing wasn't just a trick he'd mastered. He really did have an ability to get inside her psyche and fiddle with the knobs and wires.

"You're a dream auger," Anaïs said. "You offer people the chance to experience their dreams in real life. Feel as though they've actually lived their dreams. And for a hefty price, I imagine."

"The steeper the better." Frank tapped his fingers on the clarinet keys. "That's why this trinket of yours caught my attention. Nellie says it has something to do with dreams. Desires. Now, that sounds like something that might just be happier in my hands. So one more time, sweetheart. How do I make this thing work?"

Knowing he wasn't just a dullard human changed the game. "For starters, it's not what you think it is. The clarinet belongs to a friend. The leader of a group I'm a part of. She's the one who makes it sing, not me, so I'm not entirely sure how to play it the way you want."

"You're lying. You don't play it at all. Nellie saw more. There's something else here. You've reshaped it somehow."

Yes, Nellie. She'd like to know more about her and that baby. Something there wasn't right. This relationship she had with Frank wasn't right. The dynamics were oddly imbalanced, even though she seemed to be the one with all the insight. But how much did the clairvoyant truly know? There seemed to be gaps in the woman's understanding of the situation. The trick was to take advantage of those weaknesses by matching their ignorance.

"Then it's beyond my understanding," Anaïs said. "Afraid you'll have to keep supplementing your lifestyle by working as a mesmerist and bartender until you figure it out."

The reaction came swiftly as Frank's psychic energy penetrated the glass. A heavy cold descended on Anaïs until she felt like her body was encased in ice. She couldn't move, couldn't speak. The ice filled her mind and froze her thoughts. The assault stung for only a second before her eyes rolled up in her head and things went dark.

CHAPTER NINE

The Disappearing Woman

"How did you do that?"

Tony blinked repeatedly as he slowly stared back and forth between Celeste and the wall behind her. Not with the awestruck manner of someone witnessing Fée magic for the first time, but with the curiosity of a man who needed to know how the trick worked. She'd thrown off her glamour and now stood in full view before him again, but he kept checking the wall, going so far as to run his hand over the bricks in search of some hidden doorway she'd escaped inside. As if her magic were limited by the physical constraints of his profession as Tony the Great.

"Is that the sort of trick you were expecting?" she asked, hoping for the help he'd offered earlier.

"Uh, yeah, that'll work." He gave his head a quick shake to snap out of whatever thought process kept looping through his head. "So, this thing Frank has gotten his hands on is real? Not just some prop?"

"Real and very old." Celeste made sure to stand toe to toe against the man and his gun. "And I plan on getting it back." Tony retreated a step, as though he wasn't certain what she was capable of anymore.

"But if we're going to trust each other, you better tell me exactly what it is you expect to gain from this partnership."

Celeste lowered her defenses just enough to dip into his aspirations again so she could hold them up against the words coming out of his mouth.

"Frank is the one who told me to kidnap your friend." Before Celeste could open her mouth to object, Tony held his hands up in surrender. "I know, I know. Thing is, there's something different about Frank you ought to know." He tapped his temple with his finger. "And I don't just mean up here." A door rattled deep inside the darkened hallway, making him pause. The noise distracted him, putting him on edge, as though the sooner he could get out of the alley with her, the better. "He can do things other mesmerists can't. He does this thing with his eyes."

"His eyes?" Celeste was intrigued.

"He can make you feel things. See things. It's uncanny." Tony looked over his shoulder and stared down the alley, only this time Celeste noted a small shiver travel underneath his collar. His demeanor changed, morphing into something that reminded her of a caged animal that yearned for the freedom of the open meadow underfoot. "Anyway, enough talk. If you want to see your friend alive again, your best chance is with me."

"You still haven't told me what you want."

"What do I want?" Tony's face hardened, aligning with the framework of aspirations Celeste was sensing. "I get your help gouging out the man's eyes so he can't manipulate anyone else ever again, that's what I want."

Celeste wasn't sure if he meant the threat against the man literally or not. For now, she didn't care. She just needed to get inside the club, find Anaïs, and retrieve the staff so she could end this nightmare and maybe, just maybe, find a way to return to the sunny shores of California someday. Besides, Tony was being straight with her, and that was enough to extend a little probationary trust.

"Agreed." Celeste held a finger over her lips to warn Gideon to hold his fury until she returned with his mistress. They could decide later which side everyone was really on. "Let's go."

"Just one more thing." Tony lowered his voice. "I need you to follow my lead in there. No matter how strange or uncomfortable things might get."

Uncomfortable? Something told her this wasn't going to be as simple as it had sounded a minute ago. Celeste nodded, but she called for Sebastian to jump into her purse.

The delivery door led to a brick-lined hallway that reeked of damp wood and coal dust. A single overhead bulb held in a wire cage lit their way as Tony led Celeste through a mazelike intersection of interconnecting hallways lined with narrow wooden doors. The third door down on their left, they passed a young woman in tights and a tutu. She wore a silver headdress with an array of stars radiating around her head like a halo. The makeup around her eyes had been drawn on in exaggerated lines that gave her an otherworldly aura up close.

"Hey, Tony, boss man is looking for you." The woman nodded toward Celeste. "Who's this?" She looked Celeste up and down as though she were a new species of rat that had invaded the city. "You bringing another new act on?"

"Could be," Tony replied in a sparring voice. "Place could maybe use some new blood around here."

"Oh, I don't know. I never get tired of your old tricks." She winked at Tony before disappearing into her dressing room. She left the door invitingly ajar, but Tony pushed past until they came to a room at the end of the hall near a stairwell.

"You're in here," he said to Celeste.

"In here for what?" On the other side of the threshold was a dingy room with peeling floral wallpaper and yellow water stains on the ceiling. There was a rack of feathered costumes hung on a bar suspended from the rotting beam and a vanity with a mirror that had six light bulbs embedded in the frame. Only five of the vanity lights worked, leaving the sixth to stand out like a missing tooth. The place reeked of mildew and cheap perfume.

Tony sorted through the rack of costumes, sliding hangers aside until he hit on something he liked. "This'll do." He shoved the costume at her and pointed to a screen where she could go change. "When you're done putting it on, meet me at the top of the steps."

"You want me to wear this?" While Celeste complained, Sebastian scampered out of her purse to investigate an interesting hole behind the baseboards the minute Tony headed for the hallway.

"No matter how uncomfortable," he reminded her. "And don't forget the headdress." He ducked out with a smug smile on his face just before closing the door.

"Uncomfortable" didn't describe it. The low-cut costume revealed more than the most risqué bathing suit Celeste had seen on display at the Côte des Basques. She shook her head at the gold glitter and sequins on the leotard, the dark fishnet stockings, and the spaghetti-thin straps that held it all up. "Maybe we can do a quick alteration," she said to Sebastian, thinking of the costume department at West Coast Studios in Hollywood. "What would Rose do?"

The stoat pulled his head and whiskers out of the hole in the wall at the mention of their first protégé. He circled Celeste, prancing with his back arched, until the glittery costume hung on her frame in a swell of glamour. The sequins had been swapped out for expensive gold beading and the useless wet-noodle straps widened by adding decorative cap sleeves over the shoulders. A short gold skirt had been attached to the bottom of the leotard. Only a modest improvement, but she'd take what she could get. Now the only question was why Tony had insisted she put on the ridiculous costume in the first place.

Feeling somewhat self-conscious, Celeste kept her arms folded over her middle when she met Tony at the top of the stairs. "Why am I wearing this, and where's Anaïs?" She assumed she'd been gussied up in glitter to blend in with the array of female performers hurrying up and down the staircase in a blur of feathers and sequins, but after seeing the wicked grin spread across his face, she wasn't so sure.

"You'll see." Tony led her down the stairs in hurried steps. "Nice gams, by the way."

Live jazz reverberated in the narrow hallway, full of screaming trumpets, deep bass thumps, and hot snaps on the snare drum. Heat rose off the bodies of the performers who passed them going up on the stairs. Everyone in the place seemed to move in a rush, with their makeup dripping and armpits sweating. At the bottom of the steps, Celeste got a glimpse of what looked like a stage positioned in front of a room full of cocktail tables, where people in silver gowns and black tuxedos slurped brown concoctions from crystal coupe glasses. She didn't know which had lit up the audience's eyes more, the stage lights or the bootleg booze, but everyone's face practically glowed.

Celeste was still getting her bearings backstage when Tony spun around and leaned close. "Don't look, but there's a door to my right that says 'Private.' That's where your friend is." Celeste tried to push past, but he caught her by the shoulders. "Not yet," he said. "Not while the place is hopping."

Celeste blew a drifting feather from her headband out of her face. "But you said you'd get me in."

"And I have. But if you want to stay alive, you'll plant your feet right where you are and not move. Not one inch, not even when I get you a glimpse of your friend. You stay right here. Promise?"

Celeste moaned internally. If she made a promise, she had to keep it. "All right. But see if she's okay. Will you do that?"

Tony nodded, then knocked on the door. The man she'd seen out front, the one with the brooding eyes and heavy brows, sat in a chair with his arms crossed. He waved Tony in, as though waiting for his help in solving a conundrum. Celeste didn't have to wonder what the man's problem was. Anaïs sat slumped on her side inside a peculiar glass box like a fish in a drained aquarium. A band around the top was painted red with gold flourishes, tigers, waterfalls, and palm leaves. In the center of the exotic panorama, it read Tony the Great in bold swirling letters that now hung over Anaïs's head.

For a split second, Celeste nearly followed her instinct to barge into the office and flash-blind both men with a pulse of light from her palm. But she'd given her word, and Fées Gardiennes were bound by their promises. Besides, she still didn't know where the elder staff was or who actually had it in their possession. She didn't even know if it was still on the premises, but she surmised it must be if Anaïs was still being held alive. "Of course, just because I gave my word doesn't mean you are required to abide by the same promise," she whispered to Sebastian, who'd nestled inside her headdress à la Dorée's mouse, Bastian, who used to curl up inside the elder Gardienne's hair to nap. The stoat tumbled off her head and chased after Tony before the door slammed shut, leaving her to fend for herself in the bustle of backstage activity.

While left on her own, Celeste marveled at how much nightlife was tucked away underground and out of sight of the world above. It had to be close to midnight, yet the club was full of young people ready to leap out of their chairs to dance the Charleston the moment the music began to play loud and sassy. Celeste felt the urge too, subtly sliding her feet to the tune backstage. In contrast to the carefree jazzy gyrations of the couples on the dance floor, a pockmarked man, holding a clipboard and smoking a cigar, paced back and forth behind the scenes, threatening to blow his top if his next act didn't line up to take the stage.

Tony emerged from the private office holding a top hat and wearing a pair of white gloves. His cheekbones were even more pronounced than before as he lifted his head to search the area. "Ready, Felix," he called with a wave to the cigar-smoking grump. "Now, if my lovely new assistant will just follow me this way." He hooked his arm around Celeste's elbow and led her to a platform containing a table with props on it. There was also a box similar to the one inside the office, only this one was tall and narrow and made of wood. Just the right size to fit a flummoxed Fée Gardienne who was out of her element.

"Assistant?" Celeste tried to resist, putting the brakes on with her feet. "You want me to go out there? Dressed like this?"

"Would you rather end up in a box like your friend?" He shook his head and whispered, "She's fine. Still breathing, anyway, and apparently not talking. Now just follow my lead and smile and we'll get through this just fine. Oh, and Frank is still in there, but he always comes out to catch my act. If you see him lurking, try not to look him in the eyes."

The pair hopped on the platform. As soon as "The Charleston" ended and the dancers took their seats, they were wheeled out onto the stage while the band played a little introduction music. Tony had his routine down. He ran through a standard catalog of tricks. He opened his performance by asking an audience member to pick a card, which he guessed after sorting through the deck. Celeste wasn't sure how he did it, but she was certain it didn't actually involve magic. Next, he made a woman's watch disappear and then reappear just as he'd done with Anaïs's pendant. Then he made the audience gasp as he tore up a twenty-dollar bill belonging to a cynical man in the front row. The man watched with his arms crossed, then nearly rolled out of his seat laughing when Tony restored the bill perfectly after dipping it in his glass of champagne. All the while Celeste followed the magician's instructions by smiling and gesturing to the props he picked up. Halfway through the act she'd actually begun to enjoy herself after hearing the audience cheer for Tony the Great. The lights and laughter were intoxicating.

And then it was time for the finale.

Tony wheeled the narrow box front and center on the stage and announced he would now make his assistant disappear. While Celeste dutifully stepped inside the box, waving goodbye to the crowd, he took the opportunity to give her one final instruction. "I'm going to spin you around three times. When you hear me say the word 'voilà,' do that disappearing trick of yours again before I open the box. I'll spin you around one final time, open the box to show the audience you're back, and then we'll take our bow and get your friend out of here."

It sounded so simple. But then out of the corner of her eye, Celeste spotted the man with the brooding eyes standing in the wings watching the show. Eyes that bored straight into her just before the box was shut. He had his hat and coat in his hands. Was he leaving? Just getting some fresh air? Celeste felt the box spin, so she braced her hands against the sides. Was the brute coming back? She nearly missed her cue thinking about what he might have done to Anaïs, but the "voilà" registered and she went full shimmer. When Tony opened the box, the audience let out a collective "ooh" at her disappearance. The thrill of hearing their reaction was almost enough to make her stay until the end of the trick. But before he could close up the box again for the big reveal, she jumped out, making a bet she could get to the door marked Private before Tony or Mr. Brooding Eyes knew she was there.

CHAPTER TEN

Spiked Drinks and Chilled Blood

Anaïs rubbed a sore spot on the back of her head from where she'd hit it when she'd briefly passed out. Her blood had thawed again, but if the situation didn't get sorted out soon, she was going to go full loony. She stretched her legs out and straightened the stocking on her right leg. She was about to fix the other when a furry face peered at her through the glass, whiskers twitching.

"Well hello, you." Sebastian circled the tank, sniffing the rivets and the seams as though trying to sort out a way to get it open. When he got behind her, he saw the mug of chicory coffee that she'd been keeping perpetually warm ever since she got her spark back. "My little secret," she said and winked.

The stoat had to have been sent by Celeste. Which meant the pair had followed her back to the bookshop. Sneaky. "Let me guess," Anaïs said to Sebastian. "She still thinks I had something to do with stealing the elder staff." She shook her head at the absurdity. "Listen, you didn't see which way that big, tall brute went, did you? I'm about to float away in here if I don't sneak out to the little girls' room."

The stoat tossed his head toward the main room just as a group gasp rose up from the club audience. Applause broke out again. The decibel level swelled just before the door opened and shut quickly.

"I thought you might not be far behind," Anaïs said when a bedazzled Celeste entered in full glamour. "Glad to see you dressed for the occasion. What have you been doing? Getting shot from a cannon?"

Celeste glanced down at her costume as though she'd forgotten she was wearing it. "Glad to see you're not dead," she said in response. She added a harrumph as she put her hands on her hips and traced the glass tank with her eyes. "How did this happen?"

Anaïs tossed a hand at her. "Oh, you know, a spiked drink, a little ice to chill the blood."

"You seem remarkably calm, considering you're locked in a glorified icebox."

"And you're still shimmering inside that costume." Anaïs sat up, eager to learn more. "Don't tell me that was you who caused all that gasping and clapping out there." She looked Celeste over again. "Did you go full glamour in front of an audience?"

"I'm in disguise," Celeste said, showing off the beaded leotard. "I was told it was the only way to sneak inside and save you from that Neanderthal who just walked out of here." She steadied her stance and held her sapphire pendant. "Now slide back while I get you out."

"Not on your life!" Anaïs dropped the smart-aleck attitude. "I'm staying put right here."

"What?" Celeste tested the thickness of the glass by tapping against it with her knuckles. "Why?"

"Listen, there's something going on. Something big. I can't quite figure it out yet, but that man who just walked out of here is real trouble. For you, for me, and certainly for everybody else."

"What kind of trouble? I mean, besides the fact that we allowed the elder staff to be stolen right out from under us in a foreign country."

"That's the thing. I don't know yet, but I need to find out. My gut tells me it's important." Anaïs scooted closer to the glass. "Look, don't worry about me. They thought they knew what they were doing, keeping me on ice, but honestly, it's not nearly cold enough anymore. They actually offered me a hot cup of coffee." She produced the steaming cup proudly. "Been keeping a spark alive for when I need it."

"That reminds me." Celeste reached in her bodice and pulled out a ruby pendant. "Here, thought you might like this back." She handed the necklace off to Sebastian, who scrambled up the side of the tank and dropped it through the bars into Anaïs's hand.

"A snake in a tuxedo knocked me out and stole it when he dropped me inside this thing." Anaïs hung the pendant around her neck and raised her left eyebrow. The glass on the tank wiggled like a sheet of gelatin. "There, see, I can get out anytime I want, but I don't want them to know that." She transformed the glass back to the way it had been.

"Well, what am I supposed to do, just leave you here? How do I know you'll—"

Anaïs raised her brow again. "Not run off with the elder staff?"

"I meant how do I know you'll be all right." Celeste used her own pendant to change out of her costume and transform into an all-black outfit. The perfect getup for spying on people in the middle of the night.

"I *promise* that's not my intention." Anaïs crossed her heart, then assured Celeste she'd be fine on her own. "I've dealt with his type before. Good tail, by the way. I didn't even see you following me." Anaïs sat up straighter when the truth hit her full in the face. "Hey, neither did Gideon. How'd you do that?"

"You must both be getting slow in your old age," Celeste said as she winked at her stoat. "Just so you know, Gideon is waiting for you outside, ready to tear Tony to shreds if he doesn't produce you soon."

"Tony? The guy with the knockout drug? How do you know about him already?"

"We met in the alley on my way in to rescue you." Celeste paused while the audience groaned. Loudly. "He promised to get me in the back way so I could rescue you without getting shot."

"Out of the goodness of his heart?" Anaïs didn't think so. "You struck a deal. So what did he want in exchange?"

"Oh, he just wants me to put out his boss's eyes." Celeste scooped up Sebastian. "Says he has some kind of ability to make people see and do things."

"The guy is a dream auger, Celeste." Anaïs didn't know if the newly minted Gardienne understood, but the way she hugged her stoat a little closer suggested she'd at least heard the rumors. "He uses a sort of hypnosis that allows people to experience their wildest dreams. As if they're living it. Somehow he creates an entranced reality for them in their minds. Almost like a hallucination, if I'm not mistaken. But it requires him drilling down into their minds. A real wild ride, from what I've heard. And one they happily pay him for."

"But if he can get into someone's mind like that . . ."

So she had heard the rumors. "He can access a whole hell of a lot more than just their dreams. Their deepest secrets, their secret ambitions, maybe even get in there and do a little mind control. Someone like that could do a lot of harm if they weren't led by the right moral obligations, if you know what I mean." Anaïs chewed on her lip while digging up old recollections. "There was a man in Barcelona rumored to be a dream auger. A few of us tried looking him up after the war but never could find out where he lived. An acquaintance"—she couldn't bring herself to say Edward's name out loud—"said he knew a man who'd tracked him down once. He'd had his memories of the war sucked right out of his head. Last anyone heard, the man ended up in an asylum quacking like a duck."

"And if this one has the elder staff?"

"Oh, he has it." There was a scuffle outside the door. Anaïs pressed a hand against the glass and spoke quickly. "But he doesn't know what to do with the thing. Not yet. But with his ability I'm afraid of what he might be capable of if he ever figures it out. Might not be just one guy who gets his brains sucked out. Could be a whole city of dupes." Anaïs craned her neck to watch the door. "They're coming back. You better go."

"But . . ."

"Don't worry about me. I'll get out when the time is right. Like I said, there's something I have to figure out first. There's more going on here than just a dream auger reaching for more power."

Anaïs didn't have time to explain about the woman and child before Tony and the boss man burst through the door, grumbling about the night's take and the disastrous performance at the end of the act by the new assistant. "I want her fired," Frank said as he sat down with his lockbox full of cash. Celeste and Sebastian took their cue and shimmered out of there behind their veil of glamour.

CHAPTER ELEVEN

Promises, Grudges, and Chance Encounters

"She did promise." Celeste scratched behind Sebastian's ear as they walked up the back stairs toward the dressing rooms. "I think she's on the up-and-up now, but we do seem to attract trouble wherever we go," she said, wondering how she'd ended up in a speakeasy in a foreign city in the middle of the night. A normal-enough evening for Anaïs, perhaps, but she and Sebastian were usually tucked under the sheets asleep by now. The stoat sighed at their ongoing plight before sinking to the bottom of her handbag.

The club's upstairs hallway was still a jumble of feathers and sequins despite the late hour. And though several performers had changed into their street clothes, ready to call it a night, they weren't necessarily headed home. It was long past midnight, yet the city remained wide awake. There were other clubs to go to, restaurants to visit, and movies to see. Hearing talk of an exciting new moving picture playing at the Embassy Theatre in Times Square gave Celeste a case of the blues as she sought the alley exit. For a few hours she'd managed to put a certain Hollywood producer out of her mind. But now Nick West's face was fresh in her thoughts again. She'd had only the briefest taste of his lips, but she knew she wanted more.

Celeste found her way back to the delivery door that led to the alley and ducked outside. Luckily, there was no one waiting on the other side except Gideon, who frantically flapped his wings while hopping from light post to light post. She waved and he flew down, landing on the lid of a trash can.

"She's all right," Celeste said to the rook. "But she isn't coming out. Not yet. You probably already sensed that, since her magic isn't too impaired. She's playing at something, so we'll just have to wait and trust her."

Gideon shook out his feathers, cawed, and flew off. He was a polite-enough bird, once you got to know him, though too long of a stare from the rook could still rattle Celeste's mood. She brushed off the feeling and considered going to the Embassy Theatre to see the movie everyone was talking about, but she had no idea where Times Square was. She was adrift in a sea of the unfamiliar. "Back to the room?" she said to Sebastian.

Celeste walked to the end of the alley, expecting to turn left toward the hotel, when a black Model T roadster pulled in front of her, blocking the way. The top was up, but the driver was plain to see behind the steering wheel.

"Get in." The way Tony said it felt more like an order than an invitation. When she adjusted her posture to show she wasn't going anywhere on demand, he added, "Please. We need to talk."

"Sorry I ruined your trick."

"I've never been booed before." He shook his head as though sweeping the incident clear of his thoughts. "Anyway, get in."

What was it about this man that made Celeste trust him? She knew he worked for a hoodlum, carried a gun, and maintained at least semi-criminal aspirations. Yet there was something pure at his center that her intuition recognized. Some good intention he thought he'd buried a long time ago, but the feeling told her it was merely dormant. Or maybe disguised as something else.

She slid onto the front seat and closed the door. "Where are we going?"

Tony responded with a wrinkled brow, as though he hadn't thought that far ahead. "We just gotta move." He put the car in gear and rumbled away from the only part of the city Celeste had any acquaintance with. Again, he nervously watched over his shoulder, looking for threats in the rearview mirror. She thought he might say something more about what he was afraid of, but he kept his attention on the traffic as he maneuvered through another neighborhood.

Celeste found herself checking the side mirror too. She watched for whatever trouble might have followed them, until Tony slowed in front of a corner store. A florist. At one thirty in the morning. "Feeling a sudden need to stop and smell the roses?" she asked.

Tony ignored her remark as he slowed the car to a crawl and drove past the shop. He was checking the windows, looking for some hidden bogeyman inside. Apparently, some thread of danger had been woven through the city that remained invisible to her eye. Whatever the threat, it pulled at everything in Tony's world with the tension of a single thread about to unravel the whole thing.

"Things look all right," he said, parking the car across the street. "Let's go inside."

"What, here?" Celeste had to wonder what he hoped to find at a florist's shop in the middle of the night. It was only after they'd entered through the front door that she remembered she was in a country where it seemed half the shops weren't what they pretended to be. The stores wore masks to fool the prudish eye during the day. But if one knew the password, they were gifted secret passage to an underground den filled with music and booze.

A heavyset man in a pin-striped suit sat reading a newspaper at a table covered with empty vases and drooping roses. He looked up with bloodshot eyes as they walked in. "Heya, Tony."

"Heya, Big Mike. How's the family?"

"Little Mikey's gonna be ten next week. Can you believe that?"

Both men shook their heads as Tony tossed down a dollar bill and slid a long-stem rose out of a vase. "Pete's is a safe place," he said to Celeste as he opened a refrigerator door at the back of the shop and gestured for her to walk through a display of silk flowers propped up in metal buckets. On the other side awaited a hidden room. The music wasn't as loud as the speakeasy they'd just left, and the lights were dimmer. There was no band, and no acts rushed on and off the stage, just men and women tucked away in booths made for two who sipped from crystal glasses while a piano player accompanied their conversation with easy notes of slow classics. Tony handed the rose to the hostess, who led them to a booth in the back where a wooden partition provided ample privacy.

A fifty-pound weight seemed to fall off Tony's shoulders as he slid across the leather seat. He smiled at the waiter and addressed him by name as he ordered two Manhattans. Celeste lied and said she wasn't hungry, so he ordered a steak for himself. The drinks arrived and Tony slid into the corner of the bench seat with his back against the wall and one arm extended.

"We struck a deal, you know."

Celeste stirred her drink with the toothpick with the cherry on it before taking a sip. "You still want me to put your boss's eyes out?" she asked, looking over the rim of her glass.

Tony seemed to realize she'd taken the request literally. He tapped a finger on the table as though trying to figure out the right tack to take with her. The waiter brought out his steak, and he sat forward again, unfolding his napkin and placing it on his lap. "Frank and I met six years ago. We worked the vaudeville circuit together. He was a normal guy. Friendly enough. We had a lot in common with our acts."

The scent of charred meat made Celeste's stomach squirm as her eyes couldn't help staring at the pomme frites that were stacked on the side of the steak. Tony took a bite of his steak, then slid his plate forward briefly to offer his American french fries.

"Frank had some impressive card tricks, but he mostly did a hypnotist routine with audience members. I had my magic routine. Escape artist stuff too. Getting free from lockboxes and chains." He waved a hand like it was a normal way to make a living. "We did all right."

The fries were hot and salty, just the way Celeste liked them. "So, what happened that's got you so jumpy?"

Tony got that cagey posture again, glancing around before cutting his steak. "I'm not jumpy. I'm just cautious. I don't know what's what anymore in this world. I thought I understood magic until she came along."

The mention of a *she* had Celeste's french fries hitting like a cold lump in her stomach. "She?"

Tony sawed through his meat violently. "Nellie worked the circuit with us for a year, doing private tarot and palm readings." He stopped cutting and pointed his knife while he spoke. "Look, I know what I do is an illusion. I know how to make things appear and disappear for the saps and suckers. But it's misdirection. With Frank and Nellie there's something else going on. Like you and your friend." He dropped the knife and pushed his plate away. "That disappearing act of yours isn't just a trick, is it?"

Celeste had to be careful. There were topics that weren't for general consumption. The sisterhood of Gardiennes had survived for centuries because they'd learned to keep their magic in the shadows, working behind the scenes to affect the lives of their protégés. She'd been raised by magical beings, certainly, but even she didn't always understand how it all worked. She was never quite certain if she'd been born with the ability to do magic or the sisters had instilled it in her with their lessons. All she knew was that she'd been set on that path of destiny the moment she was plucked up as an orphan and taken to live in the cottage in the woods.

"It's not a trick," she said and dabbed a french fry in a small bowl of mayonnaise that the waiter had brought out. Likely the work of Sebastian's subconscious summoning.

Tony's eyes watered as he exhaled in a shudder of disbelief. "So magic is real? And Frank and Nellie have it too? I mean, I always knew she was different. Special."

Celeste had caught a glimpse of Frank in the club but hadn't witnessed his unusual talent for herself. But if what Anaïs had said was true, and the dream auger's ability had progressed past initiate level, Tony had reason to keep looking over his shoulder every five minutes. A dream auger, once given access to a person's mind, could wade through their thoughts, ideas, and fantasies. A person's most secret inner world was exposed to him. Gardiennes were trained to take great care with a person's ambitions, wants, and desires. They didn't meddle, they merely observed the energy rising off them. But a dream auger could interfere. And it sounded like this one knew exactly how to do just that. "Tell me about Nellie."

"She's the one who warned Frank and me about you and your friend. Nellie knew you were coming to the city. She knew about whatever that thing is you were carrying." Tony leaned forward. "And what it might mean if Frank could get his hands on it."

"How?" Neither she nor Anaïs had planned their arrival in New York, so how could this woman have predicted it?

"Nellie has always been . . . different. She gets flashes, calls them insights. Her body goes slack, and you think she's having a seizure or something, but then she comes around and . . . and she just knows things. Things that are going to happen."

A psychic, a dream auger, and a magician. It was beginning to sound like an inevitable recipe for disaster. "So, this woman knows who we are?" Celeste dipped another fry. "But she doesn't know what we brought with us. Or at least not what it's for." Tony nodded, but she could tell he was holding something back by the way his eyes looked away. "What? What is it?"

"It's possible she knows more than she's telling. She has the baby to think about. Information might be her only protection. Her one bargaining chip."

Celeste was beginning to feel like a diver who'd gone too deep, running out of breath. "Tony, what are you all involved in? Why steal from us? Why kidnap my friend?"

"Why leave her behind?" Tony smirked, knowing he'd answered her question with a question.

"You answer first," she said and sneaked Sebastian a fry dipped in mayonnaise under the table while Tony looked over his shoulder.

"It's Frank. He's got this crazy talent. He can hypnotize someone so they actually believe they're living out their fantasies. They dream of being a boxer? They wake up squinting, convinced they've been punched in the eye. They want to be a race car driver? They swear they can smell gasoline on their clothes the rest of the day. Because of the way he hypnotizes people, he's grown a following of true believers. But he's after a bigger payday."

"How does he do it?" Celeste asked. She'd heard the rumors about dream augers, about the way they snagged your gaze with the dazzle in their eye. How they hooked you with a fleck of mystery shining in their irises. Then drew you in with a snake's stare while they got inside your head, leaving you hypnotized and rendered spellbound. Could the elder staff intensify that sort of talent?

"I don't know." Tony picked up his fork and slid the steak around on the plate. "He gets inside people's heads. They end up revealing things. The stuff you'd normally never say out loud to anyone. When we were still doing the vaudeville act, he'd leave people in the audience with their mouths hanging open in awe at the way he got them to confess things. At first, it was funny. He'd pull out some bank teller from the audience who, under Frank's influence, would confess something like he always wanted to be a ballet dancer. And then the poor sap would pirouette across the stage. Or he'd convince some woman she had butterfly wings, and she'd flit around the arena flapping her arms in front of everyone. But it was later, after the show, where he really made his reputation. All kinds of people would come backstage to congratulate him. They'd strike up a conversation, and he'd tell them how he could make their wildest dreams come true. Only they'd never have to leave their chair. They could live in the dreamworld inside their head. Experience their deepest desires as if they were real. Smell their lover's scent on their skin again, feel their feet leave the ground and fly. Whatever they fantasized about."

Tony sat back in the booth. His body went slack, weary with what Celeste suspected was firsthand experience. "After the first few audiences had seen his act," he said, "word started to get around. Some big fish started coming to the show. Rich men in their top hats and silk suits, each with a woman in diamonds on their arm. They wanted a taste of the fantasy life and were willing to pay good money to get to live out their dreams. In private. Most did it on a lark at first."

"And later?"

"Oh, they crawled over each other to throw money at him after he'd delivered. Like opium freaks waiting for their next hit." He pointed to his temple. "But it's all in here. He tricks the mind into believing it's experiencing the most outlandish encounter, even though the person is sitting still in an armchair with their feet propped on an ottoman the whole time. They snap out of the trance, and no one can convince them they haven't been making love in a field of buttercups or tap-dancing on a Broadway stage. Of course, once word got out among the elite about what he could do, he made a killing, charging three, four times as much. Enough to set up the French Drop and pay off the cops six months ago. And you'd think that'd be enough. But then he got this idea to up the ante."

Tony rubbed the back of his neck while tilting his head from side to side, as though all the stress in his life had congregated in the muscles there.

"About three months ago he changed his act. Frank had me pick up a guy from uptown and bring him in for a reading. I'll never forget him. The strangest man I ever met. Skin like candle wax. Like maybe he'd been burned in the war or something. And his eyes. The way they tracked every movement in the room with the cold intensity of a reptile." Tony shook his head at the memory. "I took the man to their meeting place, then left so Frank could do his thing. When I came to check up on him an hour later, Frank was sitting there in his chair staring at the wall and rubbing his chin in thought. I asked if he was okay. And he tells me he's been sitting on a once-in-a-lifetime opportunity for months and didn't even know it. Until he'd read that guy's dreams. Something he saw. Something about himself."

Tony lost his easy posture as his body tensed up again. His head swiveled to his left, double-checking the clientele inside Pete's place out of habit. "After that, he started wearing this creepy mask that he'd picked up in a curio shop when we were still touring the show last year in London. His subjects would come out of their hypnotic trance in the same good mood as always, but then they'd get this weird look on their face like they were worried they'd pissed their leg in front of everyone or something. But Frank? He just smiled, because he'd somehow figured out a way to get at their secrets without them willingly spilling a thing. All this crazy stuff these guys were doing."

Celeste's intuition was humming with dread. "What kind of stuff?"

Tony shied away from sharing the details with a guilty shrug. "The kind of things that people get blackmailed for. Usually with other people. And wouldn't you know it, pretty soon I'm mailing letters off to these rich guys, with Frank threatening to go public with the info unless they pay. Believe me, some of these guys were so rattled, they agreed to cough up the dollar bills on the spot. Half my job working for Frank anymore is going around collecting money from drop-off points."

"Is that why you're always looking over your shoulder?"

He blew out a short breath. "It wasn't enough to go after rich men. Recently, he started going after his rivals. At least in his mind that's what they are."

Were there other dream augers? Celeste knew the probability was incredibly low. "You mean other hypnotists were doing the same thing?"

"No, not that. I mean the club. The girls. The booze. He had a couple of splashy gangster types come to him for a reading. Got it in his head he could blackmail them the same way as the others. Make them give up a little territory so he could maybe expand his business. Maybe buy another club. Gain a little real estate on the west side and control everything that flowed in and out. But, believe me, those guys don't scare so easy. Instead of paying, one guy sent him a dead cat with its mouth stitched shut in a box as a warning."

Sebastian crawled into Celeste's lap. She didn't know if it was to comfort her or himself, but as always, she was glad he was there.

"Anyway"—Tony tossed his napkin on the table—"the whole encounter with the disfigured man changed Frank, and not for the better. He hasn't been the same after that. He still does a show at the club a couple nights a week, but it's changed. It was like he started taking pleasure in the pain he could cause others. Embarrassing them, humiliating them. He had this enormous gift, but now he wields it like a ball-peen hammer. And he uses it against anyone he wants."

Hearing Tony describe the change in Frank's demeanor left Celeste uneasy about the strange man who'd visited. Someone with knowledge of the occult perhaps, or with a dream auger's unique skills. She wished she knew what was in the dream the man had shared and how it involved Frank and the mask. And did it have anything to do with the elder staff?

"And now he seems hell-bent on flexing that power even more." Tony looked around before speaking again. Celeste swore he shivered inside his jacket. "After the fellas who run the west side told him to get lost, he's grown even more reckless. Says he's found the perfect mark. A way to flip the power in the city so the rewards start landing in his lap instead of some crooked cop's or a west-side mob boss's."

"What's a mark?" Celeste dabbed another french fry in mayo and slipped it to Sebastian while his little heartbeat thundered away on her lap.

"A mark is a patsy," Tony explained. "Someone you can manipulate into giving you what you want. Sometimes with bribes. Sometimes with threats. They're pawns. Used for your own gain. And Frank's got a big one in his sights." He downed the last of his drink, wincing slightly as he swallowed. "When Nellie told Frank about you two coming to the city, he got really quiet. Like he'd seen a ghost or something. But that's when he said it was time to make our move. To get our fair share. Go after whatever it is he's got planned with this mark of his." He set his glass down gently and slid it forward. "That's when he sent the kid to watch for your train at Grand Central. Soon as we knew you'd hopped off, we set the plan in motion. Gotta say, you two made it easy. You stuck out like a pair of daisies in a rose garden." He smiled like the fox who'd caught the fattest hen in the yard. "You still don't recognize me, do you?"

"Should I?" Celeste shook her head. "Wait, are you saying we've met before?" She knew they hadn't. *Had they?*

He held his hands out like he was gripping a steering wheel, then pantomimed crashing into a wall, complete with sound effects.

"That was you?" Celeste could hardly contain her shock at how diabolical their plan had been. Sebastian squirmed on her lap, no doubt from the guilt of not having sniffed this man out earlier. "How did I not know?"

"I've been in vaudeville most of my life." He shrugged. "A mustache, a little gray at the temples. A lot of fake blood. You can make an illusion as real as you like with enough practice."

Celeste nearly choked on her french fry after hearing the confession skirt a little too close to the magic she conducted as a Fée Gardienne.

"We even found an old jalopy to smash up," he added. "The timing was the hardest part. Traffic was hell this morning. If you'd have made it inside the hotel, I suppose we would have had to rob you at gunpoint to get the . . . thing." He allowed himself another quick smile at her expense before settling back into his solemn posture. "Obviously, Nellie was right about your arrival, so now Frank is ready to execute the rest of his plan. As soon as he gets what he needs out of your friend, there'll be no stopping him." He frowned then. "By the way, you never said why you left her there. I thought the whole point of me getting you inside was for you to help her escape. He'll wear her down in there. She will give in."

"Oh, I wouldn't count Anaïs out just yet," she said. "My friend is made of sterner stuff than that." Tony looked to the side briefly, as though storing the name away for later, while Celeste reflected on how easily the word "friend" had left her mouth, considering how recently she'd believed the woman had been out to kill her. "But I'm not so sure about you." Before he could protest, she held up her hand. "I know all about who you are and what you likely get up to. Only, I'm beginning to suspect you don't want that anymore." At their first meeting Celeste had believed he did want it. On some level he'd wanted it all then, but there was hesitation now. The development of a conscience? Guilt?

Tony attempted to release the lingering tension in his body in one rolling twist of his neck and shoulders. "Yeah, before tonight, maybe I did want to take it from him. The club, the money, the girls. He's been selling me short ever since we left the circuit. Treating me like his trained monkey, while he goes out to get measured for another silk suit. So, yeah, I've thought about taking it from him from time to time."

"So, me putting his eyes out—and I'm still hoping that's purely metaphorical—is about simple revenge?"

"Nah. It's more than that. You see, Frank doesn't care if innocent people get hurt in his scheme. Even the people closest to him. It might even be part of the plan. Causing pain seems to have become the main attraction for him." Tony leaned in and stabbed the steak with his knife. "He needs to be stopped. And I was fully prepared to handle things with my bag of tricks." He opened his jacket slightly to remind her of his gun. "But then Nellie saw something sparking in the future. Something big. She thinks that whoever you and your friend are, whatever your *gifts* are, that's how we stop him before he executes this crazy idea he's got running through his mind. It's something to do with a city big-timer, that's all I know. Said he'd share the rest when he knows the magic object he stole from you will do what he wants. In the meantime, he's got a bunch of patsies lined up to keep his regular enterprise going."

It was Celeste's turn to slump against the back of her seat. Frank knew what he'd taken from them. Or at least enough to know the elder staff's potential power. But how? How did a vaudeville dream auger turned gangster know about the history of the Fées Gardiennes?

Celeste wished she knew more about this stranger who'd come to see Frank. This man with the skin like candle wax. Such a disturbing yet familiar image. So many men had come back from the war with unimaginable injuries. The image put her in mind again of the Skulk they'd fought at the studio lot in Hollywood. He'd been disfigured by a blast of intense light and confined to an oily pool of bubbling asphalt when they'd left Los Angeles. Thoughts of the murderous Infortunii she'd once befriended ruined her appetite, and she pushed the rest of the fried potatoes away. Besides, she needed to get back to her hotel room. Chasing after Anaïs had left her with no time to dig through her books to read if there was anything more to be learned about the staff and its power. Or what the relic might be capable of in the hands of a dream auger.

"I'll help you," Celeste said. "I don't know how, because I won't put a man's eyes out, but I will help you stop Frank from hurting anyone. I promise." And with that her bond was made.

The message rippled through Tony. The relief showed in his eyes by the way he stopped checking the front door every few seconds. His body calmed. His shallow breaths relented. He left a generous bill on the table, said good night to the waiter, and escorted Celeste to the exit.

Celeste was just checking on Sebastian to make sure he was snug in her handbag before she reached for the refrigerator door to leave. Before she could give the handle a push, the door opened. A pair of men stood on the other side, one with a gray streak in his hair and a scar across the jaw who was full of relief at the sight of a bar, and the other who wore a dazzling smile that could've stopped traffic on Hollywood Boulevard.

Her heart did a loop the loop at the sight of Nick West entering the secret tavern. In the dead of night. In the middle of New York City.

She'd only arrived in the city less than twenty-four hours ago herself. What was he doing here? Was he truly standing there or had her mind somehow conjured an image of him, as it had at the train station? How lovesick did a woman have to be to see a man's face everywhere she went? But then she caught a whiff of his hair and skin, still tinged with the scents of orange blossoms and Ivory soap, and knew he was real. Their eyes met, and before she could stop herself, she blurted out a hopeful, "What are you doing here?"

Nick stopped and gave her that smile again, only this time the effect hit across the bow, landing deep inside her where the walls were down. "I'm sorry, miss. I seem to be at a loss here. Have we met before?"

Celeste's heart did another swan dive, remembering he didn't recognize her. He couldn't have if he'd wanted to, even if his eyes lingered on her in the most curious manner. She'd erased herself from his memory after their one brief kiss. The disappointment of knowing she couldn't touch those lips again sucked the air right out of her. She shook her head. "Sorry, I guess I thought you were someone else."

"He gets that a lot," said the other man with a rough-around-the-edges brogue that jabbed her intuition in all the wrong ways. "You've no idea." He slapped his hand on Nick's back with a laugh, then led him to an open booth.

And while Celeste could have reversed the memories, she'd been drawn once again into an impossible situation. One that demanded she not rekindle the spark she and Nick had felt in California. Not yet. Not while the survival of the sisterhood required her full attention to return the elder staff to Paris. And so, while the handsome movie producer turned around to give her a wistful look of what might have been had there been more time than just a passing glance between them, she exited the tavern with the man carrying the gun in his jacket and a chip on his shoulder.

CHAPTER TWELVE

No Such Thing as Coincidences

Anaïs woke the next morning inside the private office, warm and swaddled in the down comforter she'd conjured out of her stockings the night before. Once she'd been sure everyone had abandoned her for the night, she had transformed the glass tank into a canopy bed. She turned her shoes into a bedside lamp on one side and an alarm clock on the other, just in case she overslept. The ice was left to melt in the tub Frank's flunkies had packed it in, though she'd shrunk it down to the size of a small bucket.

There was a narrow, smudged window in the office that looked out at the street level above. From what Anaïs could tell, the sky was still a grimy gray outside. Not the time of day she preferred to be awake, but Gideon had flashed an image in their shared psychic eye of bringing her fresh rolls from the bakery down the street for her breakfast, so she threw off the covers. She supposed she ought to get things squared away before anyone arrived, seeing as how she was supposed to be shivering inside a glass island surrounded by ice water at its base. But cabaret workers tended to work late hours, so there was still a little time. She nearly cackled at the notion of the utterly uncharming Frank finding her swimming in a warm comforter and silk pajamas instead.

Anaïs had just tied her robe around her when Gideon rapped at the glass. She slid the window open to greet him. "Hello, my pet. Did you get along all right?" There was no real reason to ask. He'd always been a clever bird. Resilient and loyal to a fault. But she always felt the need to dote on his emotions whenever she'd been away from him for very long.

Gideon bobbed his head and scratched at the pavement. He held a paper sack in his beak that showed a grease stain on the bottom from all the buttery goodness she hoped it held inside. The rook dropped the baked goods in her hand and tried to hop inside to be with her.

"Not yet," she said, peeking inside the bag. "I've got a little more digging I need to do today, so you better stay clear for a little while longer. Hey, what's this?" The bag contained two dried-out cannoli that had gone hard from being day-old. She held up one of the sweet treats to show him the dented shell and a filling that had formed a yellowy crust where it had congealed.

Gideon's whole body bobbed up and down in distress. Apparently, the bakery owner didn't like birds diving inside his store and had chased him away with a broom before he could snatch any of the warm buns just out of the oven. He'd found the bag of cannoli sitting on someone's kitchen table and snatched it through an open window before they'd noticed. After the look she gave him, the rook shook out his feathers and tucked his beak under his wing, pretending to preen while pouting instead.

"There, there, it isn't the end of the world. I'm sure someone was saving them for their own breakfast, but they ought to know better than to leave something tasty like cannoli by an open window. The fault lies entirely with them." She gave her rook a scratch under the chin and told him he was a good bird. But if he wanted to be an even better bird, he'd keep watch for the boss man and his sidekick and let her know when to jump back in the tank.

Gideon flew off, leaving Anaïs alone with her day-old breakfast. There wasn't a Gardienne who didn't occasionally regret that food meant to be eaten couldn't be conjured out of an old teacup or silver spoon.

Though rare, the possibility of the ingested food reverting into the original object was too dangerous a proposition. Drinks were usually safer, as they tended to swoosh through the body quickly, but no one wanted to find a transformed teacup lodged in their lower intestine.

With a resigned plop, she sat at Frank's desk and ate her dried-out cannoli while perusing his day planner. She didn't recognize any of the names in his appointment book until she'd gone back several weeks. She'd been skimming over the entries, trying to glean what she could from the limited information, when a familiar name jumped out at her. It was just as easily a coincidence. After all, anyone in New York could be named Leopold Lombardi, but it just happened to be the name of the wealthy man she'd married one of her earliest protégés off to before she'd wised up about arranging marriages for young women as an easy fix for improving their lives. She intended to check up on her protégé, knowing the couple had recently arrived in New York City to spend the summer making the rounds on the social circuit.

She glanced at the entry again. There were several asterisks beside the name and a short note that read "Pick up at Sixth and Thirty-First." Uncertain what it meant, she sucked the cream out of the last bite of pastry shell, closed the appointment book, and crumpled the paper bag. She didn't bother sweeping away the crumbs from his desk when she was finished.

So, was it just a coincidence? There was usually no such thing in the world of Fées Gardiennes. She tapped her fingers against the desk, weighing the idea of flying the coop before the boss man returned so she could drop in on Mrs. Lombardi. There might be more to be gained, information-wise, by reinfiltrating her protégé's world to discover what connected her husband to this speakeasy goon with the odd twitch in his eye. Then again, she had to stick close to the elder staff. If she were the one Fée Gardienne, in all the sisterhood's time on earth, to lose the damn thing, she'd never forgive herself. No, it was better to keep dangling the mysteries of the ancient relic in front of the baboon in the hopes of finding out where the loose lips were that allowed him to know about it in the first place. And, no, she didn't think Edward could have been the source of her troubles this time. She'd never shared that kind of information with him. At least she didn't think so. She really did need to stay away from the sangria.

As long as she was staying, Anaïs decided she ought to go give the rest of the club a proper search. Just in case the ape was dumb enough to have left the clarinet case behind. After all, it would require only the flick of her eyebrow to open the office door or any other locked room in the place.

She pressed her ear against the wood and listened for signs of workers. Nothing rattled. No one cleared their throat. Not even the scratching of a mouse behind the walls. If the boss man thought he could contain a Fée Gardienne with a little ice and a knockout drug, he was only half right. She could have a quick look around, then shimmy back into her helpless damsel in distress mode before anyone noticed. She had just arched her brow to escape when Gideon squawked out his warning with the message resonating in their shared thoughts.

They're back? So soon? Anaïs had to quickly restore the final details in the room, folding up her bedding, changing out of her silk pajamas, and installing the glass walls behind her as she climbed back inside the tank. A small puddle of melted ice water greeted her hip as she scooted backward.

A baby whimpered on the other side of the door. A key turned in the lock. Nellie walked in carrying Hazel in one arm and a grocery bag in the other. "Good morning," she called from the doorway, as though allowing Anaïs a moment to wake and make herself presentable before she came all the way inside the office. Such an odd courtesy, considering they were keeping her in a glass cage. Nellie placed the bag on the desk before bending to set the baby girl on the floor. "I've brought you something for breakfast. And I know you've got to be dying for the chamber pot to be emptied."

"I, uh . . ." Anaïs wondered how Nellie expected her to pass a commode, even a small one, through the locked bars of the tank's lid. Or did she feel confident enough to open the cage door by herself? And why were Nellie and her baby even there so early? Surely a place like this didn't get hopping until the afternoon. Though she supposed there was some urgency in squeezing as much information out of her as soon as they could. "I'm fine."

"Oh." Nellie looked up, surprised, then went back to emptying her paper sack.

On the floor, Hazel gazed up at Anaïs with her dazzling green eyes. The baby smiled, showing a few tiny white teeth, and the padlock on Anaïs's heart flicked open.

"Did you say it was her birthday today?"

"Uh-huh," Nellie said while busy unloading two small bundles wrapped in greasy brown paper.

Anaïs felt a desperate need to give the child something, even though the notion was absurd. She and Dorée had come up with their plan for getting Celeste to California by playing off Anaïs's reputation for being a tinge jaded when it came to domestic matters of marriage and children. Oh, how easily Celeste had swallowed the story of her cursing a baby to death! But there was something about this child that stirred her emotions toward a generosity of spirit that she generally guarded with claws out.

While Nellie removed what looked like homemade egg sandwiches from their wrappers, Anaïs lifted her ruby pendant away from her chest. With a little swing of the chain, she turned the dust motes in the air into soap bubbles that floated in front of the girl. Her chubby little hands grasped at the bubbles, and she squealed in delight when one burst against her nose. The exchange had Anaïs smiling like a simpleminded, lovesick fool.

"What on earth? Where did those bubbles come from?" Nellie placed a sandwich and a bottle of cola in a basket and lowered them into the tank to Anaïs. "Did you do that?"

Anaïs wasn't quite sure how to answer the question. If she said no, that introduced a whole new mystery into the morning's affairs.

If she said yes, the jig was up. Tempting. She went with a shrug. And then a wink at the baby behind Nellie's back. Her reward was another squeal of joy.

Nellie sat in the desk chair and handed a small piece of fried egg to Hazel. "I'm pleased to see you two getting to know each other better," she said. There was a wistful tone to her voice that puzzled Anaïs. Well, everything about the woman puzzled her, but this was different. It sounded personal. Sad. Resigned.

"She's very well behaved." It was the highest compliment Anaïs could bestow upon another person's child.

"She won't be any bother."

Again, the resignation underlying Nellie's every word hit like a dropped tin pan in Anaïs's ear. But enough of this chitchat; there were real situations at stake. "So, what's the master plan for the day?" Anaïs asked, sniffing the sandwich she'd been given.

Nellie patted Hazel gently on the head. "Oh, we're going to have cake and a special present later."

"I meant about me." Anaïs rapped her knuckles against the side of the glass case. "When's the guy with the menacing stare coming back? I'd like to get out of this fish tank and get on with my day."

"You mean Frank?" Nellie sat up straighter. "Are you ready to tell him how the object works?" Her face paled and her eyes tensed. Anaïs might even have described it as panic. "I didn't expect . . . I mean, I don't know where he is. He usually doesn't come in until later."

"Calm down, I was only curious how much longer this was going to take. Oh, fiddlesticks, enough of this charade." With her patience dried up, Anaïs made the glass in front of her vanish, stepped out, and handed the sandwich back to Nellie. "If he doesn't think keeping a woman locked up in a cage for information is an urgent-enough matter to show up for in the morning, then there are certainly more important things I could be doing with my time."

Nellie gawked with her mouth slightly open. She scooped up her child and hugged her close with one hand held protectively over her head. "How did you do that?"

Understanding that her actions had breached the standard behavior that concealed Gardienne magic from dull human eyes, Anaïs gave a little shake of her head. "It's a trick box made for an escape artist. I've had all night to figure out how the cage works." She fanned out her dress to give it a fluff, then ironed out the wrinkles with a puff of breath and a lift of her brow.

"You need to get back inside. If he finds out . . ." Nellie looked over her shoulder to the door. "He has plans. He'll never let you leave."

"Sorry, sister, I've got an errand to run uptown. But don't you worry, I'll be back later to collect what he stole."

"This isn't how it was meant to go. You're supposed to stay and show him how to use the wand."

Anaïs put a hand on one hip and took a step closer to the woman psychic. "Those shadows you see are just that," she said. "Flitting silhouettes of an uncertain future. The real gift is in the interpretation of the vision, not in the seeing." With that she turned and walked out the door, veiling herself in glamour to go unseen should anyone else get in her way. She really was overdue on checking in on her protégé, Mrs. Leopold Lombardi.

CHAPTER THIRTEEN

Masquerade

Celeste hugged her pillow and stared up at the ceiling. She'd barely slept a wink all night. First there was the incident with Anaïs, then her deal with Tony, and then later running into Nick at the tavern. What was he doing at a bar at three in the morning? Who was that man he was with? And though she was still relishing in the glowy aftereffect of seeing Nick again, none of it made any sense.

Sebastian tugged at the sheets, urging Celeste to get out of bed. She sat up, hoping the change in posture would shake loose some rational thought. She couldn't stop second-guessing herself over whether she should have undone the glamour she'd cast to make him forget her back in California. Had she ruined her one chance of reuniting with him? What if she never saw him again because she didn't seize the moment? She nearly flopped back down on the bed to hide under the covers, but Sebastian wouldn't have it. He, and surprisingly Gideon too, forced her to stand by nudging up against her back with nose and beak.

"All right, all right." Celeste stood and put her arms out. The pair chose a sapphire-blue ensemble with a pleated skirt and matching blouse from her trunk. It didn't quite suit her mood, but she didn't have the heart to argue as they slipped the sleeves over her arms. Her hair was curled, her cheeks rouged, and her teeth brushed with a bit of tooth powder. "I suppose," she said as she stood in front of the mirror, "I don't *look* like an assassin, at least." Though murder was possibly the main event on the day's agenda, should she have to uphold her end of the bargain she'd struck with Tony.

Gideon shook out his feathers and cawed out that weirdly human laughing noise in his throat, making Celeste eternally grateful she couldn't read the bird's thoughts. She checked her outfit one more time in the mirror, then grabbed her handbag. "Time to go," she said to Sebastian. The stoat hopped in, while the rook snickered before flying out the open window. Tony was supposed to pick her up in front of the hotel soon. Part of her agreement to help him stop Frank was to find out more about his diabolical plan. If she could figure out what the dream auger was up to and with whom, she might be able to sort out how he intended to use the elder staff.

The simple black roadster pulled up to the curb in front of her hotel right on time. Tony didn't bother to get out. No romantic aspirations there! Instead, the doorman opened the car door for her so she wasn't left standing on the sidewalk like a dope. She gave the doorman a Gardienne smile as a thank-you, which ought to have him finding a lost bill in his pocket later.

"I appreciate a woman who's on time." Tony pursed his lips, making the angle on his cheekbones devastatingly attractive as he watched for traffic before pulling out in the road.

"Why wouldn't I be on time?" Celeste didn't wait for a reply as she watched out the window, taking in the hodgepodge of city buildings they drove past. Apartments, hotels, shops, and restaurants. Each stone building cut from a different quarry yet complementing each other like a mosaic of American street life. "So where are we going?"

"There's a place across town where Frank likes to do his thing. He doesn't bring the dream-reading clients to the club. He likes to keep the business separate from his extracurricular pursuits."

Celeste didn't like the tremolo of fear in Tony's voice. She lowered her guard just a smidge to take a reading on him again. There was deception there, as though he might be trying to hide his true self from her, but that same sliver of integrity he kept behind a stone wall still stood at the center of his ambitions. Some motivation she trusted with all her heart. She said no more as they headed toward Lower Manhattan by taking Seventh Avenue to Bleecker Street. When they turned again, he eased on the brakes long enough to point down the long avenue called Broadway. "That's the Woolworth Building. Tallest building in the world. Something, isn't it?"

Celeste was amazed at the sheer height of it. The skyscrapers were nothing like the buildings in Paris or Brussels. Those were old cities content to sit like hens on their population centers, low and maternal. But in this city, everything appeared to be in competition with itself to grow bigger, faster, and more expensive. Something akin to the growth spurt of a teenage boy, which she supposed was what America really was beneath all its bluster. No longer a toddler, the nation had grown sharp, permanent teeth and an attitude that attempted to project a rising superiority. *So much to learn,* she thought, with a shake of her head.

The car wound through a narrow street until the atmosphere around them grew distinctly Chinese. Wontons, noodles, and chop suey were the main offerings, according to the signs that hung over nearly every doorway they passed. Jewelry, tea, and shoe stores filled out the rest of the crouching shops. There was such an affectation to the place compared to the part of the city they'd just come from. She was intrigued and mystified at the same time. Tony finally stopped the car on Doyers Street, a crooked alley with shops and houses crammed into ramshackle buildings that appeared as though they were held up by little more than the shared tension of leaning against each other.

"What is this place?" Celeste was having second thoughts about this reconnaissance trip they were on but gave her purse a pat to let Sebastian know they'd arrived at their destination.

Tony did that quick look over the shoulder before also glancing up at the windows of the second floors above them. "It's Chinatown," he said, then pointed to a low-hung sign that wavered on its chain. "That place there has the best dumplings you've ever tasted in your life."

She'd never had the opportunity to eat a dumpling before, but she took him at his word. "Is that where we're going?"

Tony shook his head. "Tobacco shop three doors down." He turned in his seat to face her. "This is how we do this. The client is gonna get dropped off in front of us. My job is to make sure he isn't carrying."

"Carrying?"

Tony opened his coat, reminding her of the gun he kept strapped to his side.

"I see." Celeste took another glance out the window, wondering if she should be worried. She could defend herself against most things, but bullets were quicker than her magic. "Why would someone bring a gun to a session with a dream auger?"

"That's the thing. Like I said, Frank isn't the nicest guy anymore. He's made enemies getting in the club business. Crossed some people he shouldn't have. Maybe forgot to grease the right palm." Tony's eyes scanned the sidewalk on both sides of the street. "The fella he's hoping to manipulate could fix all that for him. It's why they're meeting here. It's neutral territory. Leastwise, the Chinese tongs don't mind letting us do a little business here for a small cost."

"What are the tongs?" Celeste was getting the bends from her deep submersion into Tony's world.

"They like to refer to themselves as brotherhoods. Others call them gangs. They run the gambling houses around here. Prostitution trade too. But we don't bother them, and they don't give us any trouble. We keep things copacetic."

Considering Celeste was part of an elite ancient sisterhood herself, caught up in an illegal situation, she supposed she could relate to the existence of these Chinese tongs. "So, what is it you want me to do?"

"After the guy shows up, I'll be expected to escort him inside to see Frank. You follow us, only do that thing of yours so no one sees you. Then just sit and watch. You'll see what I mean about working the guy over." A car pulled up in front of them. Tony's head spun left. "He's here. You better . . . disappear."

Celeste veiled herself in glamour. Tony got out of the car, shutting the door before she could scoot out behind him. Since it might look suspicious to open the car door on her own side, she was forced to climb out the window to avoid an awkward scene. By the time she caught up to her partner in crime, she'd nearly missed getting inside the front door of the tobacco shop. She gave Tony a jab in the back with her elbow to let him know to slow down. He'd just started patting down the man's coat and had to cover up the stiff groan she'd caused by coughing into his fist.

Tony thanked the man and his assistant for their cooperation, then extended his arm toward a painting of a dragon on the wall. "This way, Mr. O'Brien."

Nothing in this city was what it first appeared, so Celeste wasn't surprised when the artwork on the wall of the cigar shop led to a private parlor decked out in red velvet sofas, gold silk curtains, and even a live peacock sitting on a perch in the corner. What did catch her off guard was the client's face when he took off his hat and turned around. The gray streak in his hair and scar across the jaw were unmistakable. It was the same man she'd seen enter the tavern with Nick West the night before.

Celeste's stomach churned uncomfortably in reaction to the coincidence, because genuinely random events were rare in her circle of experience. Worried about the implication, she clung close to Tony as O'Brien took his seat on the red sofa opposite the peacock.

"This going to take long?" O'Brien checked a watch he kept in the breast pocket of his suit coat. An expensive one, judging by the tailored fit and fine detailing at the cuffs and collar. He seemed impatient for a man about to spend a lot of money for a unique once-in-a-lifetime experience. Perhaps he didn't understand what he was in for. Or why he was really there.

Celeste was desperately curious to see what would happen with the dream auger. Sebastian, too, as he poked his nose out of her handbag, sniffing the air. She supposed it wouldn't hurt to have him take up another position on their mission, so she shooed him away with a quick finger across her lips to keep him quiet. A moment later, a woman dressed in a gold formfitting silk gown with a high collar and side slits escorted in a bear of a man through a back door. Up close, Frank was tall and brutish with broad shoulders, and he had a face that appeared to have been hit one time too many, as his nose sat slightly to the right above his upper lip. With a different demeanor he might have still been considered handsome, but his inner demons had him wearing a constant snarl. He entered the center of the room, looming over the woman and the box she carried in her hands.

So this was the dream auger. Not how Celeste had pictured one in her imagination prior to this encounter. She'd expected more elegance, more finesse, but he'd walked in with a hooligan's swagger. She took a moment to sink into her power and take the temperature of his inner aspirations. Almost immediately she was met with ice—in his veins, heart, and dreams. Nothing but icy blue contours with jagged edges. An impenetrable wall of non-emotion. Her eyes snapped open. Had he somehow protected himself from her scrutiny? Did he anticipate a Fée Gardienne might attempt to evaluate the content of his own dreams and desires? She worried he knew she was there. Holding her eye steady on his, she waved her arms. She waited for a telltale sign he saw through her glamour, but if he did, he never let on. Instead, he greeted O'Brien with a handshake and a forced smile that made his lip arch over his right canine tooth.

"Sorry to keep you waiting," he said. "Just doing some final preparations for our session. Please, have a seat." The men squared off on opposing chairs as the woman holding the box moved to stand between them.

"So, this thing you do with the dreams." O'Brien had the same uncouth arrogance wafting off him as Frank, but his coarser tendencies were layered beneath a gilded veneer that only a lot of money could buy. One paid for by what Celeste suspected came from underhanded success later in life. "People tell me it makes you feel so good it ought to be illegal," he said with a wicked grin that reminded her of Anaïs when she was in one of her moods.

Frank answered with a bootlicker's laugh. The kind designed to let the other person think they were funny or in charge when they were anything but. "I've heard people describe it as transformative." He glanced at Tony when he said it, his hooded eyes casting both parry and thrust with one look. "I think you'll find it worth your while."

O'Brien merely pursed his bottom lip. "I've never been hypnotized before. I don't want to end up jumping around the room like some baboon." He pointed his finger like a loaded gun at his assistant to indicate there'd be hell to pay if his request wasn't respected.

"Occasionally, as you can understand, the euphoria of a dream can lend itself to a physical outburst," Frank replied, attempting to keep his mark at ease. "Some people laugh or sway as the dream progresses. Some might say a few words as if talking in their sleep, but I've never had anyone leave the chair."

O'Brien seemed to roll the potential consequences of making a fool of himself around the inside of his mouth, running his tongue over his teeth. "I can't deny I'm curious to see what all the talk is about," he said. "Members at the Metropolitan Club have been gossiping about your talents for months."

"Best to begin, then." Frank gestured to the woman to open the box. "You've come here because you have a fantasy or dream that you've nurtured. Perhaps for years. One that you like to return to over and over again. But no matter how much you think about it, no matter how much the dream entices you to enter, turning that desire into reality eludes you. It might as well be a wisp of breath carried on the wind in your waking hours."

O'Brien nodded slowly, preserving a healthy dose of skepticism as he wagged his finger at his assistant to pay the money. "Sure, there's maybe something like that I've been thinking about lately."

"But men like you are accustomed to having your every dream fulfilled. You are a commercial developer, if I'm not mistaken. You have a vision for how something is to be built. You draw up plans. You instruct people how to implement your every whim." Frank reached in the box and withdrew a wooden mask. Celeste took a step closer, drawn inexplicably to the grain of the wood and the slightly shimmery vein running through it. "Think of my unique talent as the bridge that will connect your dream to a unique experience of reality." He paused, smiling reassuringly. "Hopefully without you ever leaving the chair."

O'Brien gave in, settling into the seat and loosening his tie. "Right, but what's the mask for?"

"I like to think of it as a way to maintain separation between our egos," Frank explained. "In a sense, our minds will meet. But we don't want my presence to interfere with your experience, so I wall off my face behind a mask so it's just you and your dream in the encounter."

Celeste wasn't so sure that was the reason. Something about the mask was setting off alarms inside her head. But it was only when Frank slipped it over his face that she got an inkling of the trouble she was in. The mask was round and plain with a carved nose and slits for the eyes and mouth. There was no paint or stain, just a vein of inlaid gold running over the oak face like a scar cutting across the eye slits. A vein uncannily similar to that of the elder staff.

Celeste knew not to ignore her intuition. Something was definitely amiss, but curiosity overrode her better sense. She was desperate to see what this dream auger could do. How the mask worked and how O'Brien would respond to the integration of their minds. Frank folded his hands in his lap and inhaled deeply. Celeste inched closer, careful not to make a sound. She wanted to observe the dream auger's eyes. She wanted to understand how he was able to create the bridge he talked about. Was it a psychic connection? Pure intuition? Hypnosis?

Or was there an actual magical bond that took place between him and the other man?

"And what about your man and them two? Will they know what my dream is about?" O'Brien asked, giving a nod to his assistant and the woman holding the empty box.

"I can ask them to leave if you like, but I assure you no one will know what you're dreaming about except for me. And my memory of it will only last during the time we're connected."

Celeste was certain that was a lie, but how would the other man know what was what?

"So, shall we begin?"

O'Brien's eyes flitted from object to object in the room, eager to look away, but Frank told him to gaze straight into his eyes. The hook was set. O'Brien didn't look away again. The woman who'd presented the mask dimmed the lights until the room was lit only by the glow of three candles flickering on an end table. While everyone settled, Celeste noted again just how finely tailored O'Brien's suit was. His shoes were made from impeccable leather, and his hair was trimmed to perfection. There was no way to know what went on inside his head, but she had to wonder what a man of such obvious money and power felt he was missing in life that he had to consult with a dream auger. Or with a Hollywood producer, for that matter.

Only a moment had passed when a connection between the men manifested in a faint aura. A breath of cloudy energy exchanged between them. Perhaps not visible to Tony or O'Brien, but it was just detectible to Celeste's eyes in the candlelight. Frank spoke softly, reassuring his subject repeatedly, letting him know it was okay to relax. To close his eyes now if he wanted. To let go and dream.

O'Brien's eyelids fluttered closed. The hard scowl he wore on his face to warn others how intimidating he was had gone slack. His mouth hung slightly open as his chin fell. His hands were crossed in his lap to show he was relaxed, but his left heel tapped constantly.

The dream auger leaned in slightly. His eyes remained open and blinking normally at first, but after the connection was made, he closed them while holding his hands in a steepled pose against his chest. Celeste remained vigilant, wondering what was going on in either of their heads. What information was Frank gleaning from the exchange of energy? Who was in control of the images in O'Brien's head? Were those particles of dreams floating in the aura between them?

O'Brien giggled. The man's eyes were still closed, but he was talking to someone in his dream state. Mumbling, really. His arms lifted, with one being more extended than the other. He seemed to be taking someone's hand. He swayed in the chair with his arms held out in front of him as though embracing someone in a dance pose. His face tightened in serious concentration. His chin jutted forward, and he rotated his body in the chair, lifting his arms dramatically before bringing them down again. So much for not acting like a baboon.

Celeste had seen enough. It was a classic case of misdirection. When the session was over, O'Brien was going to wake feeling a rush of ecstasy he wouldn't be able to stop talking about. Meanwhile, the vault in the back of his brain that held all those juicy secrets he didn't think anyone else knew—about his predilections, his extramarital acquaintances, his illegal businesses—would have been emptied by the dream auger while he'd been off dancing a waltz around some Viennese ballroom. If Tony was on the up-and-up, Frank would use the stolen information to later blackmail the man he'd just given the ride of a lifetime to. But how? How did he make the intangible tangible? And he must manifest their wisps of hidden secrets into physical proof, or why would anyone succumb to his threats?

Frank leaned back in his chair. He'd gotten what he'd come for. Celeste was certain of it, and she was disgusted. She let out an involuntary sigh as he gave O'Brien permission to wake up. The dream auger's head lifted sharply at the noise she'd made.

She'd forgotten she was veiled.

He looked straight at where she was standing. He was as startled to see her as she was to see him staring at her. She didn't know what to do, so she darted to her right. His eyes followed her through the mask. He really could see her.

"Where'd you come from?" he asked, his body straightening with alarm.

"What do you mean? I've been here the whole time," Tony said, even though he was slightly out of range of where Frank was staring.

O'Brien opened his eyes and let out a whoop of pleasure. "That was just as vivid and real as everyone said. I was dancing on clouds with Mae Murray in my arms. What a thrill! I could have been in the movies myself, you know. Got a studio I'm thinking of investing in, so who knows what dreams may yet come true. I always knew I could dance and sing with the best of them."

Frank paid him no attention. "Not you. Her. Don't you see her?" Frank snapped his fingers at Tony. "Get her!"

Tony feigned ignorance better than she could have imagined. "Get who?" He shrugged and stared at the space where Frank had pointed.

"There! She's right there." Frank slipped the mask off and stumbled backward. His eyes searched the area between the chair and sofa, blinking in confusion as though he could no longer see her.

"Who?" Tony played up his ignorance again as he and O'Brien's assistant made a half-hearted search of the area around the sofa in a way clearly meant to humor Frank.

O'Brien got out of his chair. "What the hell is going on here? There's no one there. Get who?"

Frank slipped the mask back on. "She's right there." He lunged at Celeste to grab her, but a sharp bite on his ankle by a spirited stoat caused the big man to stumble. Frank crashed against the end table, catching himself on his knees as he cursed against the pain.

The mask had fallen askew and was barely hanging from one of Frank's ears. In an impulsive move, Celeste grabbed it off his face, hid it under her glamour, and ran. She didn't know why she'd felt compelled to nab the mask, she only knew it meant something, and she had to take advantage of the opportunity while he couldn't see her. With the stolen goods tucked under her arm, she ran for the door, burst through the dragon painting on the tobacco shop wall, and jumped in the back of Tony's car three doors down. Sebastian leaped in after her, and the pair huddled together, curled on their sides, panting until they caught their breath, while Frank blew over the street like a windstorm searching for them.

After an agonizing wait of what felt like an hour, Tony returned to his car. He sank against the driver's seat, eerily quiet before starting the engine. A moment later, his fist smashed against the steering wheel, followed by a raw, unintelligible outburst, though Celeste interpreted the emotion plainly enough. The car pulled herky-jerky into the street as Tony took out his aggression on the other drivers, swerving from one lane to the next. When she was sure they'd cleared the streets of Chinatown, she sat up and threw off her veil.

"Well, that made for an interesting morning."

Tony slammed on the brakes, barely avoiding getting hit from behind. "Jesus! Have you been there this whole time?" He pulled into a parking lot around the corner and stopped the car. "Frank was this close to making me drive him back to the French Drop in *this* car. What would you have done then?"

"Was he looking for this?" Celeste grinned and raised the mask to show him her stolen loot.

"I'm not sure you realize what you've done." Tony was back to glancing nervously over his shoulder. "Why'd you steal that thing?"

"Same reason he stole the relic from us, I suppose. A little insurance, maybe. Plus, I want to know what it does."

"What makes you think it does something?" Tony asked, but by the time he finished asking the question, he saw the answer for himself. "Ah, because he could see you when you were doing that trick of yours."

Celeste had been too scared of being discovered in the back seat of the car earlier to look at the mask in detail, but she studied it now. She ran her hand over the tiny vein of gold that snaked across the eye slits. It gave off the slightest of vibrations, though that could have been the gold and wood reacting together, she supposed. "And you say he picked this up in a shop in London?"

Tony exhaled. "Last year, yeah. A souvenir from an odd little junk shop, you know?"

"It was just sitting in a shop?" Celeste recalled what Anaïs had said about a black market for magical relics and thought it possible.

"As far as I know. The thing is, Frank brought the mask home and then left it sitting in a trunk until a few months ago. Then all of a sudden he started using it at his readings. Said it helped him focus."

"And that was right after he met with the waxy-skinned fellow."

"Yep." He drummed his fingers on the seatback. "So what does it do? Is it cursed or something?"

Celeste understood Tony was a practitioner of "magic" and therefore had an innate curiosity about such things, but if she was right about the mask, this was strictly Gardienne business. And she was almost certain the similar crude craftsmanship meant it had something to do with the elder staff. The gold veining wasn't identical, but it was awfully close. But how? How had this dream auger come to discover its supposed power? She needed more information. She needed Anaïs. Not a thought she would have entertained a month ago.

"No idea," Celeste answered honestly. "You better take me back to my hotel. I have a feeling your boss is going to be looking for you. He'll be wanting your help in finding me and the mask. And I need to see if there's a way to figure out where this thing came from."

"What about your friend?" Tony checked his watch. "I haven't heard an update. Should we swing by the club and check in on her?"

Celeste appreciated his considerate nature, but Anaïs was more than capable of taking care of herself. And if her fellow Gardienne could work her situation to their advantage and retrieve the elder staff, all the better. Besides, part of her was anxious to get back to the hotel room and figure out why the mask spoke so strongly to her. "She's as tough as she looks. She'll be all right. It's better if you drop me off at the Hotel Chelsea."

Sebastian tugged on her sleeve and made a little snarl sound in the back of his throat, but she shooed him off before Tony took notice. The magician locked eyes with her in the rearview mirror before smiling and putting the car in gear. Such a handsome man. Definitely Anaïs's type. It would be a shame if their paths never crossed again.

While Tony drove, Celeste nestled into her seat and let her mind drift back to her near encounter with Nick the night before. She'd been so caught up in that morning's events she hadn't had time to reflect on the significance of seeing him arrive at the tavern with the same gentleman who'd appeared at the tobacco shop in Chinatown. The same man Tony had been telling her about while he ate his steak. She'd had it drilled into her head so many times that there were no coincidences, it would be negligent of her not to scrutinize the incident more thoroughly.

"Did you know O'Brien would be at the tavern last night? Is that why we went there?"

Tony narrowed his eyes at her in the rearview mirror. "Uh, yeah, he's a regular there. Didn't think you'd noticed him." He stopped at a light and watched the traffic before maneuvering a right turn. "I wasn't sure he was going to show up last night. He was later than usual."

"Were you planning on warning him?" That would have seemed a logical solution to preventing Frank from gaining access to O'Brien's dreams and the leverage he needed to blackmail him into whatever it was he wanted. And yet Tony hadn't approached the man. He'd thrown his luck in with her instead. Though she understood the difficulty of trying to explain the situation to someone not magically inclined.

"No. You saw the guy. He claims to be a 'developer' but he's just a racketeer. Frank's had me watching him for weeks. No idea who the man he came in with was, though."

Celeste admitted nothing about Nick, though she was worried about something O'Brien had said earlier about investing in a movie studio. When she'd left California, West Coast Studios was in a jam with their investors after a string of accidents had left people whispering about curses. They weren't far off the mark, since a Skulk had been responsible for the sabotage. But why would Nick entertain the interests of a con artist? Did he believe O'Brien was a legitimate businessman?

Tony lifted his chin to see her in the rearview mirror and caught her lost in her thoughts. "So what are you thinking? About the mask? I mean, if Frank could see you through the eye slits, it must have some kind of power, right?"

"I can't really be sure yet." Celeste shook her head as she looked over the mask again. It gave off an energy that felt inexplicably old. The wood was chipped and discolored in places. Well worn, as though hundreds of hands had caressed the edges over the years. The gold vein running across the cutouts for the eyes was mostly intact, but here and there a section was dented or a tiny piece gouged out. She hadn't a clue what power the mask held or how Frank was able to see through her glamour when it was pulled over his face, but there were ways to detect an object's magical origins. All she had to do was get back to her hotel and make a quick trip to the corner market.

CHAPTER FOURTEEN

Room 823 and Compound 606

The cab crept uptown along Fifth Avenue, barely keeping ahead of the lumbering double-decker bus moving beside it. Anaïs was headed for the Plaza Hotel, which was the last known destination she had for her protégé, Mrs. Angelica Lombardi. She really ought to have kept closer tabs on the newlywed, but the woman had settled into her charmed life so easily and happily that Anaïs hadn't given it another thought after the couple sailed away for another summer in America.

No, that wasn't quite true. The matchmaking she'd done for Angelica had proved a constant source of second-guessing herself. She'd always felt there was more she could have done to promote the young woman and her talents. Angelica was a skilled pianist, generally even-tempered, intelligent, attractive, and ambitious. Lombardi had just been so wealthy and gregarious that she supposed both she and Angelica had been swept off their feet while securing the young woman's footing on her star path. But she'd always wondered if she'd released the young woman too quickly into the arms of a charismatic gentleman. Then again, Gardiennes didn't make mistakes when it came to their protégés. Or so she'd been told.

It was Lombardi's connection with the dream auger that had her second-guessing herself with renewed gusto. Gideon had his doubts too as he swooped from a terraced roof to a sky-piercing spire along the avenue, following the taxi as soon as he'd detected Anaïs was on the move. Had Lombardi sought Frank out? Or was it the other way around? She wagered she'd recognize the answer when she saw Angelica for herself. The truth would shine in her face.

Though Anaïs had never witnessed a dream auger in action herself, the rumors she'd heard made them out to be like spiders, sitting in the middle of their web of connections. One step on the wrong filament by a subject of interest, and you became lunch to one of these two-legged bloodsuckers. They'd get inside your head, clean out all the incriminating information they could find, and then the blackmail would start. Intimidating letters would purport to know the mark's deepest secrets and threaten to reveal all to the newspapers. Or perhaps the threat involved notifying a spouse. Or the authorities. For a protégé to be involved in something so suspect was almost unheard of. They were under the protection of their Gardienne. They ought not to fall victim to such plots. Unless and until the Infortunii came for their appointed spoils under the guise of the downfall effect. But that was almost always years later, after the success had time to bloom and thrive first. And dream augers were *not* Infortunii, despite the obvious commonalities.

The cab pulled to a stop in front of the Plaza Hotel. Seeing the austere face of the building for the first time put Anaïs in mind of the heat and opulence so aptly described by that peculiar author acquaintance of Gertrude's. The one who reeked of gin and lime. He wasn't a protégé like some of the others who hung about her salon, but he seemed to have an intuition that persuaded him to stay close to the elder Gardienne, as though he could feel the charm and grace oozing off her for his benefit. It hadn't helped. His latest novel hadn't impressed the ruling literary class, though Anaïs had enjoyed reading about the delectable rise and fall of its ritzy characters.

After paying the cabbie, Anaïs had Gideon wait atop the building while she entered the grand lobby of the Plaza Hotel. As she strolled through its interior, with its crystal chandeliers, luscious palm trees, scrumptious velvet divan de milieu, and a total of ten elevators waiting to take guests to the top, she took a moment to devise a plan. She had no intention of making a direct approach to either the front desk or the Lombardi couple. She wished to remain discreet. Unseen. Observant. If nothing was wrong, it was best if no one knew she'd ever been there. But first she had to learn what room the couple were occupying for the summer.

While the desk clerk spoke to a gentleman in a suit that cost more than some people's annual salary, Anaïs slipped behind a palm tree and veiled herself in glamour. As inconspicuously as possible, she removed a piece of hotel stationery from a sideboard and flipped it over in her hand, transforming the blank slip of paper into a sealed letter addressed to the couple at the hotel, complete with a cancellation stamp from the post office. Of course, if anyone looked too closely, it would only say "New York City" in dark ink, but she took a chance no one was paying attention to that sort of detail. She slipped the letter on the front desk when no one was looking, then waited.

Less than a minute went by before the vigilant clerk noticed his error and popped the wayward envelope in the cubbyhole for room number 823. *Hmm, less than halfway up.* Not the penthouse, she noted, as she stepped into the elevator behind a couple hooked arm in arm. Of course, the operator hadn't noticed her enter the contraption, so she had to push the button for the eighth floor herself while he closed the gate. The couple got off on the fifth floor, which led to an awkward moment when the elevator stopped again on the eighth floor, and Anaïs had to pop open the gate herself. She left the operator crossing himself inside the ornate box of wood and mirrors as it plunged back down to the lobby to pick up the next guest. Sometimes a little collateral harm was unavoidable.

Room 823 was quiet as Anaïs pressed her ear to the door. It was ten o'clock in the morning, so either the couple were early risers and had already left to shop and run errands, or they were late sleepers and hadn't yet dressed for the day. She considered waiting in the lobby to see if they came or went, but she didn't have time for dillydallying. Not when the elder staff was still in the hands of a goon and the entire sisterhood of Gardiennes was in peril. Using her pendant to unlock the door, she decided to peek inside the room just to be sure. But before she could turn the knob, a room service trolley wheeled its way toward her, pushed by a handsome young man in a white button-up jacket.

Anaïs never looked luck in the face twice, so she pressed her back to the wall until the waiter entered the room, then ducked inside behind him before the door closed. Her hunch about the couple being late sleepers proved true as she found Angelica and Leopold still in their boudoir attire, awaiting their breakfast. They sat down at a small bistro table in front of the window overlooking the park as the waiter laid out their silverware and a breakfast that consisted of a soft-boiled egg and toast for the gentleman and baked bananas and a croissant for the lady.

So far things appeared normal, though there was something peaked about Angelica's complexion. The spark that had drawn Anaïs to the vivacious young pianist had been dulled in half. The blush was noticeably absent from her cheeks, like a hydrangea that had wilted from too much sun.

Angelica let her arms rest at her side as the waiter spread a napkin on her lap before doing the same for her husband. "Thank you, Arthur," she said in a small voice.

The waiter lit a candle, straightened the rose in the crystal vase, then poured each a cup of coffee. "Anything else, sir or madam?"

"That will be all." Lombardi was short with the server. He didn't even bother to look up at the poor young man, who left without an added gratuity, which was so common in the American city. Especially in a ritzy joint like this one.

Anaïs moved like a serpent through a jungle, not making a sound, as she eavesdropped on the couple's breakfast conversation. Something was amiss, and she intended to find out what.

"Any plans today, my dear?" Lombardi paid more attention to his soft egg than to the other human in the room, neglecting to lift his gaze to receive her reply. "There's a new art exhibition at the Met I thought we might like to visit."

Angelica poked her silver fork at the caramelized banana. "I don't think I'm feeling up to it," she said. "I may stay in and read a book today."

"Not even to check in on the Van Gogh paintings? You know how you love gazing at the cypresses."

"Hmm."

Definitely not the vibrant and talented young woman Anaïs was familiar with. But what had dimmed that beautiful light that had once made her shine apart from the others to catch a Gardienne's eye?

Lombardi's cheek twitched at his wife's response. "I can't be expected to continually apologize," he said.

"And I can't be expected to bear the public humiliation for what's happened to us," she said as she dropped her silverware, letting it clatter against the plate.

So, something had happened. Anaïs leaned in closer. The line of tension between the married couple had been drawn taut. The slightest pressure could trigger an explosive fight. But why? What could have invaded the bliss enhanced by Anaïs's magic?

"How many times do I have to tell you?" Lombardi pleaded. "There was nothing to be done. If I don't pay the man, my whole life will be ruined. Reduced to moneymaking fodder for every newspaper between here and Calcutta."

"And what about me?" Angelica held her napkin to her mouth as though she might be ill. "How am I to endure this treatment?" She pushed her plate away as tiny pinpricks of sweat dotted her forehead.

"Salvarsan is the best treatment available. The doctor assured us you'd see improvement eventually. You just have to soldier through it, my dear. And show a little gratitude that there is at least a potential cure."

"You mean until we can't afford the doctor fee anymore." Angelica threw down her napkin. "All because you had to go see that con man.

That hypnotist who picked your pockets clean." She went into the bedroom, slamming the door behind her.

Anaïs was dumbfounded. Known in some circles as compound 606, Salvarsan was a drug used in the treatment for syphilis. Far from a cure-all, the side effects from the dosage were said to be almost as bad as the disease. What was happening? It was far too early for the downfall effect to have overtaken Angelica. The couple had been married only two years. And yet there were money troubles, marital strain, blackmail, and a dangerous health issue. The link to the dream auger couldn't have been clearer. Frank had met with Lombardi, dug around in his subconscious, and found something worth blackmailing him over. "Despicable," she whispered.

Lombardi looked up. "What was that?"

Anaïs froze after speaking out loud. She was slipping. She waited for Lombardi to shake his head and go back to his newspaper, then summoned Gideon to create a distraction at the window. It took a moment for the rook to find the correct one, but once he beat his wings against the glass and squawked maniacally enough, Lombardi rushed to the window to shoo him away. Anaïs touched her ruby pendant, sending a wave of protective magic over Angelica so that she might not suffer too much from either the malady or the cure. She made her exit while the husband cursed the damn bird to go back to the park and leave decent people alone.

Halfway down the hall Anaïs threw off her glamour to wait for the elevator. No need to give the operator two heart attacks in one day with her veiled mischief. When the elevator arrived and the door opened, she had to step aside to let a male passenger out. It was only when she lifted her head to make polite eye contact that she recognized the man's face. Nick West in the flesh. He stepped out and greeted her with a nod. Her face flushed as she entered the elevator, hoping he hadn't recognized her. And yet she saw the slow, curious turn of the head to look over his shoulder just as the door closed. Anaïs bit her lip, knowing his presence in the city was no accident.

Oh, Celeste, what have you done to that man's heart to have him cross our paths here?

CHAPTER FIFTEEN

Signs of Malediction

The Hotel Chelsea was nearly abandoned at midday. Celeste rode the elevator up to her room with the wooden mask tucked away inside a common shopping bag. After Tony had dropped her off out front, she'd made a quick trip to the corner grocer to pick up a few supplies. Marjoram for boosted insight, some bay leaf and thyme to help with wisdom, and a little garlic and fresh rosemary for protection, just in case. She'd had to ask the man behind the counter to fill out her list, which led to him asking if she was making a roast for dinner. She nodded quickly to appease his curiosity, then stuffed her bundle of dried herbs in her shopping bag.

Celeste set the mask on the velvet chair by the fireplace while she unwrapped the herbs and transformed a pair of slippers into a pestle and mortar to prepare. She hadn't done any herb work in a while, not since Cassiopeia had insisted three years ago Celeste make a poultice to check her salamander for signs of malediction after he'd accidentally set her work shed on fire. That incident had turned out satisfactory, but with Sebastian watching from his pillow on the bed, Celeste had second thoughts about her ability to remember *exactly* what was required. "You're right," she said. "I'd better double-check my ratios."

Celeste returned to her trunk to look for her instruction book but found herself drawn to the *History of Gardiennes* again. Her intuition snagged on the book, convinced the mask and staff were related somehow. They were just too similar in appearance and construction, even though they were made from different wood and had completely different purposes.

She opened the book and skimmed the index to see if there was any mention of distinguishable masks throughout their history. Nothing was indicated in the subtitles, so she hovered her hand over the pages to see if anything spoke to her on an emotional level. About three-quarters of the way into the book, a slight ruffle tickled the underside of her hand. Just about at the same page where she'd left off earlier when reading about the elder staff.

A chill broke out on Celeste's skin. Two pages past where she'd read about the elder staff, there was a footnote at the bottom of a section on other noteworthy relics of the era, some of which were recovered by Hugh Capet himself after they'd been stolen from a monastery. Among them was a mask made to hide the disfigured face of a long-dead priest, which the king gifted to a wandering stranger who'd given a witty reply in answer to a question on the deteriorating weather. The wanderer had stated there was no such thing as bad weather, only inadequate clothing to meet the conditions. It was said the man was "spritely of mind yet hideous to look upon," and so Hugh had awarded him the mask so that he might not offend the eye of those who would do well to hear his counsel. The footnote concluded by indicating, once again, that most historians of the sisterhood credit this event to interference by the Infortunii at the monastery.

Celeste checked in with Sebastian. "It couldn't be the same one. It just couldn't. Could it?" Doubt flooded in almost immediately. There was simply no way a thousand-year-old mask would suddenly turn up in New York. "Then again, there is a nearly one-thousand-year-old enchanted staff sitting somewhere in the middle of Manhattan."

Celeste slowly closed the book and set it aside. While she was reaching for the volume on herbs, a spasm of hesitation hit her. What if the mask *was* old? What if it *was* related to Hugh Capet and the elder staff? What would happen if an individual as corrupt as the dream auger got his hands on both the mask and the staff at the same time *and* he somehow figured out what to do with them? But before she began conjuring doomsday scenarios, she first had to know if the mask was even something to worry about.

The instructions for a fogging mixture were clear enough. She had all the right herbs. All she had to do was crush them in a particular order, going from greenest to woodiest, and get a blaze going in the fireplace. Sebastian took care of the fire while she did the grinding. The book mentioned boosting the potency of the mixture by attaching a few rhyming couplets as she applied the herbs, so she centered herself before the fire. It was getting warm in the room with the windows closed, but she didn't want any of the fogging smoke escaping before it had a chance to penetrate the mask.

Sebastian scampered a good two feet behind Celeste as she placed a sprinkle of each crushed herb onto her palm. When she'd arranged them in equal piles in a circle on her hand, she leaned forward and blew them into the fire. As a fragrant smoke rose off the logs, she invoked her magic to meld with the smoke's properties. "Earthy herbs and swirling smoke, reveal what's hidden in the oak. Spell, hex, curse, or enchantment. If they be there, find attachment."

She picked up the mask and held it near the fire until the smoke enveloped all the nicks and crevices in the carved oak. If the herb smoke worked as it should, the grain in the wood ought to reveal any malediction affixed to it by changing color. Even if the mask did prove to be centuries old, she supposed any one of the Merlin types Anaïs had warned about could have manipulated the energy around an object over time. But a spellcaster who could enchant a mask to let the wearer see through Gardienne glamour? Of that she wasn't so sure.

Celeste watched as the smoke infiltrated the vein of gold that cut across the eye slits. Something was happening. Some chemical reaction. The properties of the gold mixed with the herb smoke until the inlaid material glowed bloodred. "So, there is a trace of something there," she said.

Sebastian stood on his hind legs and began chittering wildly. A warning that Celeste didn't know what she was dealing with. Perhaps he was right. The mask began to vibrate in her hand. She didn't want to let go. Her curiosity to know why it reacted like it did grew almost overpowering. She wanted to put it on and feel the wood's grain against her skin. She wanted to inhale the scent of the oak, sense the energy of the others who had tried it on. Her vision blurred as her mind fell into a trance, and she brought the mask to her face.

CHAPTER SIXTEEN

A Little Smoke and Cognac by the Fire

Anaïs stepped off the elevator and walked to her room inside the Hotel Chelsea. By the time the cab had dropped her off at the curb, she was convinced the only way that Angelica Lombardi had succumbed to the downfall effect so soon was because the Infortunii weren't abiding by their obligations. The unwritten agreements that the Gardiennes and Infortunii had lived by for centuries to maintain the balance that was so crucial to the work each did in the world had been violated for the second time now. Their corrupt behavior was the reason the Gardiennes had needed to come to America in the first place. They'd had to confront the rogue Skulk on the loose in California who'd ended up murdering a young woman after the Infortunii weren't able or willing to control one of their own. What she didn't know was if this new level of interference with Angelica was part of a breakdown in the natural order of things or one simply designed to influence *her* protégés, given her ongoing hostile relationship with the Skulks.

The Hotel Chelsea was noticeably quiet in the middle of the day, yet a faint trace of smoke lingered in the hallway. Perhaps from a pipe or cigar. Anaïs entered her room, then went to the window to open the sash wide, while thoughts of Skulks churned in her head. Her personal history with the Infortunii since becoming a fully minted Fée

Gardienne had been wrought with aggression and threats. She, like all brand-new Gardiennes, had been shadowed by Skulks from the start, as they watched and schemed while waiting for the opportunity to bring their influence to bear.

Anaïs threw her purse and shawl on the bed, forced to remember the one particularly antagonistic Skulk who'd made a true nuisance of himself shortly after she'd set up her very first protégé as the first woman chocolatier in Brussels. Mary's sweets were tenderly made to be individual pieces of art. And her ganache was to die for! So she'd gotten the enchanted nudge from Anaïs, and yet she might never have reached the pinnacle of her destiny if that Skulk had had his way. He'd had no appetite for abiding by the rules either. Not once his misogynistic tendencies had become inflamed after seeing a woman find success in the male-dominated profession of chocolate making. Anaïs had needed to ditch him fast to protect her ward, which may or may not have caused a small kerfuffle.

Gideon flew in the open window and perched on the bed's headboard. He'd heard her thoughts and bobbed his head in agreement.

"Do you remember how that Skulk crept up behind me, always watching and waiting with that awful snaggletooth poking out of his mouth." Anaïs shook off a shiver. "He was out of bounds, that one."

The Skulk hadn't acted yet, but Anaïs had had enough of her and her protégé being stalked. To throw him off, she'd traveled from Brussels to Paris, and then backtracked to Bruges on an old horse path, and yet he persisted. The Skulk began sending letters listing all the terrible things he had in mind for her protégé's downfall. Then one night he got close enough that Anaïs could feel his cold, fetid breath at her back while crossing a bridge, so she gave him a hard shove to send the message to back off. He fell into the canal and had his head bashed in by a passing barge. The incident had caused an uproar between the Gardiennes and the Infortunii, but it was decided the Skulk's death was an accident, so Anaïs got to continue her Gardienne work.

After that, her reputation morphed into something verging on malevolent. She was rumored to flirt with the dark arts because of the murderous heart she'd been born with. She didn't mind the gossip in the least. It was like being given a coat of armor with no one in the occult world ever wanting to test her mettle. But at the same time, the incident had made her the target of Infortunii ire. She'd had to work twice as hard after that to protect her potential protégés from unwanted attention, but this business with the Lombardi couple was over the line and years too soon.

Anaïs gave Gideon a scratch on the head. If it *was* the Infortunii who'd infiltrated her protections over the couple prematurely, then how did it involve Frank and those hypnotic eyes of his? The connection to Lombardi was no coincidence. They were listed in his day planner, *and* Angelica had specifically blamed their troubles on a hypnotist. But if it wasn't the Infortunii behind the misfortune, then this dream auger was more dangerous than she'd first thought.

Anaïs looked at her watch and wondered if Celeste had returned yet. She wanted to share what she'd discovered and hear her thoughts on the matter. Yes, she'd come around to the idea the young woman might make a fair Gardienne after all. She'd been on the right track by looking back at their history and the origin of the elder staff after it had been stolen. Anaïs was almost certain there was some sort of trade in ancient magical relics at play. Perhaps the dream auger thought he could pawn the staff to a collector and use the proceeds to improve his club. The French Drop could certainly use an upgrade in its aesthetic.

Anaïs knocked politely on the connecting door between her room and Celeste's before giving the knob a twist. She was about to call out a "hello" when the scent of burning herbs hit her in the face. Across the room, Celeste sat leaning before the fireplace. Was she performing a fogging? And what was the object in her hands?

Anaïs approached. "What do you have there?" When she got no answer, she came around to get a better look. "Celeste?"

The young Gardienne appeared to be in some sort of trancelike state as she raised a crude wooden mask up to her face. Celeste's eyes were wide and unfocused, as though her thoughts had skipped a mile away. Her skin had the sallow complexion of one about to lose her stomach contents, and yet she would not turn away from the object in her grasp.

Quick to trust her intuition, Anaïs swiped at the mask seconds before it touched Celeste's face. The mask rolled on the floor, and the Gardienne stirred out of her daze, surprised to find Anaïs standing beside her with what must have been a look of pure terror displayed in the whites of her eyes.

"What do you think you're doing?" Anaïs kicked the mask away from reach.

"I . . . I'm not sure." Celeste stood, seemingly as bewildered by the near calamity of messing with magic she didn't understand as her fellow Gardienne was.

Anaïs flipped the mask over with the toe of her shoe. "Where did you get this thing?"

"I stole it from Frank, the dream auger. He was wearing it while doing a reading."

The walls and floor trembled as Anaïs stood with her fists at her sides and a snarl curling on her lip. Celeste backed up a step as a Lalique vase on the mantel vibrated dangerously close to the edge before gently righting itself.

"You stole it? From the dream auger?" Anaïs gripped her pendant and arched her eyebrow. The side table next to the velvet chair collapsed and was transformed into a lead box with a padlock and chain. The mask flew into the box, the lid slammed shut, and the padlock clicked into place, punctuating what she thought of bringing home wayward masks and attempting to try them on while conducting magical experiments alone.

After agreeing to sit and listen to Celeste explain what had happened and how she'd come to be in the same room as Frank and his latest subject, Anaïs didn't exactly calm down. She lifted her brow instead, opening the adjoining door to call for her rook. Gideon flew in and nestled on the mantel beside the delicate vase.

Anaïs stared at the lead box currently keeping the mask secure. "Why'd you steal it? Were you compelled? Did it feel like you were under some influence that told you to take it?" She jumped out of her chair to feel Celeste's forehead, wondering if a hex or curse could be detected through the temperature of her skin.

Celeste blushed and pulled away. "No, it wasn't like that. I was veiled, and yet he could see me. But only when he was wearing the mask."

That set off an alarm. Only the Infortunii and other Gardiennes could see through their glamour.

"And did you notice?" Celeste pointed her thumb at the lead box. "The mask has a vein of gold running through it. Just like the elder staff. It can't be a coincidence, right? Both objects here in the city at the same time."

Anaïs warily approached the box she'd conjured. She glanced at Gideon, who bobbed his head to have a peek. She undid the padlock and pried the lid up just enough to get a glimpse of the mask inside. Celeste was right. There was an uncanny resemblance to the crude but distinct way the gold had been inlaid as though poured into a crevice hot and then instantly frozen. "Do you remember what the smoke told you about it?"

"It clung mostly to the vein where it crosses the eye slits. That's why I was curious to hold the mask up to my face. I wanted to look through the eyes myself and see if they'd been enchanted. But then something took hold of me. I felt myself going under, like I wasn't in control anymore. Almost like I was hypnotized. I suppose I'm lucky you walked in when you did."

"I can't argue with that."

"But that's not all." Celeste retrieved the history book and pointed out the section mentioning a mask and a vague reference to someone who was "hideous to look upon."

"A Skulk?" Anaïs blew out a long breath and sat on the bed, letting her face fall into her hands. She hadn't wanted to believe it, but the evidence was mounting that the mask might be the genuine article. "There's another source that mentions a mask like this one," she said. "*The Chronicles of Elsbeth the Enlightened.*"

"I've never heard of it."

Anais nodded. Few Gardiennes had taken the time to reach for the books on the upper shelves of the cottage library. "It's a handwritten book that describes things a little differently. In it, she describes how the king had been forced to play arbiter once the Infortunii learned about the gift of the elder staff. They'd threatened chaos, including ransacking monasteries and abbeys, if they didn't receive equal favor. So Hugh Capet bestowed upon them a plain wooden mask that purportedly gave them the ability to alter their appearance and find more acceptance in the world, without actually giving them his court blessing. Apparently, he couldn't stand the sight of them either. Despicable creatures beneath the veneer of humanity they wear now."

"So it's real?" Celeste wiped her hands against her dress as though trying to rid them of any trace of Skulk energy she might have picked up after touching the mask.

Anaïs didn't blame her one bit. After the news had sunk in about what they were likely dealing with, she shared the revelation she'd made after her morning excursion to the Lombardis' hotel room. "I had begun to suspect there might be Skulks in New York," she said. "My protégé's wealthy husband was a client of Frank's, and now their finances and health are failing. But what if it's this dream auger channeling a little Infortunii bad luck because of the mask? Maybe the damn thing is cursed. You felt it yourself, didn't you?"

"I couldn't put it down," Celeste said. "But that might just be how a Gardienne reacts to the energy. It could be something entirely different for a dream auger. Who knows what power he feels when he wears it."

Anaïs pressed a hand to her stomach, knowing he had powers enough when he wasn't wearing a mask. So what did the mask do for him? What control did it give him?

The younger Gardienne flopped down on the velvet chair by the fireplace. She looked defeated. Anaïs was sorely tempted to tell Celeste about her run-in with Nick on the elevator earlier at the Plaza to cheer her up, but the moment wasn't right. She didn't need the young woman scattering her attentions when the possible annihilation of the sisterhood hung in the balance.

Anaïs understood how mere talk of Skulks was enough to knock a little breath out of any Gardienne, but she wasn't accustomed to feeling beaten. There was a streak of pride within her that wouldn't allow her to be bested by this dream auger. Not when he was so obviously using his craft for ill-gotten gain. She wondered if he even knew the consequences of his meddling.

"So, you're saying the dream auger put this mask on to do his mind reading." Anaïs rubbed her chin just below her lower lip, wondering again how it enhanced his power.

Celeste reached down to scoop up her stoat and hold him in her lap. "He said it worked like a barrier between his ego and the other man's while he was reading his dreams."

"But why? He shouldn't need any help in that regard. A dream auger's talent is innate."

"There's more." Celeste nuzzled her chin against Sebastian's neck. It was something Anaïs had seen her do since she was a girl. Whenever the world of magic got to be too overwhelming for her, she'd bury her face in the animal's fur. She supposed she'd always done something similar with Gideon, scratching his neck feathers when she needed comfort. Perhaps it's what youngsters did when there was no mother to soothe away the fright with a calm arm around the shoulders. "Tony says he doesn't just read their dreams. He reads their deepest, darkest deeds like he's breaking into a vault at the back of their consciousness, and then blackmails them with the information."

"You'd think he'd have to have physical proof to do that, but it coincides with what I witnessed today with my protégé." Anaïs stood and crossed to the bar Celeste had conjured for herself. "But here's the thing. He shouldn't have been able to do anything to my protégé or her husband. Not while under my protection. It just doesn't happen. He's not a Skulk." She poured herself a glass of cognac and found it surprisingly good. She tugged on her ruby pendant, transforming a stand-up ashtray into a second velvet chair so she could sit by the fire too. "It's possible Frank could have found the mask on the black market," she reasoned. "There are markets in Cairo, London, Algiers." She swirled her cognac, absorbing the glow from the fire as Gideon hopped over to sit above her shoulder on the chair. "If the Infortunii did lose track of the relic—after all, they no longer require any aid in physically transforming their appearance—it's plausible the mask could have found its way into one of the specialized markets. Hell, one of their own kind might have even sold it for a small profit. There is no honor among Skulks." Anaïs snapped her fingers in a eureka moment. "Or maybe Frank stole it from them like he stole the elder staff from us! And they're too thick-skulled to admit it or ask for help."

"London." Celeste suddenly sat up. "Tony said Frank bought the mask as a souvenir while they were touring London in their vaudeville show. After that, he put it in a trunk for months. But he recently brought it back out and started wearing it at his readings. Said he'd discovered a way to change their lives after doing a reading on some guy who gave Tony the heebie-jeebies."

"Then there can be no more doubt." Anaïs sipped her cognac, letting the burn help fuel her desire for retribution. "I couldn't get the elder staff back before I left the club. I assume Frank had taken it with him. He still doesn't know what to do with it, but I think this dream auger found a way to channel whatever malignant power still resides in the mask. And now that he's become dependent on that power for his livelihood, I dare say, he must be missing it very much."

"He was livid." Celeste couldn't control the mischievous smile that took hold in the corner of her mouth before sobering again when another worry seemed to cross her mind. "But if he has the mask, why steal the elder staff too?"

Anaïs tipped her half-empty glass toward Celeste to show she was onto something. "And between the two relics, which would he prefer to have in his possession? The one he knows how to use to blackmail people or the one that frustrates him because he isn't smart enough or threatening enough to compel it to do his bidding?"

"I don't follow. Doesn't he want them both?"

"Yes, but he doesn't know what to do with our elder staff. He only suspects it will enhance his abilities the same way the mask did." Anaïs swirled her cognac and inhaled the aroma. "But he hasn't even seen it in its true form. That's why he kidnapped me to figure it out. I can't say for sure, but Nellie could have been the one to tell him about it. She must have had a vision. About us. About the staff. About coming to New York. Could that be how he knew to buy the mask in the London shop too?"

Celeste confirmed that's what Tony had told her. "She's seen some grand plan that involves all of them. And us. But what could a dream auger do with both relics?"

"Well, that's just it. He *had* both, didn't he. But thank goodness he didn't know what he was doing. You can always rely on a dolt to be a dolt."

Celeste let her stoat loose to go lie by the fire while she curled her legs up on the chair. "Frank's entire livelihood of blackmail and corruption depends on that mask."

"I'd wager it lets him create a wormhole into men's souls through some residual Skulk magic. He must be desperate to have it back."

"So, we do a trade," Celeste said, suddenly getting the bigger picture. "We offer the mask in exchange for the elder staff. He can't possibly say no. He needs that mask to do his dirty work."

"Exactly!" Anaïs's mouth nearly watered with anticipation. "And we're going to use Tony to set it up for us. After all, he owes us one."

At last, they had a map forward. And if everything went according to that plan, they could still make their steamship on tomorrow's tide. Anaïs swallowed the last sip of cognac. She'd never been so anxious to get on a boat and leave a port behind her.

CHAPTER SEVENTEEN

Better Make the Deal

Celeste and Sebastian walked down the alley behind Frank's speakeasy. It was still daylight and far too early for any of the performers and patrons to be milling about inside, but Tony's car was parked a block away, so she had high hopes she'd find him inside. The delivery door where she'd entered before was locked, but a swing of her pendant on its chain transformed it into a beaded curtain. She parted the strands of beads and entered the dark hallway fully veiled in her glamour.

The dressing rooms at the club weren't completely abandoned. A janitor was busy sweeping up cigarette butts in the hallway and dumping them into a metal bucket. The sight of him gave Celeste flashbacks of Charlie, the affable janitor at West Coast Studios who'd turned out to be a murdering Skulk. The janitor ducked into a dressing room, so she took the opportunity to shake off a shiver and bolt for the stairs to go find Tony.

Things proved quieter on the main floor. The stage was empty except for a piano and a stand-alone microphone. No one mixing drinks at the bar. No one barking out threats if the next act didn't get in position. Celeste threw off her veil, remembering her impromptu debut as a magician's assistant the night before. She'd enjoyed herself more than she could have guessed. Tony, and all those young men and women rushing between the dressing rooms and the stage every night, got to experience that intoxicating thrill of the audience's approval over and over again. A type of magic of its own, she supposed. But the lights were dim now and the chairs empty.

Ahead, a beam of light seeped out beneath the office door where Anaïs had been held in a glass tank. People were talking in low voices inside. A man and a woman. And there was a baby who cooed and squealed in a happy outburst before being playfully hushed. Celeste crept closer, pressing her ear against the door. It was Tony. He said something softly to the baby that she couldn't make out, but when he spoke to the woman, she heard everything.

"I'm going to get all of us out, I swear it," he said as though he'd promised a thousand times before. "We just need a little more time."

"That's what you keep saying, but he's getting worse. Our situation is getting worse." The woman paused long enough that Celeste imagined her imploring Tony with her tearful eyes. "I have to think about little Hazel. She has a full, beautiful life ahead of her. As her mother, I owe her that chance."

The words were so tender, so full of hope, Celeste couldn't help but swallow a lump in her throat. Was this the woman Anaïs had told her about? Nellie, the clairvoyant supplying all the information about them?

"Of course you do." Tony's voice was softer and gentler than she'd heard him use with her. "And she'll get that life, I promise. But it's that damn mask." Celeste leaned in even closer. "Ever since he started using it, he's been impossible to reason with. And now that it's been stolen, he's like some hophead ready to tear the world apart until he gets his fix."

"You should have seen him when he found out the other one had escaped." Nellie laughed conspiratorially. "I don't think that old tank will ever hold water again."

"Yeah, it's beat up pretty bad, but I think my days as an escape artist are finished anyway. Isn't that right, Hazel?" There was cooing and baby talk that caused a strange vibration inside Celeste's chest. "At least she didn't escape with the magic wand, or he'd have murdered half the people on the street." Tony let out an exhausted sigh. "They're quite a pair, aren't they?"

"The women? If it weren't for them and the vision I had, I'd have run away already."

Celeste tensed. What could the woman have seen? What else was to come? She needed to get inside and talk to Tony. She'd been sent there to propose they enter into an exchange, the mask for the elder staff, but now she worried she was intruding on something more personal than she'd anticipated. Should she knock? Come back later?

"They'll do the right thing," the woman said. "In fact, I believe they're here already."

Celeste sucked in a breath. The door opened and the same red-headed woman she'd seen arriving at the club the night before invited her in with a wan smile. Nellie. It must be.

"It isn't what you think," the woman said. "I smelled your perfume. Gardenias, isn't it?"

Celeste was still impressed by her deduction. "Yes, it seems to follow me around."

"Celeste?" Tony had been playing with the baby girl on the floor. He stood up, seemingly embarrassed to have been caught in such a quaint domestic scene as though it tarnished his tough-guy image. "What are you doing here?" He checked the backstage area with his usual paranoia while he threw on his suit jacket.

"I believe she's here with news." Nellie stepped aside to allow Celeste to enter.

Tony looked past her to the darkened staircase that connected to the bookshop above. "We may only have a few minutes left before Frank returns."

"I'll be quick." Celeste entered, closing the door behind her. "You're right, I have news. We think we understand about the mask. Where it's from and how he got it."

"London," Nellie said, glancing at Tony. "He got it in an occult shop just off the Strand."

"We suspected as much. It's actually very old and very powerful. You can tell him that."

"Why?" Tony looked from Nellie to Celeste for explanation.

"Because we're ready to make an exchange," Celeste said. "If he's as anxious to get the mask and all its power back, as you were just saying, then he can have it."

"If he gives you the 'clarinet.'" Nellie glanced at Tony and then the baby.

"Exactly."

Tony rubbed the back of his head and exhaled. "What if we don't want him to get it back. What if the mask is the problem. Remember that little deal we made last night?"

Nellie put her hand on Tony's arm. A gesture meant to show she shared his concern. It was a good question. Celeste had said she'd help deprive the man of his power. Or at least his power over Tony and this woman with the strangely electrifying eyes. "Is she yours?" she asked impulsively, kneeling in front of the baby. She knew it was rude to ask so bluntly, but the dimensions of the relationship between Tony and the woman were suddenly important to her.

Tony's cheekbones sharpened as he sucked in a breath. "Are we playing at that game again?"

Celeste smiled at the baby. "No, just wondering what's truly at stake."

"She's Frank's." Nellie knelt beside her child. "It was a mistake. Him, not the child. He doesn't care a whit about her or me. Tony has been more of a father to her than Frank ever has, but he won't let her go. Or me either. So you might say the balance of Hazel's life is at stake."

The baby stared at Celeste as though mesmerized by the sight of her. Babies, she'd been told, still carried a trace of stardust in their eyes when they were born that helped them see through the mundane. It faded as they grew older, but Hazel was still young enough to see the aura that radiated around a Gardienne in its glittering brilliance. Celeste had the faintest memory herself of seeing the sisters standing around her at the cottage when she'd first been brought in. Their shimmering glow had enveloped her, making her feel safe and secure. Of course, a Gardienne never lost that particular skill; she just learned to temper her vision to give the eyes a rest on occasion.

"She likes you," Nellie said.

Something inside Celeste relaxed, as if the child's opinion meant something crucial to her. She took a quick temperature of the woman's hopes. Her dreams were all about her child. About how Hazel would look in ten years, how she would giggle when she received her first pet, and how smart and polite and happy she'd be. *Someday.* It was confusing. Celeste understood the sacrifice of a mother's love, but it was like Nellie had sawed her own dreams down to dust to carry these premonitions for her daughter. But then Celeste saw something that hadn't been completely smothered. There, at the edge of the woman's aspirations, awaited a shimmering, otherworldly energy Nellie longed to embrace. Celeste caught only a glance at the glimmering through her psychic periphery before it was gone.

Celeste shook off the odd encounter and produced a letter from her handbag as she stood. "Tell Frank you received a message while he was out." She wiped off a spot of Sebastian's saliva before handing it to Tony. "We're demanding a trade. He can pick the place, but it must be tonight. We're not leaving without the, uh, clarinet."

"And then what? You get what you want and leave?" Tony scanned the letter. "Frank needs to be stopped. Nellie and Hazel need to get out of here. We all need to get out of here."

"That can still happen." Celeste nodded toward the note. "Once we get what we came for."

"You don't understand. With that mask, he's a different person. Power hungry. Angry. Conniving. It's like he feeds off other people's misery. If he gets it back, we'll never be free of him."

"Help us get our relic back, and when it's safe, we'll make sure you're safe. He can't hope to win against two . . . of us."

A bluster blew through the club outside the door—a table base scraped the floor, bottles and glasses rattled, and the thud of a heavy body leaned back in a creaky chair.

"Hey, Tony, get out here," boomed a man's voice.

Tony protectively scooted Nellie and Hazel away from the door. "It's him. He's back. You better do your thing," he said with a nod toward Celeste.

"Give him the note. Make sure he accepts the deal, or I don't know what will happen." With that Celeste disappeared under the guise of her glamour, drawing a laugh from the baby and a gasp from Nellie.

Tony straightened his tie and walked out of the office. Celeste followed, remaining in the shadows in case it wasn't merely the mask that helped the dream auger see her. Frank kicked a chair out from beneath the table, indicating Tony should sit. He poured a glass of bourbon and slid it toward him.

"What we got here is a total goddamn trainwreck." Frank threw his homburg on the table. "First the dazzler escapes. Then my mask gets taken right off my fucking face. Can you believe that?" He shook his head at the human lump sitting on his other side. "And now we're hearing there's word on the street that the Mancuso brothers are holding a grudge 'cause of the little arrangement I tried to finagle with Luca after his reading. They already sent a dead cat to get the message across. What more do I have to do?"

"About the mask." Tony pulled the letter out of his jacket and slid it across the table to Frank.

"What's this?"

"We had a visitor while you were out. The women sent over a messenger. They want an exchange."

Frank ripped the envelope open. He read the letter and frowned before staring at a blank spot on the wall. He turned the paper over, then held it up to his nose, sniffing. "Definitely from the tomato. It's got the whiff of her perfume on it."

Celeste clapped a hand over her mouth. The only thing on that envelope was Sebastian's spit.

Frank swallowed a gulp of bourbon, wincing. "So, they want a trade."

"It says you name the place." Tony tapped his fingers nervously on the table, ignoring the bourbon.

"Yeah, I can read." Frank stared a long time at the note. He had to be wondering what was to be gained or lost if the offer was legit. "Where's Nellie?" he asked. "Nellie, get out here!"

The woman came out of the office, carrying the girl. The baby started fussing and squirming in her arms. Hazel reached for Celeste, who stood only a few feet away, though no one in that room ought to know that, including the child.

Frank handed the note to Nellie. "Got any insight on this? Is it some kind of trap or something?"

"What is it?" Nellie shushed the baby and rocked her in her arms while pretending to hear about the note for the first time. Hazel continued to cry and stretched her tiny hand out toward Celeste until the Gardienne thought it might be best if she ducked out the back.

Frank slapped the table. "For God's sake, can't you shut that kid up?"

Nellie threw the note down in protest. "Why don't you make up your own mind for once, instead of always relying on me." She had started to walk toward the office when Frank lunged out of his chair and grabbed her by the hair. He yanked back, forcing her to return to the table. Tony snatched Hazel out of Nellie's arms just before Frank forced her face down against the note on the table.

"Frank, don't." Tony turned Hazel's face away.

"Let's try that again," Frank said, applying pressure. Nellie grimaced, baring her teeth as she rode out the pain, refusing to cry out.

Celeste scanned the club for something she could use to stop the assault. A decorative sconce on the wall flickered. She clenched her fist and pointed her anger at it until it exploded. But rather than letting the shards of glass fly in all directions, she aimed the sharpest fragments at Frank, avoiding Nellie and the baby. A jagged piece sliced across his cheek, drawing blood. He let go of Nellie, cursing the building for its faulty wiring.

"I'd say that's your sign," Nellie said, lifting her head. "Better make the deal."

CHAPTER EIGHTEEN

Every City's Got One

An hour later Anaïs put down the receiver. "That was the call. He's willing to trade."

Celeste poked her head through the adjoining doorway between their rooms. "Where? When?"

"Tonight, at seven." Anaïs glanced out the window. "They won't say where. Not yet. Said they'd send Tony to pick us up in a car out front and take us to the location when it's time."

Celeste bit her thumbnail with that look on her face that something was bothering her. "Tony is counting on us to do something," she finally blurted out.

"Us?"

"Well, me." Celeste entered the room and flopped down on the chaise lounge. "I promised I'd help him stop Frank from hurting people. And if we give him the mask back, he'll keep blackmailing people. And maybe get Tony, Nellie, and the baby hurt in the process. You should see the way he treats her."

Anaïs thought of her protégé and the sad trouble the young woman had found herself in prematurely. "There's no way we're giving the mask back. If that thing really is an Infortunii relic, it's got no place in a dream auger's hands."

"But we have to trade. How else will we get the elder staff back?"

Anaïs paced in front of the window thinking, a finger pressed to her lips. "Frank may try the mask on to make sure it's the real thing. He'll know instantly if it isn't authentic."

"Why couldn't we simply overpower him and his goons with a few improvised cages," Celeste said excitedly. "Snatch the staff and shimmer our way out of there."

"Depends on how many guns they bring. Even we can't out-glamour a spray of bullets." Anaïs raised an eyebrow, getting an idea. "But we could maybe do a swap. After he tests the mask to make sure it's the real McCoy, he'll be less wary."

"How? He's not going to let it out of his sight once he gets his hands on it again."

Sebastian stood on his hind legs as though volunteering for the job as thief. Not to be outdone, Gideon flapped his wings to remind everyone he was the one who could fly out of there with the mask in tow.

"Tony is a magician." Anaïs stopped and sat against the windowsill. "He's also an escape artist. How good, I have no idea."

"They call him Tony the Great."

"Do they now? Then what if we made a replica out of, let's say, that ashtray." Anaïs picked up the very thing on the end table beside the chaise lounge.

Celeste sat up and put her feet on the floor. "A little misdirection. A swap, one for the other. Tony could do it."

Anaïs turned the porcelain ashtray over in her hands. On the third flip it transformed into a reasonable re-creation of the wooden mask, but without the ominous energy emanating from it. "What do you think?"

"I think it could work, but we'll have to get the word to Tony beforehand."

"He's the one picking us up, so we can go over it with him on the way over. He can keep it under his coat. The switch ought to be easy enough for a man with his skills." Anaïs opened the window and checked the sky. The sun hadn't sunk behind the buildings yet but would soon. "We still have a little over an hour. I'm just going to sneak out for a minute and check on the ship to make sure we're all set to sail home tomorrow. I'm anxious to get out of here, and I don't want any surprises. Back in a jiff." Anaïs picked up her shawl and headed for the door before Celeste could object.

Gideon swooped out the open window, catching up to Anaïs on the street below. He was in the mood to play his game of pretending not to know her, so he flitted from tree limb to lamppost to shop sign while she sank deep into her intuition. She wasn't really off to check on the ship. She'd already sent Gideon to inspect the dock earlier. No, she was looking for some insurance in the form of a little extra information. Something to settle a nagging suspicion that wouldn't let her be.

From the start, something had been off about this trip. A feeling of misadventure that had dogged their every move since arriving in California. She'd first attributed the feeling to the level of deception she and Dorée had needed to maintain while Celeste flushed out the Skulk at the Hollywood studio. But now? The theft of the elder staff, the infraction of misfortune affecting her protégé, and now this mysterious mask that had found a dream auger—something was amiss. The truth of it skittered on invisible synapses hovering in the hot summer air.

Anaïs headed west toward Tenth Avenue, then turned south, following an instinct that told her she was getting closer to her goal. The buildings lining the streets grew a little grubbier, a little less polished. The people's clothes lost the shine of silk and worsted wool, as the workers opted instead for the practical durability of cotton and hardened leather aprons. To her astonishment, a freight train ran down the middle of the street, jockeying with cars and horse carts while children darted in and out of traffic. This corner of the city was drenched in chaos. Just the place she was looking for.

Gideon soared ahead and landed on a sign above a little café with a picture of a coffeepot on it. Below, the restaurant's windows were smudged and splattered with so much dirt from the road that it was difficult to see inside. Anaïs had to agree with her rook's assessment—the place certainly looked the part of an occult enclave. She crossed the street in a mad dash to beat an onslaught of delivery trucks newly loaded with crates barreling her way. She entered the café to find two stragglers sitting at the counter. One read a newspaper, the other munched on a thick sandwich using both hands. Behind the counter, a woman scrubbed a soup pot with a rough rag while eyeing her newest customer with an appraising look.

Anaïs closed the door firmly behind her to announce she knew exactly what kind of place she'd walked into. The two men twisted around to see who'd entered, then went back to minding their own business. It took all of three seconds for the woman behind the counter to give her a nod toward the restroom in the back, suggesting she'd passed scrutiny. The men each took a second glance as she walked past them, but neither look lingered on her as she passed through the door with a sign that read To the outhouse.

Indeed, the disaster of a toilet was located inside a small enclosed courtyard in the back where scraggly weeds grew up around the base of the wooden structure. Anaïs cringed and hesitantly opened the outhouse door. She expected to come face-to-face with a hole in a wooden bench and a smell to make her eyes water before finding passage through a secret panel, but she was pleasantly surprised to find it wasn't an outhouse at all. Instead, she found herself staring at the top of a marble staircase. A neon sign above read The Charmstone with an arrow pointing down. The stairs loomed like a gaping corridor into darkness, but with each step a small light came on at her feet until she reached the bottom. There, she was greeted by a combination martini lounge and occult shop that apparently specialized in shriveled dead things tied up with string. Anaïs wouldn't be having any of that. Not around Gideon and Sebastian. But she could see there were a number of other temptations to lure the eye.

The Charmstone showed itself to be an oddly nostalgic refuge with perhaps a dozen patrons inside. The Victrola in the corner played a recording of Enrico Caruso singing "O Sole Mio," while a Siamese cat licked its paws on a cushion beneath the brass speaker horn. Two women dressed in men's tuxedos flipped over tarot cards while sipping gin, a man in an apron stood at a worktable grinding herbs with a cigarette hanging out of the corner of his mouth, and a woman in a silver turban braided what appeared to be human hair into jewelry while her body swayed to the music. Still, not the craziest place Anaïs had ever stumbled into.

A man dressed in a morning suit and spats approached. "Welcome to the Charmstone. Am I correct in assuming you've not been in before?"

"Yes, that's right." Anaïs made a quick sweep of the shop side of the establishment with her eyes. Besides the desiccated specimens, there were herbs, amulets, oils, and candles filling the shelves.

"Is there something special you're looking for today?" The gentleman walked halfway around her as if sniffing out her magical credentials.

Anaïs wasn't one to get tongue-tied, but she'd not been in a shop like this in some time. The question tripped her up briefly as she realized she ought to buy something. "I, uh, I suppose I'm looking for . . ." She stopped herself there. There seemed little point in pretending. She didn't need any of their trinkets, and she didn't have much time. What she wanted was information. "Actually, I'm in need of a clairvoyant," she said. "Someone who really knows their stuff. Have you got anyone on hand for a quick consultation?"

"Well, let me see." The man scratched along his jawline as he looked over the room. His eye landed on the two women reading tarot, but there was a perceptible shake of his head as he passed them over. He seemed to consider the woman braiding hair, then pursed his lips, unconvinced. He lifted his chin and searched farther in the back, where the electric lights didn't quite reach. "Ah, yes, follow me. I think we might have what you're looking for."

He led Anaïs to a table tucked in a cave-like niche. A single gentleman sat at the table sucking on a pipe while reading T. E. Lawrence's *Revolt in the Desert* by candlelight. She was instantly charmed.

After introductions were made, the shop owner left to tend to his other customers. The gentleman sitting at the table, who went by the name Thomas, dog-eared the page he was reading and closed the book. "So, you need to know which horse to bet on? What the sex of your baby will be? Or maybe if it will rain tomorrow. It will."

"Clever. But no, that's not why I've come."

Thomas gestured with his hand for her to sit. Anaïs paused a moment, deciding if she could truly trust him. He puffed out a plume of smoke and said, "Sit. You haven't got much time, so we might as well get started."

Ah, so he had at least some intuition. Anaïs stared at him for a hard second before searching through her purse. She hesitantly removed a velvet bag. Inside was a diamond pendant the size of a quail egg. Dorée's, entrusted to Anaïs a moment before the eldest Gardienne had departed this life. She held it up by the chain, waiting for the man's eyes to bulge out of his head. He merely peered at her through the smoke and smiled.

"I've heard about your kind," he said, eyeing the stone. "Thought you ladies usually stayed in the shadows. Doing your work without people noticing. What brings you out now?"

"I want you to tell me what you can see about the owner of this necklace."

Thomas asked if he might hold it. Anaïs agreed, but with a look of warning that telegraphed he was outmatched in every way, if he thought he could snatch the diamond and get out of the Charmstone alive.

Message received, he smirked and let the diamond rest in the palm of his open hand. "It's very old, this. And it's got a flickering energy." His face grew serious, as though realizing this wasn't just a lark she was on.

"Yes, but what can you tell me about the person who wears it?"

Thomas blew out a puff of smoke. It seemed to be a ritual part of his clairvoyance. Or maybe it just relaxed him. Either way, he hit the nail on the head when the answer emerged from the smoke. She almost couldn't believe it was that simple. Anaïs thanked the man, grabbed the diamond, then headed for the marble staircase with her suspicions vindicated in the nick of time.

CHAPTER NINETEEN

Sticky Brakes

Celeste looked out the window for the fifth time in two minutes. There was no sign of Anaïs or Gideon anywhere on the street below. She hadn't believed the story about checking on the ship. Sebastian could have done that in five minutes. So what was so important that she had to disappear an hour before their big meeting to finally get the elder staff back? It made no sense. And it was infuriating. She'd nearly chewed a fingernail completely off.

Celeste checked the clock on the wall. Twenty minutes to seven. "Well, if she doesn't make it back in time, we're just going to have to go without her," she said to Sebastian. She wasn't sure she meant it, but she had little choice.

Celeste grabbed the shopping bag she'd used earlier and put both the real mask and the conjured replica inside, taking careful note of which one was on top. Bag in hand, she checked the time again, which apparently flew by when you were waiting to exchange a semicursed mask for an ancient relic with an aspiring gangster. They now had only five minutes before Tony was expected to pick them up. She shook her head and decided to go downstairs to the lobby to wait. Sebastian sighed, as much as a stoat is capable, and crawled inside her purse.

As soon as Celeste entered the lobby, Tony pulled up in front of the hotel. Celeste did *not* want to do this alone. "Anaïs, where are you?" She stepped outside the front door and searched the sidewalk in both directions. Nothing.

"Ready to go?" Tony hopped out of the car and opened the door for her. *Now* he wanted to be a gentleman. When she held up a finger asking him to wait a minute, he shoved his hands in his pockets as though perturbed. "You got the mask? Frank is waiting. Don't want to be late."

She gave the shopping bag a swing to show she had the goods for the exchange. "I know we have to go, but my friend isn't here yet. She's supposed to ride with us."

"I don't think we can wait or Frank might get the wrong idea." He made a show of checking the traffic. "Things are going to get jammed up if we don't get moving." He opened the door to the back seat.

Celeste appreciated the time constraint they were in, but could she really negotiate the exchange for the elder staff by herself? She sighed and got in the back seat after Tony opened the door a little wider. A grumble in her purse let her know Sebastian wasn't keen on her going it alone, but what else could she do? Their ship was going to sail in less than twenty-four hours. Anaïs had practically abandoned her by walking out right when they were meant to get back the one thing they were responsible for delivering safely to France. No, she had to go alone.

At the last minute, she opened her purse and whispered to Sebastian that maybe he ought to stay behind and let Anaïs know she'd been forced to go on ahead. He tried to argue by backpedaling with his feet, but she opened the door a few inches to show she wasn't budging. With a perceptible shake of his head, the stoat jumped out of the car just as Tony sat behind the wheel.

The car drove away from the curb. A noticeably different vehicle from the one she'd ridden in with Tony earlier. This one had an enormous tear in the seat where stuffing poked out, and the interior smelled of rotting onions. "How far is it?" she asked.

"Not far." He looked at her through the rearview mirror. "So, you have it, huh?"

She remembered then that she had to explain to him their plan for switching the mask. "Listen, I need to run something by you. Could we pull over for a second?"

Tony's brows tightened. "Sure, but what's this about?"

"It's about what you said. Not letting Frank get his hands on the mask again."

"Right, uh, let me find a place to stop the car."

She pulled the first mask out of the bag and then the second one, holding them up for him to see.

At first, he didn't say anything, trying hard to control the expression on his face, but she could tell he was surprised. "I don't understand. Where did the second one come from?" He glanced over his shoulder to check the traffic so he could veer to the curb and park.

"A little magical mischief." Celeste set the masks on the seat beside her. "So, my magician friend, do you think you could manage a little sleight of hand once Frank verifies the mask is real?"

"You want me to switch them." He grinned at her in the mirror. "Okay, that might work. But how do you know which one is which? They look identical to me." The car swerved to the right as they drove alongside the curb. Tony hit the brakes harder than necessary, jostling Celeste so that she had to grip the back of the front seat. "Sorry, the brakes stick a little on this old car," he said and downshifted into first while leaving the engine running.

Celeste recovered, but the abrupt stop had launched the masks onto the floorboards. Now she couldn't tell which one was real and which was the copy. In a panic she picked up the pair, inspecting them for the one detail that ought to give away the true mask from the fake.

"Something wrong?"

"I, uh . . . No, just give me a minute."

With Tony still watching her, waiting for an answer while the engine idled, she impulsively brought the first mask up to her face to see if she could detect any sort of magical energy running through it like she had before, only this time she knew to stop before it got too close. Sebastian wouldn't approve of her approach, but if she didn't figure out which one to give Frank, the whole thing would go off the rails.

Celeste held the mask level with her eyes, wondering if there'd been special lenses implanted behind the slits to allow Frank to see through her glamour. Perhaps put there by a spell? But who would be capable of such a thing?

Tony tapped his fingers anxiously against the steering wheel in a staccato beat. "So, what are you thinking?" The traffic cleared around them. He accelerated slowly, pulling away from the curb as the traffic signal ahead turned green.

Celeste didn't know what to think, but she had to sort out the mess she'd made before they got to wherever they were going or they might never get the elder staff back. Why hadn't he waited at the curb? "How much farther is it?"

"Two blocks."

Not much time. Celeste leaned a little closer to the mask, eager for answers. Tentative at first, she was careful not to put the mask against her face. She just wanted to get close enough to get a good look through the eye slits, but then Tony hit the brakes again, jolting her body forward. The abrupt stop threw all her careful handling out the window. An edge of the mask touched her jaw, and a peculiar suction closed the distance between the rest of her skin and the mask's smooth wooden interior.

Celeste pulled against the mask to get it off, but it wouldn't budge. It had adhered to her face as if glued on. A claustrophobic panic flooded her arteries. "Tony, help me. It's stuck." She tried to wedge her fingers between the wood and her skin, but the suction held as her eyes were forced to gaze through the primitive slits, and the only breath she could take came through the two holes gouged out for nostrils. When Tony didn't respond, a panicked scream gurgled inside her throat.

"Just relax," he said from the front seat. "See what the mask sees. Feel what the mask feels. I promise a whole other world will emerge for you."

Celeste's heart pounded in her ears. What was happening? She reached out to grab Tony by the shoulder and make him stop the car, but something was wrong. It was no longer him. A new face grinned at her in the mirror. A man transformed, with skin like candle wax.

CHAPTER TWENTY

"Gut Bucket Blues"

Anaïs ran in her heels all the way back to the hotel with her shawl fluttering off her shoulder. She was just going to make it in time. There were still ten minutes before Tony was scheduled to pick them up. Just enough time to powder her nose and collect the masks. She punched the elevator call button three times to hurry it up. Once in, the contraption took forever to climb to the twelfth floor, but as soon as the door opened, she ran to her room to get ready.

"Celeste? I'm back. Sorry it took so long. Should we head down to the lobby?" No one answered, so she put her ear to the door. "Celeste?"

Gideon flew in through the open window.

"Where's Celeste?"

The rook shook out his feathers, unable to answer the question. Anaïs opened the connecting door between rooms and detected the slight ozone-like scent of used magic lingering in the air. The bed was made, and a room service tray still sat on the table. The history book they'd been looking at the night before was on the nightstand beside an alarm clock with a piece of hotel stationery marking Celeste's place. Closer inspection showed she'd gone back to reread the section on the origin of the elder staff and the first king of France.

Anaïs snapped the book closed. Some kick under the rib told her something was wrong. She checked the box where she'd locked up the mask. Empty. And the replica was gone too. Celeste wouldn't have left without her, would she? Another glance around the room had her eye stopping on the clock above the fireplace. Ten minutes past seven. Alarmed by the time, she grabbed her shawl and purse and headed back downstairs.

The lobby was quiet. A handful of people came and went, but Celeste wasn't among them. Anaïs approached the desk clerk, hoping he was more observant than his stifled yawn indicated. "I was supposed to meet my friend in the lobby. Short brown hair, probably wearing a sensible but smart blue skirt and jacket. Have you seen her?"

"Yes, she left about ten minutes ago. She got in a waiting car, I believe."

"Got in a car?" Anaïs ran outside. She looked left and right down Twenty-Third Street, standing on her toes to see over the pedestrians. When she didn't see Celeste, she checked her watch. Still five minutes *to* seven. How could that be? She ducked back inside and checked the grandfather clock in the lobby. It also said five minutes to seven. Had Tony arrived early? Why would Celeste leave without her? She checked the street again, then retreated behind one of the pillars framing the front door of the hotel. Her rook swooped down from their room to perch on a sculpted boxwood. "Oh, this is not good. Not good at all, Gideon. I'm going to need you to track her down."

The rook guffawed.

"I know, it's an enormous city, and she could be anywhere. But you have certain skills other birds don't when it comes to this kind of work." Anaïs stroked his head. "You have wonderful eyesight, and you're the smartest rook I know. Not to mention your magical aptitude. It'll be like digging for snails in the mud. Just look for our shining girl among the mundane city dwellers."

It never failed. The bird was exceedingly prone to respond to flattery. Not to mention his lust for snails. He spread his wings and took off to sail through the canyons of skyscrapers.

But *why* was she out there? Why had the car shown up early? Why hadn't they waited for her if they were early? No, something wasn't adding up. This mask and elder staff business had taken a diabolical turn. Celeste was just green enough to be taken advantage of. Anaïs knew the young Gardienne had trusted Tony too quickly. Maybe the whole thing was a scam.

Or maybe . . .

Anaïs had to lean against the wall for a moment. Discovering the premature downfall of her protégé had made her suspect the Infortunii weren't playing by the rules like they should in the city. But what if it was more than that? In a fit of frustration, Anaïs returned to the lobby and ducked behind a six-foot palm. It was time to do a little sleuthing of her own while Gideon swept the city blocks for Celeste. If a Skulk was involved, she'd better be prepared.

Anaïs took a moment to change into something with a little more edge to it. Something to remind her of how she'd earned her reputation with the Infortunii. A black drop-waist dress with a slash of red silk bleeding through the slits on the sleeves ought to put her in the right mood. She held her ruby pendant and finished off her ensemble with a black-and-red cloche and two-toned Mary Janes to match. She added a layer of red lipstick to her mouth, then smacked her lips together. "Time to do a little hunting."

There were the usual haunts where the Infortunii liked to hide from the sun. Gambling halls, opium dens, and houses of ill repute were the types of places they fed from. Anyplace where the human spirit could be degraded, deprived, exploited, robbed, injured, or entrapped, that was where she'd find the miscreant.

There was only one problem. As she stepped onto the sidewalk with her war paint on, she had to confront the fact that the only Skulk she knew for a fact to currently be in America was Barnaby, the leader of the Infortunii. He'd presumably arrived at the same time she'd had to oversee the events in Los Angeles, after one of his Skulks had gone rogue and started dishing out misfortune like Halloween treats. After reaching out for help from the Gardiennes in the matter, Barnaby had lurked in the background, making sure everything was done to his liking before revealing his presence in California. So was he still there? Or had he already returned to Europe? That was always the problem with Skulks. They were deceitful to the marrow.

Anaïs had no way of knowing if Barnaby had come to the States alone or if he'd brought another of his creatures with him. That could be a complication, if it proved true. Confrontations with the Infortunii were sometimes unavoidable. Toes were stepped on. Egos were bruised. Scars were inflicted. She smirked, thinking of the indignant outrage Barnaby had displayed after the incident in Bruges.

After Bruges, Anaïs was always willing to engage defensively, should the need arise, but she wasn't so certain about Celeste. The girl was still so trusting. So naive. Always searching for the good in people. Of course, Anaïs had been duped by Tony too, but she'd seen it coming. Well, most of it. She hadn't counted on the drug being quite so strong, but she'd sniffed his intentions out the moment he sat down. But how else could she have gotten a personal escort into the back of the club to find the elder staff if not for a little abduction?

Anaïs's heels clicked against concrete as she followed a thread of instinct through the city. It was remarkable how much uncanny attention they'd attracted while in New York. Gangsters, a psychic, a dream auger, and a Skulk or two were all swarming around them just as they were trying to board a steamship to France with the elder staff.

She stopped dead in the middle of the sidewalk. People bustled around her, jostling her shoulders and calling her a stupid cow under their breath, but the clarity of what she'd been missing this whole time had hit her so solidly between the eyes she couldn't move. "How could I have been such a fool?"

"I don't know, lady," said a man forced to go around her on the left. "But try doing it over there next time."

She ignored the man and ducked into a shop on the corner to buy some time to think. The place turned out to be a store that sold vinyl recordings and the portable Victrolas they were played on. She moved toward the back and sorted through a stack of records by Jelly Roll Morton's Red Hot Peppers. "Black Bottom Stomp," "Dead Man Blues," "Doctor Jazz"—she'd have to return someday to do some more exploring when she wasn't in the midst of a crisis.

Anaïs pretended to read the labels of the records she plucked out of the stack while revisiting her earlier breakthrough. With Dorée's recent death occurring on the west coast of the United States, Gertrude still ensconced in her Paris salon, and the elder staff lost somewhere in between, the sisterhood of Gardiennes was in a state of genuine flux. In the past, the transfer of power had always taken place immediately after the death of the eldest or soon thereafter, and always within the European borders where the Gardiennes lived. But this business with the Skulks had disrupted their normal protocol. Had someone sniffed out an opportunity to expose them while the transfer of power was still in a mercurial state? Anaïs sucked in a breath at the gaping vulnerability. She'd never met a Skulk whose bones hadn't been dipped in a froth of dishonesty before they were born. Or hatched. Or whatever design the devils used to emerge into the world.

Anaïs shook her head and moved to a different bin of stacked records. She glanced at some of the song titles performed by Louis Armstrong and His Hot Five and smiled at the good times she'd had dancing to them all back in Paris: "Muskrat Ramble," "Gut Bucket Blues," "Skid-Dat-De-Dat," "Big Fat Ma and Skinny Pa." It was like being on a treasure hunt. But that was before she came to America and got dragged into this pile of manure with the Skulks.

Barnaby. He must have surmised the inevitable while they were in Los Angeles. She and Dorée had openly complained that Celeste's *first* protégé was being interfered with by one of his rogue Skulks. An initiate's rise always meant an elder's demise. There could only ever be thirteen Gardiennes. It's just how the cycle worked. The leader of the Infortunii would certainly know that. But how could he have set everything in motion so quickly? That part didn't make any sense. The Lombardi business began months ago, according to the day planner in Frank's office. The Infortunii were assuredly behind the misfortune, which would place them in New York City long before the Gardiennes traveled to Los Angeles. Yet Barnaby would have only learned about Dorée's fate last week. For as much as the Gardiennes came in contact with the Infortunii, Anaïs knew very little about their fraternity or their history, which made her nervous.

Gideon needed to find Celeste now. The naive young woman could be in terrible danger. Anaïs closed her eyes, pretending to listen to a record being played on the Victrola, and sent a silent prompt to her rook through their psychic connection. Her companion responded almost immediately, giving her access to his sight. He'd perched atop a skyscraper, causing her a moment of vertigo before she adjusted to the height seen through his eyes by gripping the bin of recordings to ground her. Below, she witnessed through his eyes the usual hustle of people on the pavement walking to and fro, with one small exception. A furry brown-and-white stoat was frantically trying to cross a street without getting run over.

Get him, Anaïs said to Gideon in her mind as she mindlessly flipped through more records. She braced for the rook's leap off the roof, followed by the unnatural feeling of falling that eventually gave way to the thrill of gliding on air as she stayed connected to his vision. People on the ground put their arms up defensively and sidestepped around Gideon once he landed on the sidewalk.

"Filthy bird!"

A woman in a brown tweed skirt attempted to shoo Gideon away with her handbag, but after he nipped at her ankles with his sharp beak, she shuffled away. With her gone, Gideon screeched to call to Sebastian. The little stoat narrowly missed getting squashed beneath the wheels of a four-door Chevy speeding by. Back on the sidewalk, he chittered and ran in circles in front of Gideon in a state of panic. It seemed he'd been separated from Celeste and had tried to follow her through the busy traffic. Gideon turned his head to look at the oddly shaped triangular building not far from the hotel. Through his vision, Anaïs spotted two men dragging a woman out of a car and strong-arming her through the building's revolving door. She recognized the blue suit as the sort of ensemble Celeste was prone to choose for herself. And was she wearing the mask on her face? "What the hell is this?"

"Beg your pardon, ma'am?" The store clerk was eager to respond, coming out from behind her counter to see if she could bag a sale. "Was there something I could assist you with?"

Anaïs heard the woman but was too invested in the vision to acknowledge her. She shook her head instead and bent over another stack of records as though on the hunt for something special. She plucked out a Bessie Smith recording of "Backwater Blues" and stared intently at the label until the clerk went back to her register.

The disturbing image of a Gardienne in the crude wooden mask drummed against Anaïs's intuition. The blood in her veins took up the beat, pounding out a warning in her body when the reality of what she'd seen through Gideon's eyes finally surfaced. From somewhere in the vault of information at the back of her brain, she remembered reading about another Gardienne forced to wear a crude wooden mask during the Reign of Terror. She'd nearly died from the mask's cursed magic. "Skulk magic." Startled by the revelation, Anaïs dropped the record she'd been holding and drew a rebuke from the sales clerk.

"Those are eighty-five cents each," the woman said with a raised brow.

Anaïs slapped a bill on the counter along with a mumbled apology before she darted onto the street, record in hand. Before breaking her connection with Gideon, she had the rook corral the stoat toward the sidewalk and wait for her to come to them. Something was very, very wrong.

Anaïs clutched the record and left the shop behind, ignoring the woman calling after her about her change. She had a vague recollection of which direction the angular building was located, after seeing it on their cab ride from the train station to the hotel the day before. She remembered thinking the irregular skyscraper had the ungainly appearance of an ugly stepsister's hulking foot being shoehorned into a tiny glass slipper in the middle of the city.

Anaïs headed east. She recalled seeing a quaint park across the street from the building on their introductory drive through the city, so she kept her eyes peeled for the first sign of greenery among the sea of concrete. She'd walked a block and a half when the vision presented itself. There, on the right, stood the prow of the building, as self-satisfied as any ship traversing the ocean. The image gave her a spasm of remorse, reminded of Dorée commanding a derelict pirate ship to cross a studio backlot in pursuit of justice against the rogue Skulk. She nearly stopped, too overcome with sadness to face yet another trial, but she knew her old mentor wouldn't have backed down, not when a fellow Gardienne was in need, so she marched forward to meet her rook and whatever trouble he'd found.

Gideon swooped in with the stoat riding on his back as he met Anaïs at the park across the street from where they'd witnessed Celeste's apparent abduction. Sebastian was shivering with fright by the time Gideon dumped him out on a park bench. His fur stood up in damp clumps and his ears drooped while he got reacquainted with solid ground. Anaïs sat beside him and encouraged the little fellow to catch his breath before needling him with her questions.

"Now, why were you alone in the street, and was that Celeste I saw being forced into the building?" Sebastian shook out his fur and stared intently at Anaïs. She took that for a yes. "Is she all right? Why was she wearing that mask?"

The stoat wiped his face with his paws repeatedly, growing more frantic the longer it took Anaïs to decipher his meaning. Their animal companions were quite adept at understanding human speech, but it didn't always work the other way around unless one was intimately accustomed to the animal's voice and mannerisms, which only came with time. The gist of the message seemed to be that something bad had happened to Celeste and he'd tried to follow.

"Was she with a man named Tony when this happened?" Sebastian hissed, so she pressed on. "Did he do something to her? Is she in trouble?" He stomped his feet and chittered loudly while staring up at the wedge-shaped building. Anaïs took in the sight of the looming skyscraper and her posture shrank. She'd thought she'd been clever allowing herself to get kidnapped by Frank and his goons. She'd known what she was getting into, but now it looked like Celeste had been abducted for real. Anaïs could only assume they'd found a way to disarm the young woman's abilities as they'd done with her. Could the mask have that effect on one of their kind? Cut off their ability? Freeze their magic?

Unfortunately for Celeste, do-gooder virtue swam in her blood. Anaïs had become an amateur historian of the sisterhood after stumbling upon the record books in the cottage attic as a child. She'd spent hours hiding from her instructors while she'd read the oft-detailed entries written beside each of the Gardiennes' names that explained the circumstances of how every one of them had come to arrive on the doorstep of the cottage in the woods. Dorée had been pulled out of the ocean by a pair of sisters named Henrietta and Cora after the ship her family had been traveling on sank in the English Channel. Anaïs's own parents had been the victims of a political street riot in Brussels in 1899 that had turned deadly. Marta and Jezebel had been there to scoop her out of the baby carriage when the mayhem broke out and her parents were killed by stray gunfire. In every case, the girls were presumed dead along with their parents. But the babies—always a girl and always an only child—didn't die. They were snatched out of Death's grip at the last moment by a Gardienne to be taken away to the cottage in the woods and trained in the ways of the benevolent magic they practiced.

How a member of the sisterhood was always in the right place at the right time to steal the children away had remained a mystery to her, but the outcome was never in question. The Fées Gardiennes had survived for centuries, always maintaining their thirteen sisters, for over a thousand years by raising orphaned children who were presumed dead. In Celeste's case, the poor girl had come to them as a one-year-old with brick dust still in her hair from the earthquake that had shaken San Francisco to the ground. It was noted in the ledger that witnesses had seen her parents rush in to help victims trapped in the fire before the wall of the county's municipal building fell and crushed them both. It was Esmerelda who'd made the timely trip to see the California city advertised as the "Paris of the West" just as the tragedy had occurred, only to return home with Celeste wrapped in her arms. After meeting the babe who'd come all the way from America, the first in the sisterhood's history, eight-year-old Anaïs had pretended the girl was her very first protégé, putting her under her protection. She supposed little had changed in that regard.

"Right." Anaïs stood up. "It's time we turn up the heat on this dream auger and his cronies. We need to have a look at the inside of this flatiron-shaped monstrosity for ourselves." She opened her handbag to let Sebastian jump in, then watched as Gideon flew to the top of a streetlight, ready to lead her to her prey. "Onward," she said, then transformed the vinyl record into a haircomb, slipping it inside her bag alongside the stoat.

She walked the full perimeter of the building first, searching for the cold evidence that might tip her off to the presence of a Skulk. She stopped in front of the revolving door on the south side and reached out her hand. Her skin revolted against the abnormal chill still clinging to the contraption's brass and glass components. "I knew it!" The truth might as well have been sealed in amber. The Infortunii were meddling in the transfer of power between Gardiennes, and they'd drawn the dream auger into their scheme via some ancient relic of their own. "The lying, underhanded bastards." Their presence also meant her one chance to get in unseen wasn't going to fly. The Infortunii could peer through a Gardienne's glamour.

She supposed, given the circumstances, she had no choice but to go in guns blazing. Just the way Dorée had taught her.

CHAPTER TWENTY-ONE

Gilded City of Rot

Sweat had trickled under the mask's edge, creating a clammy suction against Celeste's skin. It adhered so tightly to her face she could barely breathe in enough air to keep from getting lightheaded. She forced herself to calm down in the car long enough to grip her pendant and transform the mask into something simple like a scarf, but nothing budged. What magic was this?

Celeste's sight had been slightly obscured by the narrow eye slits, but in between shallow intakes of breath, she saw the moment the car stopped outside the unusual triangular building. The waxy-skinned driver got out and met up with another man on the sidewalk. They grinned at their prize as they reached into the back seat to retrieve the fake mask and drag Celeste out by her arms. She struggled against their grip as she got swept through the building's revolving door.

"She's here to see a doctor," the waxy-skinned man said when a pair of women shot worried glances their way. "Terrible skin condition, but don't worry, it's only mildly contagious." The women scurried away like startled chickens while the men hauled her into an elevator.

Celeste tried conjuring cages and straitjackets out of everything she touched to trap the two brutes dragging her away to who knew where, but nothing would materialize. Her power rose in her veins only to get mired beneath her skin. The magic clogged up like a faulty drain.

"Thirteen," the driver said, after handing the elevator operator a wad of cash to go take a break and forget what he saw. The other man pushed the button and closed the door.

Celeste's stomach dropped as the elevator rose. "Why are you doing this?" she asked.

The men refused to look at her. "Just business, doll."

As they climbed higher through the guts of the skyscraper, Celeste tried again to get the mask off her face by rubbing the edge against her shoulder, but to no avail. The men didn't even try to stop her anymore, knowing there was nothing she could do. And it wasn't just that the mask had neutralized her power—it also burdened her with the most peculiar melancholy. Everything she saw through the slits became cast in red-and-black shadows until she felt almost dizzy with despair. The lights lost their shine. Pain dug into her side. Grief tugged at her shoulders. The feeling was so foreign to her being that it disoriented her and she listed on her feet, teetering toward the waxy-skinned man. He pushed her off callously, leaving her to wonder how she'd ever gotten things so wrong by getting in the car with him.

The elevator stopped and the men dragged Celeste to an office at the end of the hallway. Whatever waited on the other side couldn't be good. Nothing in the world was good anymore. The end couldn't come quick enough. While her thoughts spiraled, some small spark still alive at her center recognized it was the mask's influence. That truth gave her enough resolve to be thankful she'd kicked Sebastian out of the car when she had. At least he'd gotten away. At least he was safe.

And with that thought the mask's oppressive weight lifted ever so slightly.

The door to the office swung open and then another. The reek of cigars and something even more acrid wafted out of the second room.

Celeste felt a shove against her shoulder. Forced to enter, she dragged her feet into the space.

Two men stood in silhouette in front of a large window. They were tucked in almost shoulder to shoulder at the narrow corner of the building overlooking the park. Each had his hands folded neatly behind his back. One of the men she recognized as Frank, big and hulking with his square head, whom she'd expected to do the exchange with. She wasn't sure, but there was something vaguely familiar about the shorter, thinner one too. A sickly posture on a skeleton frame. He turned to look at Celeste as though eavesdropping on her thoughts, revealing his sallow skin and reptilelike eyes. Barnaby, the leader of the Infortunii? The Skulk who'd implored Dorée to clean up his mess in California? So, Anaïs had been right about their connection to the relic. The mask pinched Celeste's lips closed when she tried to curse his name out loud.

The Skulk leered. "So, we meet again. Celeste, was it?"

From a short distance, Barnaby was recognizable enough as the Skulk she'd met on the backlot of West Coast Studios, but as he moved closer, the red-and-black haze forced on her by the mask peeled away parts of his human disguise. He was only the second Infortunii she'd ever encountered, but she'd been given a crash course in their true appearance while in California. Where a thin, middle-aged man with slitted eyes and an expensive suit had stood, there now appeared a creature with concrete-gray skin, bulging eyes, and fanged teeth.

"Have a seat, my dear." There was a green damask sofa along the wall, but Barnaby extended a clawed hand toward the hard chair arranged in front of the cherrywood desk. A lamp with a green globe, a letter opener, and a silver bowl filled with walnuts sat on top of it. "I apologize, but I cannot remove the mask from you just yet," he said. "As you've no doubt noticed by now, it has the rare ability to render your powers mute. I'd like to keep it that way for the moment."

Celeste wobbled slightly as she eased herself onto the chair, knowing she had no choice. Without her powers, there was little she could do against a member of the Infortunii. But how did this Skulk and the dream auger know each other? What about the elder staff? And where was Anaïs?

"You must be wondering why we've brought you here." Barnaby took a seat behind the desk. He waved his clawed hand as though shooing away a fly. The black-and-red vision Celeste had been forced to view the world through faded. In the normal band of vision, Barnaby's face reverted to the sallow-skinned man she recognized. She sighed with relief, and the mask's hold gave way just a little. She might not have paid attention to the slight loosening of the mask near her chin, or the noticeable shift in the pressure against her cheek, if she hadn't already experienced it once before. Again, it seemed to happen because she'd been *grateful* for some small thing.

Barnaby waved his hand again, and the mask stopped pinching her lips so she could speak.

"We're supposed to be doing a trade," she said. "You've stolen something you had no right to take."

"No right?" Barnaby winced as the angle of the setting sun seeped into his lair. He paused to have Frank lower the blinds on the windows. Skulks were notoriously fond of dark and damp, which made the meeting in the tower all the more unusual. But perhaps even a Skulk wished to rise above the street-level filth to get a little perspective when committing crimes in foreign cities. "Do you have any understanding of the history surrounding the mask you're wearing?" he asked when the room became sufficiently shadowed in low light.

"I know it's old and that it reeks of Skulk magic," she answered.

Frank crossed his arms. "Stubborn and mouthy. Both of them."

But Barnaby waved off the dream auger's harsh critique. "No, no, it's to be expected. Our people have enjoyed a long and enthusiastic rivalry over the centuries. In fact, that's the reason this mask exists at all." The Skulk loomed over Celeste as he came around to lean against the front edge of the desk. "You see, the Infortunii were granted this ancient and magical relic in an age when the Fées Gardiennes were busy reveling in their rising influence and getting fat on wine and tarts.

They'd become courtiers in the French king's court, but they were little more than paid matchmakers who were consulted on every royal union. Summoned for every christening so they might impart favor on all the slobbering royal babies."

Celeste listened to Barnaby's rant with one ear, but she'd grown incurably curious about the slight loosening of the mask. While the Skulk went on and on about how conceited the ancient Gardiennes had become, she gave silent thanks that she had been raised in the cottage in the woods. The suction near her ear released a little. When the Skulk complained that the king of France had become beholden to Gardienne favors, she recognized the gratitude she felt to be part of such a prestigious sisterhood. The mask let go of the grip it had over her left eye. Was it really so simple? Could humble gratitude be the solvent needed to loosen the glue of Infortunii treachery?

Barnaby reached for the bowl of nuts on the corner of his desk. He popped a walnut in his mouth whole with the shell on. A hard crunch sounded before the Skulk swallowed the shattered mess. He picked his teeth clean with his fingernail while watching Celeste. He leaned closer. "Did you know the mask and the staff were made to complement each other?"

Celeste shook her head cautiously, feeling the loosening tension of the mask again.

"When Hugh Capet gifted your ancestors the staff, he had the foresight to predict the temptation for the Gardiennes to abuse their position and power under his protection." Barnaby dumped the walnuts out of the silver bowl and transformed it into the same scale Dorée had once shown Celeste in California. The one with the golden woman holding up two bejeweled pans suspended on chains on one side, and on the other the featureless form of a man carved out of lapis lazuli holding a pair of onyx pans. "The king declared balance was needed, and so he had his craftsmen devise these scales to bind our obligation to the effort of equilibrium. In essence binding the Infortunii's long history, our talents, and our purpose to that of the novice Gardiennes, who'd only recently emerged into the world. After making the scales, Capet then instructed his craftsmen to carve a mask of solid oak. Men's wood, he called it, because of its inherent strength. He presented this mask to the Infortunii. Why a mask, you ask?"

Celeste hadn't asked. She knew from the story it was to cover their repulsive faces. But she had been drawn in by the mysterious scales and talk of balance all the same. It was the same message Dorée had imparted only a week earlier. Only now her mentor was gone, the elder staff was missing, and the apparent mask Barnaby spoke about was suctioned to her face.

"The mask was a symbol of how the Infortunii presented ourselves to the world in the king's eyes." Barnaby's back straightened as he gestured to his seemingly normal-looking face. "Always hiding our true selves from sensitive eyes. But the oak represented our hardened yet necessary nature. The king added the touch of gold to show his recognition of our contributions." Barnaby transformed into his innate Skulk form. He touched Celeste's chin with his clawed fingers, tipping her face up slightly while she fought the urge to flinch. "The mask gave us the power. No, that's not quite the right word. He was a mortal king, after all. But it did give us a sort of *permission* needed to alter our appearance. We gained the right to disguise ourselves as men so we might walk in the world to complete our difficult work. Just as the Gardiennes moved with the natural grace of women."

He removed his talons from her chin. Another thing to be grateful for.

"But, of course, the scales were never truly balanced or equal. It had been just another gesture by the king to placate us so he might continue benefiting from the bounty bestowed upon him by the Gardiennes." Barnaby picked up the scales. He played with the mechanism that weighed one side against the other, then smashed the entire instrument on the floor, disfiguring the woman's arms and breaking the man's neck.

Celeste recoiled at the destruction, while the men who'd kidnapped her smirked.

"But now we find ourselves in a new age, do we not?" Barnaby continued. "The old kings are long gone. The world tumbles on. In this new era, people across continents kill each other one day and then dance on the edge of oblivion in a jazz-infused fever dream the next." The Skulk let out a long, cleansing sigh. "This city, though . . . it has a verve. An energy. Europe squats like an old woman at the window. Content to sit and watch the world go by as emerging nations grow their permanent teeth." The Skulk wiped the taste of his words out of his mouth with his tongue, seemingly recognizing he was getting maudlin. Or perhaps he just had shells stuck in his teeth. "New York has grown," he said after a pause. "Too fast by some standards. So many rich men threw their wealth at the monuments dedicated to themselves that the entire city's surface has the taint of gold. Oh, but the beautiful rot that sits beneath that gilded facade. The streets are absolutely crumbling with corruption and ill-gotten gains, bribery and fraud." He closed his eyes and rolled his neck around. "Delicious."

Celeste pitied the Skulk in that moment, to see him so taken with his own moral decay. It had her questioning for the hundredth time in her life why there had to be a downfall effect. Why there had to be suffering as an endnote to a protégé's rise. She looked at the shattered mess on the floor. What good were scales anyway if they balanced beauty and goodness equally with pain and suffering? But then the part of her that had been raised to abide by the rules of the covenant conceded that maybe there was a grounding influence to be found in hardship, however unfair or cruel the lesson appeared. No light without the darkness, she supposed.

The mask slipped a quarter inch.

Barnaby held his hand out to Frank. "I have my acquaintance here to thank for so many of the juicy details of the city's corruption. I'd only ever heard of a dream auger using the mask once before in its long history. An incident that ended in a regime change when it was over. Alas, dream augers are so very rare these days. Interesting, though, how their talents and ours meshed so effortlessly to get a glimpse into the deepest, darkest confessions of a man's soul." The Skulk stared at Celeste, peering into her eyes beneath the mask. "I am curious what he might see inside you."

Barnaby curled his finger at Frank. "The relic, if you will." The dream auger reached under the desk to retrieve the beat-up clarinet case. "The elder staff of the Gardiennes," he said, opening the case. "We do thank you for escorting it to the city in one piece." Barnaby waited for Frank to assemble the pieces, then held the clarinet awkwardly in his clawlike hands as though he didn't know which end was meant to be up. He opted for the natural orientation of the instrument as he set the case aside on the floor.

"Why?" Celeste wasn't sure how much longer she could bear to have the mask against her skin. Even though it had loosened a smidge, the covering induced a tunnel-vision-like claustrophobia. "Why would you even need the staff? It can't do anything for you that you can't already do for yourself."

"Ah, that is where your naivete has misled you on your quest." Barnaby sniffed the clarinet like a man buying a cigar. "You see, I have plans. Big plans. There's a river of corruption running in the streets below the city skyscrapers, and I intend to fish out as much profit as I can." Frank cleared his throat as though reminding Barnaby he was still there. The Skulk's eyes shifted in the dream auger's direction. "*We,*" he amended. He turned his attention back to the clarinet, fiddling with the keys. "This ancient staff is the final piece needed to set those plans into motion."

"But how can it help you?"

Now it was the Skulk's turn to pity her. "Even you must recognize that without the elder staff, the Gardienne sisterhood cannot consolidate its power." Barnaby shook his head. "I'm sure you're aware of when the Gardiennes gave up their wands in favor of gemstones. But did you know those wands were melded into the wooden staff? It is their combined energy that allows the eldest to envision a protégé's future." He gave a half-hearted shrug. "But with the eldest dead and her replacement stuck on another continent, there's no vessel to carry that power. Which means my colleagues and I are in the rare position of being able to sever that flow today so that the Gardiennes can never interfere again with their trivial distractions." He waved his clawed hand in a dismissive flourish. "All this wretched duty of watching and waiting for your spoiled charges to reach their pinnacle of *success* before we get to sink our teeth into their meat and bones. And after we destroy the bond forged between our factions, my dear, I'm going to hang the whole thing on your poor, treacherous head by being the last Gardienne to ever possess the staff."

"You're contemptible."

"I deny nothing," he said. "But before I can see to your ruin, we need this clarinet changed back into its true form."

The Skulk concentrated on the clarinet again, inspecting the reed, bell, and keys. He shook the instrument, stared down the end of it, and even tried blowing his cold, fetid breath over the mouthpiece. "The transformation isn't working," he said, slightly alarmed. "Why can't I restore it?" When it was clear his efforts had failed, he angrily gripped the clarinet as though he had a goose by the throat and thrust the instrument toward Celeste. "Change it back," he demanded.

He hadn't realized the stupidity of what he'd said. Celeste was trapped in the mask. Her magic had been subdued by some malevolent energy emanating from the inside of the carved wood. Like a Skulk signal jamming her Gardienne transmission. She shook her head slowly, letting him figure it out. She thought he might recognize the difficulty of his request and release her from the mask temporarily so she might fulfill his demand, but she'd forgotten she was dealing with a Skulk.

Barnaby's eyes turned ice blue when she refused. The mask tightened on Celeste's face again, only this time it felt like the wood was packed with ice. The cold stung her skin, forcing the gelatinous parts of her eyes to congeal and her nostrils to grow stiff with frost. She nearly choked on the cold, knowing it could kill her if he didn't let up. Instead, he leaned forward, tilting his head to his right. "No matter.

There won't be much work for Fées Gardiennes to do in the future when I'm through. How does it feel knowing it will be your negligence that leads to the downfall of the sisterhood you hold so dear? That it will be you who finally causes the privileged Gardiennes to sink into an abyss of irrelevance." Behind him, Frank and the other two men grinned like they'd just won a long-shot bet at the horse races. All of them feeding off her pain.

Barnaby snapped his fingers at Frank. "Someone ought to go check for the other one. She won't be far away. And that one could cause problems if she's figured out how I manipulated the clocks. She'll need to be handled."

"Tony should have picked her up by now," Frank said, checking his watch. He snapped his fingers at the Skulk with the melted skin. "Go check the street. I never told Tony what floor, so he'll be circling the block with her until we flag him down."

"As you wish," the Skulk answered.

After he left, Celeste was grateful there was one fewer creep in the room. The cold sting behind the mask lessened ever so slightly at the minor reason to give thanks, reacting to her thoughts as it had before. Could her freedom really be that elementary? The cold had nearly frozen her brain, but one thing a Skulk ought to know about the Fées Gardiennes was that they have an enormous capacity for remembering all the things they're thankful for. Gratitude was a natural side effect of the business. And so, while her thoughts were still warm inside her head, Celeste gathered up all the things she had to be grateful for in her life, feeling the mask thaw even as Barnaby continued to spew out his threats for the future.

CHAPTER TWENTY-TWO

A Glint in His Eye and Destruction in His Heart

Anaïs had just worked up the courage to enter the building and find Celeste when a car horn blared on the street, followed by a quick whistle. Normally, she ignored the wolfish howls that came her way, but her ire was already primed and ready to fire. She turned and glared at the driver, eager to inflict a little quick street justice before she went inside, when she recognized those cheekbones. Tony, the sweet-talking, drink-spiking kidnapper. She put a hand on her hip, recalibrating from anger to wariness as he waved at her from his car to meet him at the other end of the building. She sashayed rather than walked to the corner, willing to put off crushing him and his car by a wayward building stone falling from the rooftop long enough to find out what he'd done with Celeste.

The car pulled over to the curb. Tony jumped out, hands splayed open in a questioning gesture. "Where were you? I was supposed to pick you two up at seven."

Confused, Anaïs dropped her pendant, along with the impulse to kill him. "Didn't you pick up Celeste already?"

"No, she wasn't there. Neither were you." He guided Anaïs by the elbow, suggesting they move closer to the building to talk so they wouldn't be seen from the windows above. "How did you even know to come here? It's supposed to be a secret location."

Anaïs's first urge was to throw off his hand, but she had bigger problems to worry about. The desk clerk at the Hotel Chelsea had told her Tony had picked up Celeste. But if it wasn't Tony, who was it?

Reality dropped like a rock. The Infortunii. They'd been outfoxed by their mutability and conniving tendencies. "Let me see your wristwatch."

Tony reluctantly pushed up his sleeve to show the time. Five after seven. But it had been five after seven ten minutes ago. She realized now that Celeste had likely gone downstairs to meet him ten minutes early, believing it was seven o'clock. "The Skulks set this up. They manipulated the clocks. Probably to isolate us, which means they're expecting me to show up any minute. Damn it."

"The who the what?" Tony's eyes nearly bugged out of his head. "Who can manipulate time?"

"Not time, just the clocks." Anaïs sucked in her cheeks. There was no more doubt. "They fooled you, they fooled me, and now they have Celeste. Up there somewhere." She eyed the full daunting height of the building. "Which floor would they be on?"

"I don't actually know. I've never been in there. Someone was supposed to flag me down on the street once we arrived. They're supposed to be watching for us."

His confession only reinforced the notion they'd been set up. "I suspect they might be onto you. They didn't trust you with the information of their final location or with the clock manipulation. That means you could be in as much danger as Celeste. Come on, we've got to get up there."

"How? They could be anywhere in the building."

Anaïs called to Gideon in her mind. The rook came in for a landing on her arm, making Tony back away with his hands held up to block his face from the flapping wings and outstretched claws.

"Where does that bird keep coming from?" he asked, straightening his jacket.

"Gideon is my companion," she said. "His eyesight is far superior to yours or mine. But better yet, he has a way to get up there and have a look around without being noticed." Anaïs gave the rook her instructions, then sent him off to find an updraft. "Now, who was supposed to meet you? We need to keep an eye out for him."

Tony rubbed his chin and looked over his shoulder. "I don't know, maybe Sal. He's a heavy that Frank's been depending on lately. But it could be anyone."

"Sal." Anaïs had no way of knowing if this Sal was a Skulk or not. If not, no problem. They could dump him in a broom closet on the first floor and be done with him, but if Frank was in as deep as she suspected with Skulks, then there could be a public scene if they got caught out in the open by one. "As soon as we know which floor they're hiding on, we go in."

"And do what?" Tony looked up the length of the skyscraper. "They have guns, they have that clarinet thing they stole from you, and now they probably have that creepy magical mask back."

"But they don't have me," she said with a sly grin. "And you have a gun, haven't you? I felt it that night we danced. Before you knocked me out."

"That wasn't my call, by the way." He rubbed the back of his neck nervously. "I hope you know that."

Anaïs hadn't known that exactly, but she could see now how the drugging had been Frank's idea. She hadn't been around Tony as much as Celeste had, but she was beginning to pick up on an ember of honesty being kept alive deep inside him. But was it enough to trust him? She gave a modest shrug. "Celeste seems to trust you. Don't know if I can, but I don't really have any choice. I need to get inside this place."

Gideon spiraled down from the building's heights. He landed on Tony's car and squawked out his message as he strutted back and forth. "He says they're on the thirteenth floor. North side."

"Really. Your bird talks to you?"

"Yeah, and I talk to him too. Got a problem with that?"

Tony shook his head. "Nope. This way." He stuck close to the building's side as he walked them in the other direction to enter through the revolving door. They'd just been swept through the door's arms and into the lobby when he ducked his head quickly to the right and grabbed Anaïs's hand. He pulled her into a vestibule partially blocked by one of the floor-to-ceiling columns that lined the lobby.

Anaïs's pulse raced unexpectedly when he kept hold of her hand, blocking her from being seen by anyone in the lobby with his body. "Who is it?"

"Not Sal." He chanced a quick glance over his shoulder, then bent his head down to the right again. "It's trouble, like you said. Man in the flatcap and waxlike skin by the door. He's the one that convinced Frank to pull the mask out of storage and start using it. Said it was part of a dream he'd had."

Anaïs lifted her chin just so her gaze cleared Tony's shoulder. Definitely a Skulk. She'd seen this one before. Was it Barcelona? Madrid? He went by the name Cyril. The rumor was that he'd gone to battle with one of Desdemona's protégés during the Great War, carrying a glint in his eye and destruction in his heart. When he couldn't corrupt her young ward, he'd joined a German infantry brigade carrying flamethrowers and got burned while relishing the instrument of death's work a little too up close. Word was, he wore the damaged skin like a badge of honor.

"I know him." Anaïs reasoned the Skulk would know her on sight too, since she was probably the reason he'd been in Spain in the first place. Perhaps why he was here now as well.

"So, how do we get around him?"

Tony's breath hit her neck when he spoke, warm and tempting. She leaned in closer as sunlight glinted off a window across the street, dazzling her eye. "We roast him," she said into his ear.

Anaïs didn't have time to offer a history lesson on the Infortunii and their weaknesses. She simply explained that light, the brighter the better, could flash-blind a Skulk into unconsciousness, if done right. Over the years, she'd had plenty of opportunity to perfect her delivery. All she needed was the right angle and a clear shot.

She hesitantly pulled away from Tony and his body heat. "Follow me."

"Anywhere."

His saucy reply caught her attention. In a surprisingly good way. If all went well, who knew what amends might be made later. A thought that made her spin around in alarm. "Wait a minute. Who's Hazel's father? Are you?" She was dead serious and needed to know that instant, despite Tony's startled backpedaling about personal questions.

"You know, you're the second person to ask me that today." He pulled them back behind a pillar while the man in the flatcap lit a cigarette and swept the lobby with his eyes before leaning against the wall to wait. "No, doll, she's not mine. She's Frank's. But you may have noticed he and Nellie aren't exactly playing happy families."

Anaïs let out a sigh of . . . what? Relief? Dread? No, it was renewed determination for what still needed to happen and to see it through. "Okay." She checked the angle of the sun again. The Skulk had moved to get out of the direct path of the light, as they often did. "I need you to position yourself in front of the door so he can't miss you. If he tries to talk to you, draw him into the sunlight."

"Uh, why?"

"I'm going to need the help of the sun's rays to do this right. And I have a feeling we'll only get one chance with this guy."

Tony exhaled, then strode over to the front door with his hands in his pockets. It took a second for the Skulk to register the face, but once he recognized the magician from the club, he straightened and stubbed out his cigarette. He lowered the brim of his flatcap and crept closer to where Tony was pretending to watch for someone through the glass. He turned when the Skulk spoke to him.

"Hey, pal, remember me?"

Tony made a face and shook his head. "I don't know. Should I?"

Anaïs slipped behind the row of columns to get in front of the Skulk while the pair traded remarks. She could do the palm flash without the aid of the sun, but with people milling about the lobby, she needed a little cover.

The Skulk took a threatening step closer, pushing his hat back. "How about now?" he said, knowing the effect his face had on others up close. She worried Tony might falter, but he coolly took his hands out of his pockets and pointed at the man's face, remarking how familiar it looked, now that he'd mentioned it.

Anaïs took a compact mirror out of her purse and held it up to her face, pretending to powder her nose. The sun came out from behind a passing cloud. She angled the mirror just as Cyril locked eyes with her. The mirror caught the light. She held up her palm. A pulse as strong as sunlight emanated from her hand, hitting the Skulk directly in his face. He crossed his arms over his eyes before stumbling backward.

People gasped to see a man having what looked like a seizure, so Tony and Anaïs assured them their friend would be all right. Happened all the time. Meanwhile, they hooked their arms under Cyril's and dragged him off to the elevator. They took him up to the seventh floor, dumped him in the men's bathroom, and locked him inside after Anaïs fashioned a thousand-watt bulb to replace the overhead light to keep the Skulk subdued.

"It will hold him for a little while, but we haven't got much time." Anaïs punched the elevator button a dozen times, trying to make it hurry to the thirteenth floor. The contraption finally rocked to a stop and the doors opened. The hallway was eerily quiet, but there was a light on under the door to their right, faint but noticeable, considering most other offices appeared quiet at that hour of the evening.

"So do we have a plan for what's next?" Tony checked and rechecked the cylinder on his revolver to make sure it was fully loaded.

"Yeah, we have a plan," Anaïs said as she crept toward the door. "Try not to get killed."

CHAPTER TWENTY-THREE

A Little Misdirection . . . Just in Case

Barnaby cracked a walnut open with his clawed hand and tossed the nutmeat into his gaping mouth. He reminded Celeste of an oversized reptile in his Skulk form, but especially whenever he dropped his gaze to look at her with that predatory lust for blood. The only other person she knew who could master that look on command was Anaïs.

Celeste twitched her cheek under the mask. Her skin stung from the icy cold, but she could still detect some movement. She wasn't sure how much longer she could endure the torture of the mask. Celeste closed her eyes and concentrated, knowing she had to keep reminding herself of all the little things she had to be thankful for. She had a lovely neighbor who would take care of the lavender, roses, and peonies that would surely be in full bloom in her garden by now. Her feet were warm, despite the frost attacking her face. The Skulk didn't chew with his mouth open. Sebastian was safe. Anaïs was presumably safe. Five new things to be grateful for. The suction on the mask decreased near the tip of her nose.

While they waited for the Skulk in the flatcap to return with or without Tony and Anaïs, Barnaby picked up the clarinet again. He kicked the beat-up case into the far corner of the office as he tried to unscrew the body of the instrument and look inside. Nothing revealed itself, leaving his Skulk brain confounded. Celeste was glad to see him frustrated. The mask slipped a quarter inch along her forehead.

"Maybe try a sequence of notes," Frank suggested. "It plays like any clarinet. Maybe there's a code that makes it work."

Barnaby showed his fangs. "This isn't a damn party." The leader of the Infortunii approached Frank, holding the clarinet just a little more reverently than he had, cradling it in his hands. "Perhaps I haven't clearly articulated to you how ancient and special this relic is. What it's capable of in the hands of a Gardienne elder."

The Skulk commanded a lightning flash in the room, cold and stormy, making Celeste jump.

"This instrument of feminine power can stir the wind, peer into the future, and rock the babes from their cradles." Barnaby twisted around to face Celeste. He cracked open his hideous smile and recited in sing-song fashion, "When the bough breaks, the cradle will fall, and down will come baby, cradle and all." He made a tumbling gesture with his hand before making a splat sound with his tongue. "That was written about your kind, you know." He seemed to enjoy entertaining the room with his vulgar show. "The Gardiennes like to think they're all sunshine and light, but they have a dark side to their craft as well."

Celeste cringed at the words coming out of his grotesque mouth. *Lemon drops, fine cognac, dresses with lace and sequins, comfortable shoes.*

"What do you mean, they rock the cradle?" Frank's face contorted in confusion. "What the hell does that even mean?"

"You'll find out soon enough, I imagine." The Skulk tilted his head toward Celeste in accusation. "Isn't that right, my dear?"

Celeste inhaled sharply while Frank stared her down hard. She had an inkling of what Barnaby was talking about, but she knew better than to confirm anything. Frank, on the other hand, had apparently reached the limit of his tolerance for the Skulk's crazy talk, announcing with a dismissive shake of the head that he was going to go check on Tony and see what was keeping them.

"You'll stay right there," Barnaby said.

"The hell I will." Frank puffed out his chest, taking a step toward the Infortunii leader. "I'm not one of your lackeys you order around. We're supposed to be partners. Remember our deal? You get the wand, I keep the mask. And we both become kings of this godforsaken city. *Together.*"

Any fool knew the Infortunii weren't known for making fair deals. Celeste braced for the inevitable trouble that would come from such a challenge. She closed her eyes and continued her list of things to be grateful for. *Cloudless skies, champagne bubbles, a brilliant mind, a sense of humor, a handsome face in a crowd.* She could move her mouth and breathe clearly through her nose again. But it wasn't time. Not yet, so she opened her eyes.

Frank stared at the Skulk with his eerily hypnotic gaze. He squeezed his fist. Barnaby flinched, grabbing his left arm as if it had been poked. Maybe the dream auger could hold his own with a Skulk. Maybe that was why they were partners. But no. Barnaby's reply to the dream auger's invisible assault came swift and sudden. He picked up the fake mask, wielding it like a knife as he slung his arm around. He caught Frank in the throat with the edge. Not a fatal blow, but one that brought the big man to his knees. He clutched his neck with both hands and gasped for breath. Barnaby didn't move off the desk. He merely watched the dream auger cough and heave while he grabbed another scattered walnut.

"Like I said, I need you to stay here." Barnaby popped the nut into his mouth, then leaned forward to speak over Frank's head. "And for the record, any arrangement between us works in one direction only. We are not partners. You have no equal say. You are a means to my end. You think Luca, that mobster you tried to blackmail, was intimidating? Try crossing an Infortunii." The Skulk hissed, and a stream of ice and vapor shot out of his mouth, leaving a frost burn on the right side of Frank's face.

The dream auger winced and sucked in a breath as though shocked by the pain.

Celeste felt the Skulk's gaze swing back on her. An urge to fight mingled with an instinct to survive swirled inside her stomach, readying her to defend herself. Or flee if she must. But she couldn't let him know how much the mask had loosened against her skin. She needed the element of surprise against two Infortunii.

"My apologies for the outburst," the Skulk said to her, attempting to be magnanimous. "You have your own downfall to worry about." He pulled out his pocket watch and frowned at the hour. "They do seem to be taking their time." He nodded at his other man. "Go see what's keeping Cyril."

With the second Skulk gone, it was just Celeste, Barnaby, and a wounded dream auger who was still coughing and clutching at his throat. Was it time? Could she take them both on? Could she flash-blind Barnaby before he could freeze her out? Shackle the dream auger before he could lunge? If she didn't, the Skulk would get away with the elder staff, sever the sisterhood's Achilles' heel once and for all, and hang the fault around her and Anaïs's necks.

Celeste closed her eyes. There was one last moment of gratitude she'd been waiting to acknowledge in her heart. She thought of her trip to California, the palm trees, the mountains, the ocean. She smiled remembering the feel of the sun on her face as she drove in her convertible. She thought of the actors and crew she'd met at West Coast Studios, the first protégé she'd successfully guided onto her star path, and finally, Nick West, who'd scooped her up in his arms, stealing her heart with his self-deprecating charm from the very first moment they'd met.

The mask slipped loose and fell into Celeste's lap. Barnaby startled at the inconceivable. She raised her palm. Light shot out, a feeble, pale white from the mask's lingering influence. Still, the Skulk recoiled. He held up the elder staff at the last second, blocking the remaining blast from her palm so that the light only grazed him. He winced, but he wasn't down.

Celeste still held the real mask in her hand. She raised it like a shield in front of her, betting it held enough value to the Infortunii that he wouldn't strike. With her other hand she gripped her sapphire pendant. She transformed the desk lamp into a metal cage, building it bar by bar around Barnaby. The clarinet fell to the floor and rolled halfway toward her. The Skulk laughed at her inexperienced effort and simply froze the bars, shattering them to pieces.

She sent out a quick burst of light, just enough to distract his eye. With the mask in hand, she grabbed the clarinet off the floor and made a run for it. She'd nearly reached the door when a fog of ice wrapped around her ankles. The sting of the cold froze her blood so her legs couldn't move. Pins and needles crept up her veins, dropping her to her knees. The mask fell from her grip, but she clung to the clarinet. Frank crawled toward her on his hands and knees, his arm outstretched toward the mask. Even while choking for breath, he had to possess it.

Barnaby stood over Celeste, eyes bulging, one fang poking through his lips. He showed the other fang as he bent to swipe the instrument out of her trembling hands. "Why do you Gardiennes always behave so predictably?"

"I suppose it's because we don't look fondly on Skulks who can't seem to abide by the rules." Anaïs had transformed the door to the office into a gauzy curtain. She reached through, her palm exposed. A flash illuminated the room, bouncing off the glass and walls as she aimed a pulse of bright white light at the Infortunii leader. The impact startled him just long enough for Anaïs to storm into the room. Tony followed with his gun drawn. His hand shook as he pointed the weapon at Frank with his right hand while wiping sweat from his forehead with his left sleeve. Frank raised himself onto his knees and tried to muscle the gun away, but Tony gave him a hard knee to the ribs, and the dream auger gasped and rolled on his side.

Anaïs stood before Barnaby, hand extended in a threatening posture as he shriveled slightly under the intensity of her light. "As for the rest of your Skulk friends, I'm afraid they've been indefinitely detained in a downstairs bathroom, so don't bother waiting for them to take up the rear."

"A little shock to the eye. Is that all you've got?" Though temporarily blinded, Barnaby hissed out a plume of frozen mist. The chill washed over the Gardiennes just as Celeste got to her feet to scoop up Sebastian, who'd scampered out of Anaïs's purse. A thick fog enveloped her, veiling the office space in a mist so heavy she could no longer see her stoat, let alone anyone else in the room.

"Uh, what's happening?" Tony shouted through the fog.

Celeste tried to answer, but her voice froze in her throat. And no answer came from Anaïs either, so Celeste reached out, trying to feel her way toward Tony, achingly aware she no longer had the clarinet in her hands. She moved forward slowly with her arms stretched out, still hindered by the chill in her blood. No one else seemed to be moving, but where was Anaïs? Frank? Or Barnaby?

A hard clank of metal hitting metal sounded within the confusion as a soft glow of yellow light formed beneath the fog. Where the radiance emanated, the mist thinned. Soon, vague shapes came into view. Through the fog Celeste caught sight of Tony's profile. He was still holding his gun over Frank, his hand shaking from the effort. Anaïs stood on the other side of the room, clutching her pendant and raising that wicked brow of hers. She'd called up a warm light to match the dawn and burn off the haze. As it cleared, Celeste spotted Barnaby trying to escape. He stood by the door, tracing the bony fingers of one hand along the seal of what appeared to be a six-foot-tall entrance to a metal safe. It was enormous. Like the kind used in bank vaults, round with multiple locks and requiring two hands to turn the mechanism. Anaïs had the forethought to transform the only exit to keep the Skulk from absconding. If he moved left, the vault went with him. If he stepped to his right, the steel door slid over to block him.

Barnaby spun around in frustration once the fog dissipated. The light Anaïs had conjured appeared to wound him as he twisted his body to shield his eyes, and yet the clarinet remained in his hands. He held it up, threatening to break it. "Let me through or I swear I'll destroy it beyond recognition." He breathed ice-cold air on the instrument to make it brittle, then braced his hands around it, one on each end. "I'll smash it to smithereens. Your sisterhood will be rudderless."

Anaïs stood incredulous. "You can't possibly expect us to just let you go after what you've done. After what you've threatened the Gardiennes with?"

Celeste's voice thawed as the last wisps of mist evaporated. "Why are you doing this? Why do you always have to hurt so many people?"

Barnaby snarled, showing a tooth. "What a naive child you are. Hurting people, as you call it, keeps them humble. It's what we do. Now let me out!" When no one budged to give in to his demand, he shifted the clarinet so it rested in one hand by its neck. "Very well. You have only yourself to blame for the pain." The leader of the Infortunii smashed the frost-brittle instrument against the vault door as if he were launching a ship with a champagne bottle. The clarinet shattered into pieces.

Celeste gasped and dropped to the floor. She scooped up the splintered bits of wood and metal, needing to believe they could be put back together. Somehow the sisters would repair the elder staff. Reverse the damage with their magic.

Barnaby laughed at her attempt to save the broken pieces. "Idiot."

The Skulk's laugh died quickly, replaced by a sleazy, victorious smile. Behind him, one of the locks on the vault door jolted loose, as if the clarinet's destruction had undone the magic holding it in place. Then a second slid open. Barnaby wet his lips and sidestepped out of the way. "That's a good girl," he said in Anaïs's direction as he waited to jump through the exit the second the door swung open.

"It's not me doing it," Anaïs said. She checked on the dream auger, but he was still in a fetal position on the floor and barely conscious. "Not him either."

Celeste shook her head and took a step back as the third and final lock gave way. The foot-thick metal door creaked open an inch. Barnaby gripped the edge in triumph and pulled the door open wide enough to squeeze through, before faltering and backing away.

"Oh, Barnaby, how kind of you to open the door for me. It's heavier than it looks from the outside." A yellow glow emanated from behind the door as a frumpy woman with short-cropped gray hair stepped through. Barnaby's body shrank as the light grew and the woman wearing a modest traveling suit, paisley scarf, and sensible brown shoes came into view.

"Gertrude?" Celeste and Anaïs exchanged a look of confusion.

"Hello, my dears." Gertrude, the newly eldest of the Fées Gardiennes, toned down her radiance and took stock of the mess in the room. She entered the office, careful to step over Frank so she could introduce herself to Tony. "Hello, young man. Everything under control here?"

Barnaby made a move for the exit again while Gertrude had her back turned to him. She clutched her topaz pendant and aimed her hand toward the desk. The scattering of walnuts flew off the surface and transformed into a rope shimmering with Gardienne magic that wound around Barnaby's legs before he could slip through the opening and make his escape.

"Uh, yeah, I think we're good now." Tony begged Anaïs with his eyes for a clue about what was happening. She gave him a curt shake of the head and held a finger across her lips.

Celeste had to blink her eyes at Gertrude to make sure she wasn't seeing a mirage. "What are you doing in America? When did you arrive? How did you know we were here?"

"Ah, well, I took a ship like we all do. I've been waiting for this fiasco to play out for over a week now. All totally predictable." Gertrude let one of her chastising glances land on Barnaby.

"He's broken the elder staff," Celeste said, still stricken with guilt over the loss. "The clarinet. It was stolen from us. We nearly got it back, but now it's . . . gone." She dropped the pieces she'd collected, recognizing the futility of trying to put them back together. Not even a Gardienne's magic could repair the mess the Skulk had made.

Overcome with anger at the pointless loss, she flashed her palm at Barnaby, only to have the bright pulse intercepted by Gertrude, who stuck her arm out with such quick agility, she caught the light in one hand before it could hit the Skulk. "Let's not overdo it."

Gertrude took a threatening step toward Barnaby. "Now, what's this about the elder staff? I wouldn't like to think that the leader of the Infortunii would be so stupid as to threaten the Gardiennes' sisterhood when the transfer of power was still in medias res. That would be a very deliberately stupid thing to do."

Celeste rubbed her wrists. "More than stupid. Downright wicked. He's admitted he wanted to ruin the sisterhood so he and his hooligans can run rampant over a corrupt city, and now he's destroyed the elder staff. He ought to be strung up by his repulsive claws and hung on the side of the nearest skyscraper."

Anaïs nodded approvingly. "She makes a very compelling argument."

"I'm tempted to agree," said Gertrude.

"You cannot punish an elder of the Infortunii." Barnaby was indignant. "I am beyond reproach."

The eldest Gardienne dropped the pretense. "Barnaby. You're an absolutely repulsive creature. There was a time your kind had honor. Or, at least, respect for the rules. But your foul ambitions reek to the heavens. Did you think when you came to Dorée with your story about losing track of one of your men, and that you might require help from the Gardiennes to get him under control, that we wouldn't get just a tad suspicious about your motivations?" She paused and gestured to Celeste as exhibit A. "Especially after you put us in the position of having to send our newest initiate into the field for her first assignment while she unknowingly was expected to track down a murderer. And on an entirely different continent, I might add."

"I only abide by my nature, as do we all." Barnaby held one hand splayed over his empty heart.

The eldest Gardienne threw off her scarf as though getting hot around the collar. "It's all very plain now, Barnaby. Under your leadership, you let a man off leash in America to follow his most despicable tendencies. You manipulated three Gardiennes into traversing an ocean to stop him, and then used the entire endeavor to take advantage of a vulnerability in our procedural transfer of power, a ritual you knew was inevitable if we were sending an initiate to find her first protégé. You knew as well as anyone that if she should rise, the eldest must fall."

Barnaby slyly tested the grip of the rope by flexing his knees. "In my defense, I didn't know who or what she was until my man got himself caught and the young, sweet meat revealed herself."

Celeste nearly growled under her breath. "He got himself caught for murder, I might add." Her palms itched to attack him again.

Anaïs folded her arms across her chest as she addressed Barnaby. "But you knew if Celeste had found her protégé that Dorée's time on this earth would fade and the leadership would be in a state of limbo while the staff was in transport to the next eldest."

"Of course. I've witnessed the turnover many times." The Skulk tugged a little harder on his leg.

"But to have employed the dream auger in your scheme," Anaïs continued. "To set all this up with the mask and the club and stealing the elder staff, you had to have planned things months ahead of time. It wasn't any spur-of-the-moment decision to take advantage of the transition of power from Dorée to Gertrude." She paused as she sorted out the truth Barnaby had already confessed. "You knew you were going to steal the staff months ago. Long before we left France. To weaken the sisterhood simply so you could blackmail people in the city, make them sick, and then ruin their lives with no checks or balances from the Gardiennes. And I'd assert your motives weren't even about money. Not for you. You just like feeding off the pain."

The more Barnaby listened, the more he savored her conclusions, grinning to reveal the rotten, pointed teeth that resided behind his lying lips. "You've been to see the Lombardis, I take it. Now there's a sly one. Leopold is so upstanding and pleasant in society, but he hides a penchant for the young squalid boys. Several of whom prowl the perimeter of this building at night. Which, I might add, was the refreshing energy I was looking for when I chose this place," he said with his hand spread over his rock-hard heart again as though it bolstered his sincerity. "I'm afraid it was inevitable Lombardi might come away with a nasty case of syphilis after giving in once too often to his . . . predilections. Funny how you hadn't vetted your protégé's future husband beyond a few fat figures in a bank ledger."

Still bound, the Skulk took a baby step closer to Anaïs to spit even more bile. "You should know I took great pleasure in securing Angelica's footing on the downside slope of her—until recently—healthy fairy tale life years prematurely. But it was especially delicious watching her downfall begin knowing she was one of *your* protégés." He let the final *s* draw out as though the word had come off a serpent's tongue. "As for the rest, the blackmail comes easy when dealing with these 'respectable' types." He slipped his hands in his trouser pockets and shrugged, half proud, half humble at the outcome of his scheming.

Anaïs gaped. "You're despicable."

"What I am is a very patient man. The mask, for instance"—the Skulk tilted his head toward Gertrude as though she were a colleague he looked to for corroboration—"is an heirloom that's been kicked around the halls of the Infortunii compound for centuries. I planted that in the occult shop in London over a year ago. I had to keep sending lackeys in there to make sure no one else bought it. Then, of course, I had to arrange for a certain vaudeville act to travel to London so our dream auger here could 'discover' it. That alone took months to make happen."

Even Gertrude gawked at the depth of his confession. "You're telling me your diabolical mind has been working on this for over a year? You're even more vile than I'd imagined."

Barnaby laughed as though he were proud of the effort. "Worth every minute."

Celeste hoped Anaïs might lunge at the Skulk or bring a wall down on his misshapen head. Instead, her face transformed, infusing with glee as her eyes relaxed and she pressed her lips together in . . . what? Satisfaction? "You say the effort was worth it," the Gardienne said. "But what a shame to come to the end of such a long and deceptive journey only to discover all your planning was for naught."

"Ah, but the staff is destroyed." The Skulk stretched his hand out at the evidence scattered at his feet. "Maybe my New York plan hasn't come to fruition—yet—but you cannot deny I've weakened the sisterhood. That's all I needed, really, to get you do-gooders out of my way." He raised his hand in the air with a flourish. "And henceforth 'the world is mine oyster, which I with sword will open.'" His hand came down in a slashing motion, which Celeste took as a foreshadowing of his planned reign of terror over the city.

Anaïs put a hand on her hip and gave him the kind of sarcastic look her face was made for. "Was I born yesterday?" She raised that wicked brow of hers, then bent down to retrieve the beaten-up clarinet case that had been kicked in the corner of the room and forgotten. She shut the lid and snapped the fasteners closed. "The clarinet was, shall we say, a little misdirection on my part. Just in case. Sorry for the pun."

Barnaby's posture stiffened. "Wait, I don't understand."

"Imagine that." Anaïs extended the empty case to Gertrude, using both hands to cradle it. "Your staff," she said.

The clarinet case transformed before their eyes into the 940-year-old wooden relic with the gold vein running through it. The thirteen original wands embedded in the wood shimmered briefly as Gertrude accepted the ancient rod. Her eyes welled slightly as she seemed to accept the responsibility that came with being its caretaker. Celeste pressed the back of her hand to her mouth to stifle a sob of relief.

Given the level of animosity Barnaby had displayed, Gertrude wasted no time. She gripped her hand firmly around the staff and tapped it on the floor. A golden light shimmered all around her as the magic sought out the eldest of the sisterhood. The energy seeped into her skin, her clothes, and her hair, lifting her topaz pendant and shining a light into it as some invisible force confirmed her legitimacy as the staff's rightful caretaker. It had been suggested to Celeste while growing up that the energy was the coalesced spirit of all those Gardiennes who'd gone before, which she had no reason to doubt.

Gertrude—the stoic one, as they called her—laughed like a young girl who'd had her feet tickled with a feather. Meanwhile, Barnaby recoiled in his failure, shrinking inside his coat into an even punier creature than he'd been before. His appearance reverted from his true Skulk form back to that of the underfed, sallow-faced man in the black suit and broad-rimmed fedora.

Celeste stood mesmerized by the magic on display. She'd never witnessed the transfer of power before. Obviously, neither had Tony. He stood beside her, mouth open and eyes wide in the same apparent state of astonishment. She had to wonder if the memory would be taken from him later to preserve their low-key existence, but for now he was thrilled, as any magician would be by witnessing true magic.

The awestruck moment was short-lived, however. Celeste noted the gun in Tony's hand. It was hanging at his side, slack from inattention. And the dream auger wasn't where he ought to be. "Where's Frank?"

"Still curled up in a fetal position," Tony said with a toss of his head over his shoulder.

Celeste and Anaïs both spun around. They searched behind the chair and sofa, but he wasn't there. Gone, too, was one of the masks.

"There," Anaïs said, pointing to the vault door, which had been left open just a crack.

While they'd been enthralled by the magic on display, the dream auger had fled the flatiron.

CHAPTER TWENTY-FOUR

Shadows and Fire

Anaïs glared at Tony, contemplating if she should turn the sofa into a trunk and lock him up inside it. Knowing they'd all been distracted, not just him, she relented. It was almost humorous to think a magician couldn't keep a dream auger from doing a disappearing act. But it was Tony who knew best how Frank's mind worked.

"He'll go back to the club," he said. "He'll go after Nellie and Hazel if he feels trapped. I hate to say it, but he's not above using them as hostages to save himself. Not if he has the mask."

"My kind of guy," the Skulk said, patiently standing in his bindings. "I knew I picked him for a reason. Though I would like the mask returned. Sentimental reasons. You understand."

"Shut up, Barnaby." Gertrude had had enough. She tapped the staff against the floor. A ray of white light shot out, stunning the Skulk in a way neither Anaïs nor Celeste had been capable of. This time he was knocked out cold. He collapsed to the ground, so they quickly undid the rope and tied him to the radiator while he was unconscious.

"It won't hold him long, but at least his mouth has stopped moving." Gertrude transformed the staff into a common walking cane like the one Dorée used to carry. She pointed the end toward the vault opening, replacing it with the original door. "So, ladies, how do we get to this nightclub from here?"

The four of them rushed to the lobby and out through the revolving door, where Gideon swooped out of the sky to land on Anaïs's shoulder. The club was only a block south of where they stood. Anaïs thought she saw the big man disappear inside the shop front as they rounded the corner onto Fifth Avenue. Tony was right. He'd gone back to his bolt-hole, where he felt in control.

"Does he keep a gun inside?" Anaïs asked as they slowly approached the building.

Tony smirked. "Oh, yeah, he keeps a gun or two in there."

Gertrude stared down the avenue. "Surely he wouldn't hurt the baby or the woman."

Tony blew out a long breath. "I told Nellie to wait for me there. She'll have her bags packed and ready to go. I really don't know how he'll react once he figures out she's planning on leaving on top of his humiliation tonight."

It was past eight in the evening. The sun had sunk beneath the city skyline. Oranges and fiery reds tinted the undersides of harmless clouds. Beautiful but ominous. Anaïs shivered beneath her shawl as they approached the false front of the speakeasy hidden beneath the bookshop. It was unlike her to tremble, but she'd been given a glimpse of the shadows that lurked ahead, thanks to the man who'd been reading T. E. Lawrence at the Charmstone. She wondered how much of that future Nellie had seen and how she would react now that the time was upon them.

Celeste took notice of Anaïs's shiver and sidled up beside her to take her hand. "Sebastian and I feel it too," she said. "An uneasy churning in my chest. It isn't fear exactly, so what is it?"

"Skulk magic," Gertrude said, sniffing out the veil covering the shop. She touched her walking stick to the plate glass window. A mustard-yellow wreath of smoke hugging the front of the shop from sidewalk to rooftop revealed itself. "It's deviously activated by sunlight. See how it changes color with nightfall." She gazed at the darkening sky, then back at the door as the smoke steadily shifted into a shimmering silver that would attract the mundane eye, even if it didn't understand why. She turned to Tony. "And can you see this bookshop, young man?"

Tony checked the faces of those around him before answering. "Well, sure. Shouldn't I be able to see it?"

"Hmm, no, not before," Gertrude said. "But then you must have eaten something tainted recently that altered your vision. The woman and child likely have too, if they come and go regularly during the daytime."

Tony snapped his fingers. "The egg sandwiches? Nellie's been shoving them down our throats for weeks. You're saying they're poisoned?"

Gertrude pursed her lips. "Hmm, not poisoned, but we'll likely need to do a scrubbing later. You'll be fine for the time being." The Gardienne turned her attention back to the shop and peered through the glass. "He may already be inside by now."

Anaïs swung her head around. "Who? Frank? We already saw him go in."

"No, I mean Barnaby. He's the one behind all this," she said, pointing to the smoke on the glass. Gertrude bit her lip, thinking. "He must have dreamed this part up ages ago as well—buying the shop, selling it to this dream auger, and then keeping it hidden during the day from all but those with a magical gleam in their eye. Knowing a couple of Gardiennes would see it for what it was when the time was right. Such devious creatures."

Anaïs felt Celeste squeeze her hand as though to say she knew it was something more than Skulk magic making their hearts thump at an irregular rhythm. Could she know instinctively what was waiting on the other side of the glass?

Gertrude hooked the crook of her walking stick around the door handle to avoid touching it and pulled. The bookshop sat empty. Hopefully Sal was still stuffed in the men's bathroom sleeping it off with his buddy Cyril. With the all clear, Tony walked to the bookcase and pulled the hidden lever. The bookshelf opened to reveal the secret staircase leading to the club below. There was no saucy music swelling in the corridor this time. Instead, the distant cry of a woman screaming for help drifted upward through the floorboards.

"Nellie!" Tony took the steps two at a time and rushed to the basement before anyone could stop him.

Gertrude stared down the dark stairwell. "We don't know what kind of mess we'll find in there, but we can't let him go it alone." She transformed her walking stick back into the wooden staff. "Are you ready, ladies?"

"I was born ready." Anaïs headed down the stairs with Gideon flapping his wings just behind her.

"There's another way in." Celeste backtracked toward the door. "I'll go around and come in from the other side. Just in case."

"Careful, my dear."

The subterranean club sat eerily quiet. The lights were dimmed, and there was no band warming up on their instruments. The place ought to have been getting ready to open, but it was like everyone got the same memo to skedaddle. Tony came out of the private office where Anaïs had been held in the cage. He swept the club with his eyes, then shook his head and pointed to the back stairs that led to the dressing rooms. "Nellie and the baby have a room up there," he said.

The Gardiennes followed as Tony sprinted up the back steps. At the top, they caught sight of Celeste just entering at the end of the hallway. She shook her head to say she hadn't seen anyone. Between her and them was a series of six doors, three on each side, and all were closed. Gertrude held her topaz pendant and tugged on her ear. The noises in the building became amplified. A rat scratching inside a wall, a radiator clinking, and a baby whimpering softly behind the third door on Anaïs's right. There was another clanking noise, but the sound had come from the other side of the wall where the bookshop was located in the front of the building. Gertrude shook her head and approached the room where the baby had whimpered.

Tony whispered, "That's Nellie's room."

The eldest Gardienne listened a moment longer, then opened the door. Anaïs followed on her heels, anxious to see that the child was all right. Inside the small room she saw a cot made up with a quilt and pillow, a rocking chair, a washbasin still damp with soapy water, and an overpacked leather suitcase bulging at its sides sitting in the corner. But no Hazel. "Where is she?" The baby made a fussing noise from inside a tiny closet. Gertrude pushed back the curtain and found the girl lying in her cradle, which rocked gently on the floor as though they'd just missed whoever had set it in motion.

Anaïs rushed in and scooped Hazel up in her swaddling blankets. "Nellie was trying to hide her."

"There's my sweet girl." Tony patted the babe's head, but his eyes betrayed his fear. "Now, where is your mother?"

"I think it's fair to say she's with Frank somewhere in the building." Gertrude exited the tiny apartment to listen to the sounds in the hallway again. "Though not of her own free will, I'd wager. We've missed something downstairs."

A quick yelp echoed in the club below them. Celeste walked to the top of the stairs. "Did anyone else hear that?"

Tony rushed to check for himself. "Jesus, I didn't look behind the bar." He ran back downstairs as a glass broke and a table tipped over somewhere inside the club. Celeste followed him, though she ordered Sebastian to stay upstairs. The stoat pouted, running around in nervous circles while Celeste disappeared into the speakeasy below.

Gideon, too, attempted to fly into the stairwell, but Anaïs held him back by his tail feathers just as he bent his legs to take off. "Not so fast," she said. "You stay here and watch the child. If anything happens, call up a wind to carry you both outside to safety." The bird sighed and shuffled his feathers, while Anaïs and Gertrude went to investigate the source of the broken glass.

The sconces lining the walls were still dark on the lower floor, but Gertrude made them come to life with a tap of her staff. One by one they illuminated the space in soft yellow light that reflected off the bar and stage. Shattered glass littered the floor between the two.

Tony called out to the shadows beyond. "Nellie? Are you all right?"

There, in the corner, where the light didn't quite reach, a man wearing a wooden mask emerged from the darkness. His hand covered Nellie's mouth while his other one pointed a gun at her temple.

"Frank?" Tony held his hands up and tentatively approached. "Frank, let her go. She's done nothing to deserve this."

"Stay where you are," Frank ordered, moving the gun to aim it at the four of them while making his point. "Drop your gun and slide it to me. Now!" Tony paused only briefly before he took the revolver out of its holster. After he kicked it forward, Frank relaxed a fraction, shifting his weight on his feet. He was a man who'd grown comfortable being the bully. "Remember when Nellie told us about this part." Frank nodded as though he could see the premonition coming true in real time. "About Hazel, about the women, about you. We didn't really believe her at first, but here we are. She's a real corker, isn't she."

Celeste took a step forward to show her face in the light. "What did Nellie tell you about us?" The eyes behind the mask shifted to look at her. The gun went back to its place at Nellie's temple.

"She said you'd come. But that you couldn't leave until you got what you came for."

"What did we come for?" Anaïs ventured to ask, remembering what Nellie had told her about Frank getting what he wanted before they got what they wanted. Was this the moment she'd seen?

"It doesn't matter!" Frank's hand gripped the gun tighter. "You can't have it. I'll take everything with me before I let you leave here with what doesn't belong to you."

Nellie closed her eyes and wept as a high-pitched noise squeezed out of her throat.

Anaïs considered shackling the man's legs by transforming a nearby stand-up ashtray, but the danger of what he might do to that head of beautiful red hair while he kept his gun pressed against it wasn't worth the risk. Not yet.

"Frank, you gotta let her go." Tony kept his hands up where the dream auger could see them. "You got the mask back. You've still got the club. You don't have to do this."

"That's right, I've got the mask." Frank tilted his head back and forth and rolled his shoulders. "You have no idea how it makes me feel. That kid who grew up knowing he was different. Who could see things others couldn't but had no way of making the chaos in his mind work to his advantage. I finally got some clarity. There I was, a member of the freak show sentenced to helping old women in faded silk relive their dreams of lost loves. And for what? A few coins tossed in my hat at the end of the night. But with this . . ." Frank pointed the gun toward the mask. "With this I have power. I can see into the depths of people's minds. Beyond the ridiculous dreams. Beyond what any of your lot can see," he said with a nod toward the trio of Gardiennes. "The dark memories of deeds that sink all the way down into the safe within a person's soul. They think they've locked them away, but with the mask I have the master key. You've no idea how eager people are to pay me to keep quiet."

Tony dropped his arms. "Frank, you don't know what you're saying. This isn't you."

"It's the mask's influence," Celeste said. "I felt it too. You think it lets you see deeper into others' minds. Maybe it does. But I think it also sees into yours. It's constantly looking for ways to corrupt and exploit your weak spots. It's what the Infortunii do. It's what Barnaby does."

"She's right," Anaïs said. "Their whole purpose is to cause pain and misery. They like to think of themselves as a counterweight to the high of hedonism and narcissism, but what they really do is spread their misery like a cancer in the body so people are in so much pain that they let go of their bright potential." Anaïs took a step closer, casting a quick glance at Nellie to make sure she was okay. "You see, the Skulks crave the dark and the damp. And if too many people shine around them, they cannot find their own state of bliss that resides in gloom. That, Frank, is whose mask you wear."

Frank took his hand off Nellie's mouth but kept it pressed against the crook of her neck, where he could still squeeze her throat in warning. She gasped for air as tears trailed down her cheeks. "We were like family." He kept the gun vaguely pointed at her side while looking at Tony. "The three of us working the circuit together. Do you remember? And then little Hazel came along. Just like that, everything changed. That's when Nellie's visions became self-inflicted prophecies."

"Which visions?" Celeste asked. Anaïs thought she was being very deliberate and thoughtful when speaking to Frank, keeping her voice low while showing genuine curiosity.

The dream auger appeared responsive. "We used to dream of opening a little place all our own." He waved the gun at the club. "We'd be the boss. We'd run the show. No more touring or working for peanuts for somebody else." He paused to wipe the sweat from the side of his temple, pointing the gun away from Nellie briefly.

Celeste took a small step forward. "Then what happened?"

Nellie sniffled as her eyes and nose watered. "The visions all started ending the same way. In death." She licked a tear off her lips and implored the women with her swollen eyes. "Is she okay? Is she still upstairs?"

"Your daughter is fine," Gertrude answered. "No harm will come to her."

Nellie slumped against Frank and shook her head. "Then there's nothing left, Frank. They're here. The eldest has her staff. They have Hazel."

"No!" Frank jerked her into the dark backstage area. "They're just shadows. The visions don't have to be real if we don't want them to be."

As the couple receded, a crash exploded upstairs in the bookshop. It sounded like the big front window had been shattered. It was followed by heavy feet that didn't care who heard them. Three, maybe four people. Anaïs slowly backed up toward the entrance to listen for a clue about the intruders. One of them came halfway down the stairs. Anaïs could just see the soles of a man's black leather wing tips before he stopped and she heard the flick of a lighter opening. "Hey, Frank!" he shouted. "We know you're in here. Got a message for you from Luca. In case you ever think of threatening him with blackmail again."

There was a whooshing sound and the smell of gasoline just before a bottle crashed on the floor of the French Drop. Liquid fire covered the tile. Anaïs jumped back barely in time before the tablecloth nearest to her burst into flame. She thought to dump a vase of fresh flowers on the fire, but Gertrude stopped her. "It's oil! You'll only aggravate it with water."

"What, then?"

Anaïs's question was answered with a spray of machine gun fire issued from halfway up the stairs. She scrambled to the opposite side of the dance floor to huddle with the others after the man shouted, "Let it burn!"

"They're trying to kill us." Celeste coughed, choking on the smoky air as the fire spread. She pointed her necklace at the source of the gunfire. The spent bullet casings transformed into bricks that stacked up to seal the opening. "Back stairs!" she shouted, then hooked her arm around Gertrude's and led the elder Gardienne to the opposite stairwell leading to the dressing rooms. Tony followed, making sure they skirted past the fire unscathed.

"What about Nellie and Frank?" Anaïs made a quick search of the darkened corner where the pair had disappeared, but it was getting harder to see or breathe as the smoke thickened. She covered her mouth with her shawl, though it proved a useless mask. She rattled the door to the office where she'd been held before. It was locked. She banged on the door and called out. "Nellie! Frank! You've got to get out. The whole place is going to burn."

The blaze exploded once it found the wallpaper. It crawled up to the ceiling, hungry for more, then seized on the wooden beams.

"We have to get out of here," Tony yelled from the base of the stairs.

Anaïs rattled the doorknob. "Nellie and Frank are locked inside."

When no one inside the office answered, Anaïs opened the door using her ruby pendant, dissolving the hinges into sugar. She found Nellie huddled at the bottom of the water tank with her hands pressed against her ears. The psychic's body trembled in what looked like wide-eyed shock. Frank stood on a ladder beside the tank, readying to climb inside with her. "You can't stop us. There's a bullet for her and one for me. We won't feel a thing."

Tony burst into the room behind her. "Frank, stop kidding around. Enough already! The whole damn place is gonna come down."

"Can't do it, Tony." The dream auger slid the mask off his face and tossed it aside. "I thought we could beat this thing. But look at this place," he said, and coughed from the smoke. "All our dreams are turning to ash."

Tony took two steps toward the tank, where Nellie had hidden her face with her long hair. Frank pointed the gun and fired off a single warning shot above his head, forcing the magician to stop in his tracks. "I'm happy to make it a threesome, Tony, if you don't leave now. But you know that's not what she saw." He climbed higher and lifted a leg over the top of the tank. "Now go before I change my mind," he said, swinging his other leg over, ready to jump inside with the woman.

Anaïs backtracked out of the room, pulling Tony with her by his jacket. "It's no use," she said. "The place is going to burn down. We'll never be able to save them in time. We have to get out."

"Nellie!" Tony tried muscling into the room again when a second bullet zinged through the smoke. Only this one wasn't a warning. The bullet caught flesh. Tony cried out and grabbed his shoulder. He stumbled out of view, coughing and gasping for air.

"Tony!" Anaïs bent to see how badly he'd been hurt. Her hand came away bloody when she peeled his fingers back to check his wound.

She wrapped her shawl around his arm and tied it off tight. "We're leaving now!"

Anaïs helped Tony to his feet. The flames were creeping in. The rafters creaked and popped as if they were being eaten alive. She pointed Tony toward the stairs, then tried one last time to convince Frank and Nellie to leave. "Think of Hazel! Think of your little one."

Nellie shrieked like a madwoman hearing her daughter's name. "Take care of my girl!" she yelled. "She belongs to you now. Tell her I loved her, when she grows up and wonders about me."

Anaïs didn't know what to say. Part of her knew the truth. Knew this tragedy had to happen. Nellie wasn't the only one who'd seen the future, but the agony of the abandonment was almost more than she could bear. She stood with them as long as she could until the smoke finally overtook her. She coughed and squinted, unable to see the exit anymore. She had to save herself, but the light and dark played hide-and-seek in the smoke so that she couldn't see where to go. Frantically, she stumbled in what she thought was the direction of the stairs with her arms outstretched, feeling for something familiar.

A hand grabbed her by the elbow. "This way!"

Celeste!

A gunshot sounded. And then another.

The young Gardienne paused long enough to recognize the tragedy that had just occurred on the other side of the office door, then led Anaïs upstairs and outside to safety.

Tony staggered over to them as the pair emerged into the alley, covered in smoke and ash. "Frank and Nellie?" he asked, still gripping his shoulder and holding on to hope. "I heard more shots."

Anaïs shook her head solemnly. "Are you all right?" When he nodded and said it was just a scratch, she didn't quite believe him, but she didn't think he'd die anytime soon. "Where's Hazel? Is the baby all right?"

Gertrude stepped out of the way to reveal Gideon perched atop a baby carriage watching over her. "He did well, your rook. The two of them were out here waiting for us before the smoke ever reached the upper level."

Anaïs didn't need to be told what a loyal bird she had in Gideon. She gave him a quick peck on the head, then bent to pick up the baby. The poor child was tired and hungry. They'd have to get her something to eat soon, but first there was one small thing the Fées Gardiennes needed to do. Just to be certain.

"Have you got it?" Gertrude asked Anaïs while patting the baby's head.

Celeste and Tony moved closer to see what they were talking about. Celeste may not have understood everything about what had just transpired, but if Anaïs was right, the Gardienne's name, along with her own, would one day be written beside the orphan's name in a book kept hidden in the attic of the cottage in the woods.

Anaïs approached Tony, rocking the baby gently in her arms. "I can't take her," he said as a low-simmer panic settled in his eyes. "I wouldn't know how."

"No, it isn't that. But I want you to get a good look at her. To know that she'll be okay."

Tony was guarded as he examined the girl, cagey even, as though he had an inkling of what was happening but didn't quite believe it. His eyes stayed on Anaïs as he gently kissed the top of the baby's head.

Anaïs set Hazel back in the baby carriage. She reached into her purse and removed the velvet bag with the diamond pendant the size of a quail egg. Tony's eyes shifted from cautious to covetous as she held the necklace out to Gertrude. "Will you do the honors?"

"My first official duty as eldest." Gertrude held the staff in one hand and the necklace in the other. "Now, if I remember correctly, you have to swing it like a pendulum from right to left."

The eldest Gardienne held the pendant in front of Hazel. The sun had long since faded from the sky, but the diamond still radiated a spectral array of colors that danced on the girl's face as smoke and flame erupted behind them. Hazel's eyes were bright with curiosity about the stone and the sparkling lights. She reached a pudgy hand out and grabbed the diamond in her fist, as any child might do, but in her grasp the pendant's energy sent out a shower of golden light that enveloped the girl. Like a sparkler without the heat.

Tony stared, mesmerized. "What's happening?"

"It's her," Gertrude said, satisfied. "Our newest babe."

"She's really one of us?" Celeste smiled so wide she nearly outshone the sparkler.

"Hold on." Tony stared from the girl to the women. "What do you mean, she's one of you?"

"It means she'll be coming home with us," Gertrude said. "She has a destiny waiting for her there."

"Wait, all those stories Nellie told me about her visions. About how Hazel was meant for a different life. That she had a destiny. Those were real? I thought she meant she was leaving the city and going someplace Frank wouldn't find her, like Poughkeepsie."

The difference between his understanding of the situation and theirs brought the women back to the reality of the moment. They were standing in an alley where an illegal nightclub was quickly burning to the ground with two dead bodies and a few dozen spent bullets inside.

"We need to be on our way," Gertrude said as the sound of sirens blared in the distance.

"My car." Tony pointed toward the end of the alley. "It's in front of the flatiron."

"Ah, then you can give us a ride to the hotel, if you're not in too much pain, young man." Gertrude squinted at his shoulder. "Perhaps you ought to let me get a quick peek at that injury."

Tony obliged, removing his coat to reveal the blood-soaked shirt underneath. "It looks worse than it is," he said through gritted teeth.

"Hmm." Gertrude pressed the staff against his shoulder as though evaluating his injury. She tapped twice against his shirt, and the magician stopped wincing. "Just a scratch, as you said. Shall we go?" She transformed the staff back into a cane and started marching toward the car, letting the others catch up.

The women followed and jumped into the four-seater, with Hazel on Anaïs's lap in the front seat beside Tony. He pointed the car in the direction of the bookstore for one last look. They drove by the front of the shop slowly as a policeman waved the car forward, motioning them to keep going around the fire engines and stop gawking. They did as they were told, pulling forward, when a man suddenly jumped out of the building next door. He was thin, sallow-skinned, and wearing a fedora. A faint aura of cold lifted off him like a blue fog as he ran away with something that looked very similar to a wooden mask clutched in his hand.

"Of course the damn thing wouldn't burn," Anaïs said, following the Skulk with her eyes until he disappeared in the shadows ahead. "That mask is probably frozen to the core with vile Skulk magic."

Gertrude tapped the back of the front seat with her cane. "Language, Anaïs."

The Gardienne had to stifle a laugh. Some things never changed.

CHAPTER TWENTY-FIVE

Love Has a Magic All Its Own

Celeste couldn't stop stealing glances at the baby in her bassinet as she slept in the doorway between her hotel room and Anaïs's, snug under a blanket. The circumstances of how Hazel had come to be sleeping in their custody in New York City kept playing over and over in Celeste's head. One day ago, she'd had a mother who loved her and took care of her. Now, the baby was being prepared to sail away to another continent, where she'd be raised as a Fée Gardienne in the tiny cottage in the woods. Part of Celeste was excited to embrace this newest sister and see her grow into her role, but she hadn't expected that events would churn all her personal feelings of abandonment to the top of her heart.

Celeste brushed lint from a favorite jacket and hung it on a rung inside her travel trunk. Sebastian supervised from the top shelf, guarding their supply of gemstones and elixirs. Hazel would get her own collection of peridots, sapphires, and emeralds in a few years. Maybe Celeste would even be the one to teach her about channeling energy via the sun using the stones someday, as all Gardiennes took turns instructing the newest recruits in different facets of the job.

Anaïs had already finished packing her trunk in the adjoining room. With nothing to do but wait, she busied herself by taking final advantage of the bar hidden inside the radio before heading to the pier to check in for their journey home. She handed Celeste one of her latest concoctions. This one was called a gin fizz and smelled of lemons. "She's a sweet little thing," Anaïs said, leaning over the bassinet they'd transformed out of a hatbox. "She reminds me of you when you were a baby."

"I'd always longed to know how the babes ended up in the Gardiennes' care." Celeste marveled at how peacefully the child slept not knowing her whole life had just been turned upside down. "It always seemed slightly suspicious to me that a Gardienne could know to be in the right place at the right time to scoop up an orphaned girl so she doesn't perish in some disaster."

"I'd always wondered too. I suppose we all do at some point." Anaïs pursed her lips after taking a sip from her glass. She sat on the velvet chair in Celeste's room, followed by Gideon, who landed on the seatback above her left shoulder. "But after going through the experience myself last night, I think it's simply a matter of fate that brings us and circumstances together." Anaïs told her about Thomas, the psychic she'd visited in the occult gathering place called the Charmstone. "I'd been getting an uncanny feeling around Hazel. A strange kinship."

Celeste slipped a blouse on a hanger. "Yes, I'd noticed that unusual feeling too, but I couldn't place the sentiment."

"Well, it was only because I was carrying Dorée's diamond pendant that the thought occurred to me. The darn thing materialized in my handbag the day after she passed, so I knew she was really gone and that a new Gardienne was out there waiting. But I never imagined we'd be the ones to find her." She swirled her drink and licked her lips. "Even still, I wanted some assurance that Hazel might be the one. That's why I slipped out yesterday at the last minute. I went to look up a psychic and see if he could tell me who the true owner of the diamond pendant was. They're generally reliable enough with their insights if they can touch an object."

"What did he say?"

"He said he couldn't explain why but that an image of a *hazel* tree kept flashing in his mind. I almost spit out my teeth. I had no doubt after that that we are fated to come into this world as Gardiennes." She petted Gideon under his chin, then let him sample her drink. "It isn't random. It's our destiny. Sadly, it would also mean it's the destiny of those who bring us into the world to perish. Or maybe sacrifice is a better way to describe what they do for us."

"It's still a somewhat barbaric practice, though, isn't it?" Celeste sipped her drink, then wiped a little foam from her lips as she put the history book in the bottom of the trunk alongside the other volumes. "I mean, she must have family somewhere who'll miss her."

"As do most who've passed. Remember, any relatives she might have believe she died in the fire. She's only alive in their memories now."

The words didn't do anything to calm Celeste's agitated emotions. "Barnaby said an odd thing when I was trapped in the mask. He claimed the elder staff had the power to 'stir the wind, peer into the future, and rock the babes from their cradles.' I've witnessed the first two happen with Dorée, but why would he say that last part?" She thought she knew, but she wanted to hear it from another Gardienne. Someone who'd seen and done more in the world than she had.

The smile dropped from Anaïs's face. "Did he call us cradle snatchers? Kidnappers? Murderers? Sometimes they use the words 'baby killer' too." She took a long guzzle from her glass, then held it out of Gideon's reach. "We don't steal the children. Not really. They're presumed dead. *We're* presumed dead, if you think about it. Hell, for all I know, maybe we *are* dead." She leaned forward in her chair. "But that baby is safe now, and she'll have a grand life. Wouldn't you agree?"

Celeste nodded. She didn't know why recent events sat uneasy with her. She understood how the cottage worked: A new babe named Clara had arrived when Celeste was nine years old. Soon after, Lydia, the eldest at the time, had passed away. She knew the Gardiennes must maintain their thirteen members, though no one ever seemed to have an answer for why it had to be thirteen. It was one of those odd realities of nature, just as there were sometimes thirteen moons in a calendar year. She rationalized the off feeling as being due to too many emotions stirred up by the previous evening's violent events. Deciding to focus on the future instead, as was her optimistic way, she declared, "Well, this little one will be our first American initiate."

Anaïs swirled the last of her drink, then pointed a finger. "Actually, that isn't quite true."

"You mean there's been another?" Celeste swung her head around, curious to know which of them was different. "Who?" Sebastian lifted his head as well, as though asking the same question.

"You."

"Me?" There was an initial sort of shock that quickly gave way to the kind of wary curiosity that comes with hearing a truth but not yet wanting to believe it. "What gave you that idea? How could you know that? No one ever talks about our previous life."

While Celeste distractedly tossed a few last random items into her trunk, Anaïs told her about the attic, about the book of records, and about the details entered beside each name. "I don't know if I'm supposed to tell you or not, but I've never lived by the rules. Celeste, you were born in San Francisco. When you turned one, your parents were killed in the great earthquake that leveled the city."

Celeste had to consciously close her mouth and sit down on the bed. All her life she'd wondered where she came from. Who her people were before she became a Gardienne. Wondering who her mother was. Her father. She hadn't believed she'd ever find out, so she'd buried the emotion where it could bother her only in her most melancholy moods. But learning the truth was like opening a trapdoor in her side and letting that goblin of not knowing free.

Celeste had felt a kinship with the west coast of America ever since she'd arrived on the train for her first mission as a Fée Gardienne two weeks earlier. The sunshine, the people, the expanse of mountain and ocean—from the start it had felt like a place she *could* call home. But the information only raised more questions about this cradle business. "So you're saying a Gardienne just happened to have traveled all the way from France to California when this disaster happened? That she just happened to scoop me up from the rubble?"

"Just like we were there to get Hazel last night, though I have a theory about that." Anaïs set her empty glass aside and came to sit on the floor beside the bassinet. "We didn't start the fire at the club. We didn't give the dream auger a mask that let him see into the dark corners of people's hearts. And we weren't the ones who had a plan to blackmail the city's powerful. The Skulks did that. So, I figure the baby was always meant to be ours, but they were the ones who created the calamity that allowed her to fall into our arms." Anaïs pulled the blanket up to keep the child warm. "They accuse us of rocking the cradle, of stealing the babies who tumble free from their perch, but it's the Infortunii who call the violent wind that shakes the treetops. We're simply there to catch the babes before they hit the ground. Chalk it up to another ineffable link between us and them in this tug-of-war between benevolence and malice."

"It's still odd to think we were here in New York City for a specific reason when we didn't even know we'd be here ourselves." Celeste moved onto the floor to be nearer to the baby, thinking about the unscheduled timing of their trip. They couldn't have anticipated they would be in that speakeasy on any given evening, let alone on the one night it burned down and killed two of its occupants, though officially it would be reported as three. But perhaps events had been waiting for them, ticking away patiently on the clockface of time. Perhaps none of it could have occurred until or unless they'd arrived. And until or unless the Skulks were also there to stir up the kind of trouble that might leave a child an orphan. "Maybe we're always someplace at the right time for a reason."

Sebastian crawled up on her lap and stood on his hind legs so he could see inside the bassinet. He pressed his nose closer, curious about the newest child, then chittered softly before curling up in Celeste's arms.

"That's what I think," Anaïs said. "Things tend to work in tandem like that for us. Just when and as they should."

"And what about Mr. Cheekbones?" Celeste smiled slyly. "Is that something that's going to work out?"

Anaïs squirmed, pursing her lips and looking away. "Hmm, maybe. Tony was pretty shaken up last night. We held each other in the dark until midnight trying to make sense of the evening and what might happen today." She paused to check her watch and smiled. "He'll be here in a few minutes to take us to the pier. Better get these trunks secured."

While they set the locks on their trunks with incantations to protect their contents for the transatlantic journey, Gertrude entered Celeste's room with the walking stick in hand and her dog companion at her side, a standard white poodle named Basket who'd sat out the previous evening's adventure, not wishing to give away the eldest's presence in the city too soon. "Ready, ladies?" A bellman entered behind Gertrude to collect the trunks, Anaïs settled little Hazel in her baby carriage, and the trio went downstairs to meet Tony in the lobby.

After the group exchanged cordial hellos, and Basket was told to stay inside to help keep watch over the child, Gertrude hooked arms with Tony and escorted him outside with the luggage. There, she supervised the loading of the trunks onto the back of his car, giving a little magical boost with her walking stick so the straps would stay attached for the short trip to the pier.

"We got the elder staff back in one piece in the end," Anaïs said to Celeste, making a final assessment of their adventure in New York. "And we have our newest member to introduce to everyone when we get home. Not such a bad outcome."

"And don't forget your new admirer." As she said it, Celeste's eyes nearly teared up. She didn't think it was because she was leaving America so soon after learning her origins. Something else was off, but she couldn't figure out what exactly, so she blamed the emotion on pre-journey jitters.

Anaïs waved at Tony through the lobby window. "Gertrude has agreed to let him keep his memories about us and what happened. At least for now. Just in case I decide to come back to the city in a month or two to look him up."

Celeste smiled, happy for her friend. "If I had a man who looked at me like he's looking at you right now, I'd turn around and jump on the first return ship."

Anaïs inhaled sharply. "Oh, Celeste. There's one more thing I should tell you." She bit her bottom lip, as though still deciding if she should say the thing out loud.

Hazel stirred under her blanket, waving her pudgy fists on the verge of waking, so Celeste whispered, "Tell me what?"

Anaïs shook her head as though there was no cure for her flawed character. "I may have to add a gin fizz to the list of drinks that get me in trouble, but there's something I need to get off my chest. I didn't say anything earlier because we were still facing off against that fiend Barnaby. But I saw Nick West. Hon, he's here. In the city. Right now."

"You saw him? Where?"

"At the Plaza Hotel. We passed briefly in the elevator when I went to check on my protégé."

Celeste nodded, wondering what to do with the information. She didn't think Anaïs had told her merely to make her squirm in regret. She genuinely seemed to want to share something helpful. "I saw him the other night too," she admitted. "Briefly. He was going inside the tavern when I was walking out with Tony. Which seems to be a metaphor for whatever fleeting encounter we had in California. I thought he might . . . I mean, I hoped . . ." She shrugged. "He didn't recognize me one whit."

Anaïs gripped her arm. "Wait, you saw him too? Why didn't you tell me? Celeste, I don't think you understand. It means something to keep passing him here in a city of millions. Especially after you wiped his memories of you."

"What could it possibly mean?"

"It means that when you veiled his memory of you in shadow, it didn't work. Not completely. And not because you didn't do it right but because something stronger had already taken hold in his emotional muscle. That man is here in the city for a reason. Yes, he may say he has studio business or some financial arrangement to see to, but the truth is he's here because you're here. Somehow he felt that and had to follow. Oh, Celeste, he's in love with you, can't you see? True love. The kind that can't be wiped away with a little glamour."

"She's right," Gertrude said, after stepping inside the lobby to retrieve Basket. "True love has a magic all its own, completely outside of our control. You'd be a fool not to see it for yourself."

"But what do I do?"

"Don't be silly," Gertrude said. "Go find him and remove that veil on his memories of you. The youth these days." She rolled her eyes and called her dog to her side.

Celeste spun around like a flustered bird looking for the quickest way out of its cage. "But we're leaving. He could be anywhere in the city. There isn't time to find him."

Anaïs waved to Tony to stop loading the last trunk, then took Celeste's hand. "Hon, if you get on that ship with us, I'll never forgive you. And you know you don't want me coming after you as your enemy." She raised that brow of hers again, this time in jest, as she released Celeste's hand. "Go find him. He's waiting for you, even if he doesn't know that's what he's doing."

The enormity of what might be lost if she didn't act hit Celeste square in the chest. "I have to find him. Before it's too late." She gave Anaïs a peck on the cheek. "Thank you," she said, then wished her, Gertrude, and Hazel a bon voyage as the Gardiennes transformed the baby carriage into a travel-size vanity case and climbed into Tony's car. The magician held his hand up as he caught Celeste's eye. She held hers up to wave back, when he passed his right hand over his left and the car keys suddenly appeared in his palm, hooked over his index finger. He jingled the keys and smiled. Just the way she hoped to remember him.

The car pulled away. Anaïs stuck her hand out and gave a final wave as they disappeared around the corner. There was a brief moment of distress, but rather than feeling alone or abandoned, Celeste adopted a sense of determination. She stowed her trunk with the hotel clerk, said that she'd be back later, and then had the doorman hail her a cab. She had two leads on where to find Nick West. She started with the first.

"The Plaza," she told the driver. While the cabbie darted through traffic, she held Sebastian close to her neck, feeling his pulse thump in sync with her own racing heartbeat. She didn't know how a man she'd known for only a few wonderful, sunny days had so fully ensnared her heart, but as Gertrude had reminded her, of all the energy swirling in the universe, love alone had the power to generate its own magic.

The cab driver dropped Celeste off outside the Plaza Hotel. The place loomed like a modern take on a French château as she looked up. A tiny shiver of expectation sent an electric pulse through her body. After paying the man, she took a moment to recognize the grandeur of the street, with its opulent buildings overlooking the green expanse of Central Park. Such a privileged view in a crowded city full of steel, glass, and stone.

Celeste wasn't nervous exactly as she inquired at the hotel's front desk, but her heart was beating loud enough to flood her ears with its thumping so that she didn't quite catch what the clerk had said. She could have sworn he said that Nick West had checked out that morning and wouldn't be back. She shook her head to clear it, then asked him to repeat himself.

"Mr. West had an appointment this morning, but he's expected back this afternoon. You're welcome to wait for him in the lobby, if you like."

"Oh, thank you. Yes, I think I will." Relieved, Celeste sat in a wing-back chair near the elevator with her feet together and her purse on her lap. Sebastian snored softly inside. She'd begun to calm down after the whirlwind decision to stay behind and find Nick. The gnawing irritation in her chest had gone silent. She believed with all her heart that her own future didn't reside on the other end of a long steamship ride across the ocean. She was precisely where she was supposed to be.

The doorman opened the front entrance to the lobby. A man with a head of wavy brown hair and eyes as blue as a summer sky walked in. Celeste stood up. She waited a heartbeat for him to see her. To give her just a glimmer of recognition. Maybe the bend of a smile in the corner of his lips to show there was something there beneath the magic that had made him forget. He paused halfway inside the lobby, sent a quizzical glance in her direction, then checked in with the front desk for any messages. He glanced once more in her direction, though it was more out of confusion. As though he might have recognized her from two nights ago but was slightly unnerved by why she stared at him.

Not exactly the reunion Celeste was hoping for, so she gripped her sapphire pendant and parted the veil she'd hung between them back in California. She took a deep breath, waiting for him to collect the notes about his missed calls. He read the first two as he walked toward her, then looked up to catch the elevator. There, his gaze shifted back to her. It was hard to read the expression on his face at first. More confusion, bewilderment, surprise, and then she was certain she saw delight spark in his eyes.

"Hello, Nick."

"Celeste?" Nick scanned the lobby to see if she was with someone. "What are you doing here? Did you get my note? I tried calling last night, but the hotel clerk at the front desk seemed to think you weren't in."

Now it was Celeste's turn to be confused, until she realized his last memory of her had ended at the studio. They'd run into each other in the hallway. She'd kissed him and then removed herself from his memories so she could track down the Skulk who murdered Dolores Diaz.

"I had some business to take care of in the city," she said, catching up. "I'm sorry I didn't have a chance to say goodbye. But with the death of Dolores and the studio in turmoil, I thought it best to sneak away quietly."

"Wait, that can't be right." Nick blinked and looked to the side, as though trying to correct the memory. "That was days ago." He looked at her like a man who'd had too much to drink and couldn't remember where he'd put his car keys. "But how did I get here? How did you get here? I'm supposed to speak with the police about Dolores."

Celeste began to panic. Had she done something wrong? Had too much time gone by? She didn't think his memories ought to revert like that. Sebastian poked his head out of her purse. He chittered something about needing to join the past memory and the present together again, like plugging a lamp into a socket. Something that would make the connection real for him again.

But what?

And then Celeste understood. Such a simple thing, really. She felt silly for having overlooked it in the first place, but she knew what to do now.

She took Nick's face in her hands and kissed him. Nick reacted with a startled blink of the eyes, followed by a smile that suggested he'd like more, just as he had moments before she'd had to say goodbye to him and fade his memories. Only this time she was certain there'd be an ever after waiting for them.

EPILOGUE

1949

The crosswind of artemisia and hummingbird sage coming in off the garden was intoxicating. Celeste inhaled and closed her eyes as she leaned back on her chaise lounge. After she'd enjoyed her usual early-morning dip in the pool, the California sun did its best to reenergize her. She could have stayed there all day like that, if not for the curious nose and whiskers staring at her from the foot of her lounge chair.

Celeste wiggled her toes to acknowledge the stoat. "Yes, I know, we need to pack the trunk, but I'm enjoying a little peace and quiet at the moment." When the stoat didn't stop staring, she lifted her sunglasses an inch to get a clear view of her companion. "What's wrong?"

Sebastian chittered away, trying to impress her with his new-found skill of anticipating important moments that hadn't yet presented themselves. Then again, maybe he'd always had the uncanny ability. It had just taken her decades to recognize how intuitive he really was.

Celeste sat up and finished drying her legs off with a towel. "Okay, tell me. What should I be looking for?"

Sebastian jumped up on the lounge chair and stood on his hind legs, watching the house with his whiskers twitching. Celeste followed his gaze. It was a beautiful house. She'd always thought so. Built of yellow stone with a red tile roof and bright pink bougainvillea growing over the sharp corners. The house had always reminded her of a slice of the French Riviera. A little taste of home away from home.

The palm trees surrounding the property swayed in unison. A hummingbird flitted near the bougainvillea, and a few clouds scuttled behind the roofline, but other than that she saw nothing unusual. Her own senses had maybe picked up something tingling in the atmosphere, but she didn't have Sebastian's sensitive whiskers. "You could at least give me a clue," she said. The stoat ducked as Millie, the housekeeper, came outside carrying a tray with a tall glass of iced tea and a stack of mail.

Celeste dropped her towel over Sebastian's head to hide him. "Thank you, Millie. Anything exciting in there?" she asked, with a nod toward the stack of manila envelopes placed in front of her.

"Maybe. There's a few that have come over from that Morris agency."

The housekeeper went back inside, so Celeste removed the towel from Sebastian's head to let him breathe again. They'd been very careful around Millie for years now. The housekeeper had a sharp eye. If she caught sight of him again, she'd know no normal stoat ought to be living in Los Angeles, and certainly not for the past twenty-two years.

There were two envelopes from the Morris agency this time. Headshots of actresses. Not stars by any means, not even well known, but the second one caught her eye. "Ah, so this is what you meant," she said, holding up the photo. The woman's hopes and aspirations nearly leaped off the glossy photograph. It had been a while since Celeste had felt such a strong connection through a headshot alone. The last had been Judy, but that was over ten years ago now. And before that it had been Harlean, who'd later taken the stage name Jean to honor her mother. The photos had proved a clever means for fulfilling the requirements of Celeste's two careers. One as a casting director, which she'd taken on since settling in Hollywood in 1927, the other the job she was born to do. A profession that still called to her whenever the right prospect came along.

Celeste glanced at the photo again. The doe eyes, the straight smile, the platinum-blond hair with the perfect curl—they were all valuable commodities in the business, but it was the determination shining from deep behind the irises that gave Celeste the shiver on the back of her neck. A minute later it was a stubbled chin against her neck and unexpected kiss on her cheek that gave her the goose bumps all up and down her spine.

"Hello, you," she said.

"What's this?" Nick reached around her shoulder to take a look at the photo. "Pretty. What's her name?"

Celeste flipped the photo over. "It says Marilyn on the back, though I don't think that's her real name."

"One of yours or one of mine?"

"Mine, I think, but there might be another one in the mix for your new detective movie." She sorted through some of the other photos, taking a cursory look, and then shoved a photo of a redhead at him that mildly reminded her of Nellie and that fateful night in New York City. The night Hazel had joined the sisterhood.

Celeste's husband of twenty-one years sat beside her on the lounge chair, still staring at the first photo. He was apparently as mesmerized by the woman's expression as she'd been.

"She reminds me a little of Harlean," he said wistfully.

"That's just who I was thinking about." There was only a slight physical resemblance between Harlean and the woman in the photo—the platinum-blond hair, the pouty lips, perhaps the slightly revealing cleavage that teased of more. But the real kicker was the light in the eye the camera didn't quite capture completely and yet was still strong enough to break through the barrier of the lens. "I think I'm going to have to go see her for myself." Celeste surprised herself by saying it so matter-of-factly.

"We're leaving in two days."

Celeste nodded. They were going to France for her annual trek to the cottage in the woods to do her obligatory stint as an instructor. And to reunite with old friends and older enemies, as she liked to tease Anaïs. She couldn't wait to see her old friend. Hazel, too. And the new little one, Rita, who'd arrived back in '46 after Hazel had ascended and Gertude had passed. Nick always came along on the trips with her, though he spent his time touring the countryside and visiting little villages on his own, while she taught the new initiates self-defense against Skulks and how to recharge their magic if they ever lost their gemstones. It was always a grand trip, but it wasn't really home anymore. Perhaps it never had been.

"I know, I still need to pack," she replied. "But first I have to find out if this one is meant to be under my protection. You understand."

She had, of course, told Nick everything from the beginning. Who she was, what she did, how she'd come to be in California back in 1927 when they'd first met. A part of him hadn't believed her at first, but the moviemaking, dream merchant side of him had been engaged enough with the possibility to keep an open mind about the magic she described. It hadn't taken long for her to convince him she didn't have bats in her belfry. A quick transformation of his golf clubs into a floor lamp had done the trick. But what had been more difficult to explain over the years was the complicated and sometimes tragic outcome of the work she did as a Fée Gardienne. While she was able to change lives with her benevolent magic, often catapulting her protégés into careers that straddled the stratosphere, there was always the downside effect, which never quite squared right with Nick's sense of justice. But never more so than when Celeste had discovered Harlean and her unspoken aspirations.

Harlean had been Celeste's second protégé after Rose, but the first one in the long line of actresses she promoted in what people had begun calling the "Golden Age" of Hollywood. The poor young woman hadn't even wanted to be in the pictures; at least that was the line she gave to anyone who worked in the business when they asked her why she wasn't auditioning. It was only after Celeste had befriended her under the guise of being an aspiring actress herself and read her aspirations that it became apparent just how much the nineteen-year-old wanted a taste of the glamourous life. So Celeste had kicked one door open for her and then another, while also breaking the chains that were holding her back. After that, it hadn't taken long for the bright-eyed platinum blonde to shine and find her footing, ascending into the ether of those eternal stars who continue to glow long after they're gone. Harlean had become a favorite of Nick's. A delight at parties and a gem to work with. Then, just when her fame was reaching its peak, the Skulks showed up to do their worst. After the showdown in New York, the Infortunii were always crueler and swifter in their work whenever they came for one of Celeste's protégés. Anaïs's too.

Harlean had died a miserable death at only twenty-six years old. Then, a month later, the woman pilot, whom the world was in awe of after her solo flight across the Atlantic, fell from the sky and vanished without a trace. Not even a body left for the rescuers to find. The pilot had been one of Anaïs's. Nick took the back-to-back tragedies hard. He couldn't see how any of the fame and wealth had been worth the heartbreaking ending—for them, their families, or their fans. For a brief time, he begged Celeste not to take on another protégé. For a brief time, she complied.

And then about six months later, while walking from his office to Soundstage Six on the studio backlot, he'd spotted a girl of about eight years old on a tour with her parents. Celeste and Nick couldn't have children of their own—no Gardienne could—so he often took the time to stop and say hello to kids he met to "keep up with the youth," as he put it. While the girl's parents listened to a tour guide explain how the water tower once saved the studio from burning down, she entertained herself by playing with a toy airplane, making it rise and fall in the air in big dramatic loops. He'd asked her, "Where are you flying off to today?" The girl had replied, "I'm flying all the way around the world just like Amelia Earhart." She then declared, "I'm going to be one of the Ninety-Nines when I grow up." The brief conversation was the beginning of his evolution.

Nick learned to appreciate why the world needed fairy godmothers. Sometimes, he even thought he understood how Celeste chose her protégés. In the beginning, he'd often said the way that she cleared obstacles for people so their potential could shine was a noble pursuit. What he hadn't grasped for the longest time was the reason for the downfall effect. "Why do they have to suffer? Why can't people just be successful and happy?" he'd asked. But even as he'd said it, the aftertaste of such a trite sentiment had left him needing a drink to cleanse his palate. It was only later, after meeting the girl who'd been inspired to become a pilot, his perspective began to change. He'd seen evidence of how one remarkable and unique life, even one prematurely cut short, could touch another's on the other side of the planet, and he began to think maybe the scales Celeste had talked about found a way to balance out after all.

No one lived happily ever after. There were always hard times mixed in with the good. Most people experienced a series of ups and downs, but the main trajectory of their lives followed an even-keeled, if not predictable, course from cradle to grave. But for those who caught the eye of a Gardienne, life was like riding bareback on the tail of a shooting star. Their lives flickering brightly in the firmament for all to see, until the inevitable arc of that journey reached its apex and the swift rise gave way to a swifter decline in obeyance with the laws of nature.

Nick set the photo of the blond woman down between them. "She does have something special about her, doesn't she?"

Celeste nodded, somewhat distracted by her attraction to the woman's aura. Experience told her this one could be a supernova, but she couldn't think about what would happen to her later and the downfall that would ultimately come. Her part was to think about the rising path of destiny waiting on the horizon. And so, after a quick kiss goodbye and a change of clothes, she and Sebastian were off to meet this promising young woman. For now, Celeste and her gemstones needed to become this girl's best friend.

Acknowledgments

Readers may recall Celeste is helped at a crucial moment in *The Gilded Age of Magic* by the simple act of being grateful for things in her life both big and small. I say "simple," but the truth is there's power in gratitude. And it is with that in mind that I wish to thank all the wonderful people who helped bring this novel to life. To my agent, Marlene Stringer, for plucking my first novel out of the slush pile years ago to seeing this ninth book get published. To my editor Elizabeth, who skillfully guided yet another novel through the gauntlet. To Clarence, who knows my writing as well as anyone could and gently offers honest feedback during edits. To copyeditors Jon and Kellie, who always put the final gilding on the page with their sharp attention to detail. To Kimberly Glyder for her beautiful cover art. And, finally, to the entire team at 47North for all the hard work that goes on behind the scenes. I thank you all.

About the Author

Photo © 2018 Bob Carmichael

Luanne G. Smith is the Amazon Charts and *Washington Post* bestselling author of *The Vine Witch*, *The Glamourist*, and *The Conjurer* in the Vine Witch series; *The Raven Spell* and *The Raven Song* in the Conspiracy of Magic series; *The Witch's Lens* and *The Wolf's Eye* in the Order of the Seven Stars series; and *The Golden Age of Magic* and *The Gilded City of Dreams* in the Golden Age of Magic series. Luanne lives in Colorado, at the base of the beautiful Rocky Mountains, where she enjoys hiking, gardening, and reading a good book at the end of the day. For more information, visit www.luannegsmith.com.